HOOPER'S WAR

A NOVEL BY

PETER VAN BUREN

LUMINIS BOOKS

Published by Luminis Books
90 Rimrock Ride
Sedona, Arizona, 86351, U.S.A.

PUBLISHER'S NOTICE
This is a work of fiction. Names, characters, places, and incidents are either the product of the author's imagination or are used fictitiously. Any resemblance to actual persons, living or dead, business establishments, events, or locales is entirely coincidental.

Hooper's War graphically portrays events in wartime. These portrayals may be disturbing to some readers.

Cover design for *Hooper's War* by Brit Godish. Cover image courtesy Shutterstock.

Paperback ISBN: 978-1-941311-12-7

Printed in the United States of America

10 9 8 7 6 5 4 3 2 1

LUMINIS BOOKS

Meaningful Books That Entertain

Praise for *Hooper's War:*

"Peter Van Buren's *Hooper's War* is a powerful anti-war novel of empathy, wit and engaged imagination, vividly depicting war's commingled devastation and savage beauty. Van Buren portrays the lasting wounds suffered by innocent victims and guilt-ridden soldiers wracked by grave moral injury. As Van Buren writes, "This shit doesn't end when the war does, but only ends when we do."

—Douglas A. Wissing, journalist and author of *Hopeless but Optimistic: Journeying through America's Endless War in Afghanistan* and *Funding the Enemy: How U.S. Taxpayers Bankroll the Taliban*

"Peter Van Buren has done an interesting thing here; with *Hooper's War*, he's managed to capture the rage, chaos, disorder, but most of all, shame, of the fighting men from our most noble war effort, without apologizing for any of it. Men in extraordinary circumstances often commit themselves to bouts of magical thinking, and Hooper is no exception."

—Brandon Caro, author of *Old Silk Road*, novel of the Afghan war

"*Hooper's War* is evocative and beautiful, its writing sweeps you along, touches lives and transports you effortlessly on a sometimes poignant, sometimes stark, sometimes obscure journey; that of Hooper himself, attempting to reconcile the deep tragedy and moral ambiguity of war. These are ever-relevant themes, and Van Buren's authentic insight into human nature reveals itself like the prick of a pin. Anyone can recognize the depth of research that has gone into this book, it's something those who know Van Buren have come to expect from his work—it feels effortless and uniquely enriches each character, bringing them to life in ways that build empathy for the reader, through details or twists from the ordinary to the obscene—fluently evoking the horror of war."

—Dr. Emma L Briant, Lecturer in Journalism Studies, University of Sheffield, United Kingdom

"A bloody American invasion of Japan; the incineration by firebombing of Kyoto; an unlikely truce between a U.S. lieutenant and a Japanese sergeant. In Van Buren's imaginative retelling of the end of World War II, we learn about the stubborn horrors of war—and the fragile grace that blooms ever so fleetingly amid the chaos. 'The question isn't so much why Private Garner is screaming,' notes a doctor treating a PTSD casualty. 'It's why we aren't.' Striking words from a story of searing intensity."

—William Astore, Lt Col, USAF (Ret.), author of *Hindenburg: Icon of German Militarism*

"With its changing points-of-view and reverse timeline, Peter Van Buren's *Hooper's War* is a spiritual cousin to the movies *Rashômon* and *Memento*. The book is set in an alternate World War II, in which U.S. forces invade Japan, rather than drop the atomic bomb. With philosophical precision and wit, Van Buren has constructed a literary origami, which unfolds to reveal that the creases and lines of history are determined as much by personal chance as they are big decisions—and that war is as much our doing, as it is our undoing."

—Randy Brown, author of *Welcome to FOB Haiku: War Poems from Inside the Wire*

"*Hooper's War* is a classic war story of blood and guts spilled in Japan during WWII but with contemporary meanings. Told by both a young American lieutenant and a young Japanese soldier, Van Buren writes of the inevitable questioning of what wars do to those who fight. 'This shit doesn't end when the war does, it only ends when we do.' 'Garner is likely to just be insane for the rest of his life, mind torn apart and all that. His body's in terrific shape, not a scratch. But the question isn't so much why Private Garner is screaming. It's why we aren't, Lieutenant.'

'Besides, Garner went insane because of what he saw in Kyoto. Curing him means I'd have to convince him seeing the burned children he's shouting about was not a reason to be insane.' These are commentaries echoed seventy-five years later by our young soldiers with PTSD from the Afghanistan and Iraq wars."

—Ann Wright, U.S. Army Reserve Colonel and former U.S. diplomat

Wars and Presidents will come and go.
So, too, will parents and children and other first loves.
All will be eclipsed in memory, leaving you.
Remember this.

—Randy Brown, *Welcome to FOB Haiku: War Poems from Inside the Wire*

The Yellow-Gray Noise of Morning, Pacific Coast of Japan, American Landing Craft, 1946

THERE IS NOWHERE to go in a landing craft except where it takes you.

"I don't know what to do," I said.

"Don't say that, never, sir, that's quicksand," the Sergeant said.

Chunks of steel destroyed boys. I watched someone I didn't know ripped apart, face the color of school chalk. Your nightmares have no idea.

"Stop the boat, make the Lieutenant stop the boat, we're all gonna die, we're all gonna die," a soldier said.

Their blood smelled like copper. I steadied myself touching something too wet and soft. There was a sound that started deep and only found its way out as a scream. A head snapped back like one of those red rubber balls attached to a paddle.

"Lieutenant Hooper can't stop the boat, nobody can stop the boat. Boat can't stop the boat," another of them said.

Screeching metal-on-metal, the ramp dropped and everyone ran forward. That was all I could hear except the sing-song of "Lieutenant Hooper! Lieutenant! Lieutenant! *Lieutenant!*"

Chapter 1: The Last Day

Former Lieutenant Nathaniel Hooper: Retirement Home, Kailua, Hawaii, 2017

LOOKING BACK, the party is more important than the planning. A sad marriage fades into a thing we thought would last forever. Fighting over the covers is better than remembering the empty side of the bed. Everything comes from somewhere, so once you start winding things back you can't stop until you hit the beginning. Age is not gentle.

I think of it this way: remembering can be what's happened, but also what's to come. Like water forming on top of thinning ice.

THE UNITED FLIGHT TO Japan was a long one to make alone. Unlike those around me in the cabin, I wasn't coming for business, or as a tourist; I was coming solely for memory. As we crossed the coastline from the Pacific, I thought it might be the same view our airmen had during the war, and I imagined dropping incendiary bombs from Business Class.

There's been a hell of a lot of things written about how the war might have ended if the atomic bomb had worked, both alternative histories I hate and scholarly stuff I don't, but no one can really know. All that's a lot of ink that ends up in the same place: America, and me as a young U.S. Army officer, invaded Japan, they surrendered and we won. I was briefly known as Lieutenant Hooper instead of Nathaniel. About the only thing that might have changed had any of those "alternative histories" been true was, well, me.

But bomb or no bomb, I had done a terrible thing. I was wounded. But there's no prosthetic for a soul that's dying faster than its body. You have to heal it.

SEEING KYOTO SO MANY years after the war was like looking at an old woman trying to remember the girl. Kyoto now is a huge city, too much of it gray sprawl without charm. The city in 1946 was different. While the rest of Japan tore into the modern era, Kyoto stubbornly held on to its dowager status. If you wanted a wash bucket in 1946 Kyoto, it was most likely made by hand, of wood, down the street from where you lived, by someone you knew. Your neighbors' grandparents had been your grandparents' neighbors. Kyoto was born an old soul, a special place, even in as foreign a country as Japan.

If you are high enough up in modern Kyoto, and I recommend the ugly concrete Kyoto Tower near the bullet train station, but only for the view, you can see patches of green surrounding the temples and shrines that have been there since forever. At least they've been in those same locations since forever. After the war the Japanese surveyed the ground and rebuilt every single one of them as close to the original place as possible. Kyoto's temples are mostly made of cedar, and from time to time throughout their thousands of years of history, burned down for one reason or another or were toppled by earthquakes. Almost none of them, even at the time of our 1946 firebombing, were the original structures, so the process of renewal was not alien. Once something gets broken you make repairs and it doesn't matter that it can't ever be new again, a thought that was in Kyoto's blood. The city was at peace well before I was.

I HAD PUT OFF the visit as long as I could. But now, more than wanting someone still around to go with me to the early bird buffets, I wanted this. It'd outlasted every other ambition. I was in Kyoto because like every old man, I needed to deal with a young man's choices.

If in 1946 I'd told the truth about Naoko, and Sergeant Eichi Nakagawa, I would have been thrown into the stockade for cowardice. But by being a real coward and allowing the Army to call me a hero, I had to pay up someday, collected here, now, in 2017. If I'd told the soldiers in my outfit in 1946—Laabs, Marino, Smitty, Steiner, Burke, Polanski, goddamn Jones—that only four years later they'd be taking R&R in Japan from a new war in Korea, and then a few years after that from a war in a place they'd never heard of called Vietnam, they'd have looked at me like I had a screw loose.

I'd read how awful those first post-war years had been after the destruction of Kyoto. It had taken three weeks to dispose of the dead. To earn a little money, survivors collected up bits of bone and twisted pieces of metal to sell to the occupying soldiers as souvenirs. Many of the survivors would pose for pictures with the G.I.s, earning a few coins to pull up their shirts and show off their burns while the soldiers grinned. MacArthur soon put a stop to that. He didn't want the details of what we did exposed to the folks back home. There was that myth—that we were the good guys, that we did the Japanese a favor by immolating an entire city to wrap up the war faster.

I'd picked up a bit of an apologetic stoop over the decades, but not to worry, the only thing for me to hurry about in Kyoto was dodging the crowds getting on and off trains. Walking, I remembered the river from my last visit, in 1946, and started near there. The *geisha* quarters, rebuilt where they'd been since the 1200s, are nearby. The main intersection into town, the one we must have passed over back then, is jammed with tourists. An American standing there was as noteworthy as the McDonald's next to the central aiming point for the firebombing. For about 55 years the world knew that Ground Zero, until we Americans appropriated the term on September 11, 2001, after we were attacked from the air for the first time ourselves.

Looking around, I put the Japanese man who'd watched his wife die right there—by the vending machine, Coca Cola, of course—so that I could fix him in my memory long enough to discard him. It didn't work. The dead keep coming back. I'll have to live with him.

I MADE MY WAY to what had once been the northern outskirts of town, locating, with the help of a high school girl pressed into using her limited English, that familiar temple. You'd think after 70 years married to a Japanese woman I'd have learned more of the language.

The day was warm, late March weather before Japan's infamous humidity settles in. The cherry trees had exploded into full bloom, bursts of fragile pink and beautiful, with some new unbelievably green leaves in behind them. Once a year heaven visits earth like that in Japan. I didn't see it on my first trip, as it had been winter, and cold enough then to freeze shadows to the ground. We'd knocked down a helluva lot of trees, too; maybe some of these rooted off those branches. These days beautiful things can again seem beautiful to me.

The high school girl passed me off at the temple gate to a happy college student. For those who have never been to Japan, these young people sometimes haunt tourist attractions. Unlike the rest of the world, where amateur guides demand tips or try to sell you something, in Japan they simply wish to practice English. They wouldn't know what to do if you handed them money.

"My name is Sayako, but please call me my English classroom name, Sally," Sayako/Sally said. "Do you know this temple?"

Indeed I did, but it would have been impossible to explain. Better to let her go on with her well-practiced speech.

"Therefore, let me introduce this temple for you. It is old. You might say, ancient. It has been in this very location for a long time. Locally, it is known as a place of remembering resilience. This is, first, because the temple had withstood despite many earthquakes. Second, it is because this temple did not burn during the firebombing of Kyoto. Though, it was damaged by the artillery after the bombing. So, therefore, many small Buddha statues—do you know Buddha?"

I assured her I did.

"So, therefore, many small statues are placed here after war to remember the children who died in the firebombing elsewhere. They were roasted."

I suggested Sayako/Sally say something like "killed in the fire" instead of "roasted," and she looked grateful, jotting it down with a pink mechanical pencil into a pink Hello Kitty notebook.

"So because they were killed in the fire—" Sayako/Sally looked to me for approval and I smiled "—these small statues are here. The relatives of them come to pour the water on and pray for the souls of the killed-in-the-fire-children of Kyoto."

In any other place on Earth where such violence had been done, this conversation could never have unfolded like this. Sayako/Sally knew I was an American. She could guess my age. She knew my country had roasted children to death near this spot only a blink in time before our odd meeting.

While every nation gets its own history wrong to a certain extent, there is truly no sense in Japan that the war—either its causes or how it was carried out—was ever given proper airing. It's a family secret. The emperor in 2017 is the son of the emperor from 1946—imagine some kid of Hitler's still in power in Germany. The Japanese accepted it all like a natural disaster, something that couldn't be helped. Unlike the plaques in every small town in America with lists of soldiers who lost their lives in battle, there are few if any markers or monuments referencing the war in Japan. But while they thought they'd swept up every expended cartridge and smudged away every boot print, the grass grows too well around some random parking lot, fed by something deeply embedded. I knew they couldn't clean it all up. We'd left too much behind.

Sayako/Sally gestured to an old woman gently pouring ladles of water on one of the small stone statues. The statues did not look like children. They were small ovals, with partial faces, cartoonish egg figurines with little cloth bibs, symbolic without being ghoulish. A very Japanese touch. The old woman seemed to be speaking with the statues.

"I want to talk with her, Sally, the elderly woman there."

As nonchalant as Sayako/Sally had been in her discussion of the war's events with me, speaking to another Japanese person of a certain age about what happened was a forbidden act. My request trapped Sayako/Sally between such a taboo and the equally strong requirement of treating a guest from far away well. I could see her face as she chewed on the *koan* I'd handed her. I knew I was being selfish in even asking, but cruelly justified my request in thinking it would be Sally's penalty for not understanding what had happened in her nation's recent history.

Sayako/Sally's introduction in Japanese to the woman, complete with many physical gestures toward me, took much longer than the "Hello, may we talk?" I asked her to translate. And I suspect no matter how long Sayako/Sally lives, nothing in her life will make her happier than she was at the moment the old woman said she spoke some English and would talk with me herself.

"I've been here before," I said.

"I come often to pray for the souls of these children. I have much to discuss with God."

"What do you say as you pour the water on the statues?"

"I say 'Haruo-kun, that day of the firebombing was so hot for you.' I say 'Akiko-chan, you wished so hard for water then. Please drink now.' You must think I am silly, talking to ghosts," she said.

"I am here for ghosts," I said, and without warning to myself let out everything I had seen in 1946. It was unfair, and I was conscious that I was forcing my thoughts on the woman. I didn't know what else to do. Words were all I had. When I paused, though, she made no movement away, said none of the polite things one can say to break off an unwanted conversation. When

I was spent, she surprised me by telling her own story, everything she had seen us do in Kyoto during the war, but it was sorrow, not rage.

"I am sorry," she said, "but I have never been able to tell anyone before. My husband died in the war, and there was no one I could talk to."

"I, too, am sorry," I said, "but I have never been able to tell anyone. I outlived them all, and usually in a war that means I won. My wife was from this area, but I was never able to tell it all to her before she passed. There was no one I could talk to even once about the things I think about every day."

This was no impromptu wartime reunion. The woman wasn't a destroyer captain who had hunted me as a sub commander, now sharing a drink years removed from being anonymous enemies. It felt more like an affair, a chance encounter with a willing stranger who wanted to do the things someone at home wouldn't do. I certainly wasn't saved by this, but maybe, for the first time, I felt savable.

After the elderly woman left, there was one more thing. My wife refused to return to Kyoto herself, but insisted I do something for her, after her death. Doctors say someone can't technically die of a broken heart, but I know better. It just takes a long time. So my final obligation in Kyoto was to leave behind an old photo of two Japanese children. I'd helped take care of it for 70 years, but it was never mine. It was a treasured possession of hers, and it needed to return home, before the next change of season. They were together. It had just taken a long time.

Before Kyoto 2017, Kyoto 1946

Chapter 2: A Hero's Welcome

Lieutenant Nathaniel Hooper: Japan, Before Kyoto, Captain Christiansen's Tent, 1946

THE DOGS WERE HOWLING even before I approached Captain Christiansen's tent. They must have picked up the first vibrations from the approaching planes even I could hear now, and it must have scared the hell out of them.

"LIEUTENANT HOOPER, LET ME get you a cup of coffee," Captain Christiansen said. He was talking, little pops of condensed breath as he spoke, even as my eyes took a second to adjust to the light inside the tent. I could see he'd taken up chewing tobacco, and alternated between a cup to spit the juice into and another cup to drink coffee from. He seemed to have a good rhythm down, but the last thing inside the tent needed was more tension. Still, I'd never seen him so pleased about something to do with me.

"We all figured you were dead, and then you show up all alive outta that goddamn fight at Nishinomiya," Captain Christiansen said. "Your parents will be proud, you disguising yourself in Jap clothes and escaping from behind enemy lines. Damn, boy, I'd never have guessed you had it in you."

"Thank you, sir," I said, looking down. "I guess I had it in me."

"You need to get caught up. The morning after the battle we were going to bomb the hell out of a small house nearby the Nishinomiya train station. A spotter thought they saw someone going to hide in there. Instead, our fly-boys picked out maybe 40 Japs in a valley not far away, laid out for us all pink and naked. Pilots said there were crows starting to circle over the dead before our planes even cleared out. Forgot all about the house we set out to bomb in the first place."

"Yes, sir. Um, sorry I wasn't there." I realized I was a pretty crappy liar even if he didn't.

"Well, you're hero enough, Hooper, surviving in Japanese captivity. So let me see if I got it all, because Major Moreland is up my ass to write you up for a Purple Heart. Now, after the fight for Nishinomiya train station, you were wounded—"

"No, sir, only knocked out. Private Jones was wounded," I said.

"Jones is only worth so much to us because he's dead. So be advised, young lieutenant: we attacked the Jap train station. You were fighting the Japs and got knocked out by the Japs. Getting knocked out is being wounded."

"Yes, sir," I said. "Wounded."

"We've been chewing through the stock of actual Purple Hearts pretty fast. We'll borrow one for you for pictures." He started jotting things down. "So, you were inadvertently left behind, and defended yourself from the Japs, protecting Jones."

"Sir, no, that wasn't what happened. Frankly sir, maybe I should explain it, because in truth I was more stupid than brave," I said.

"Stupid and brave are pretty close in war." He lowered his voice and came close enough that I could smell him, coffee, tobacco juice, and old sweat. He set the spit cup and the coffee cup down, something of a relief for me. "Son, look, between us, I can well imagine Major Moreland wants to puff up the truth a bit. The homeland needs heroes. The medals aren't for you. Now, you ready to hear what's next?"

"Given what, um, happened to me, I thought I might take my foot off the gas for a couple of days," I said. "I mean, what I did, doesn't that count for anything?"

"It's the only reason I'm really still listening to you. And I'd love to give you some time off, Hooper, but I need to put ass into the fight right now. The Japs dug in a defensive line around Kyoto. We've hammered the hell out of them day and night. I bet you wished you had a piece of that."

"Of course, sir," I said.

"Now the whole damn Japanese 16th Army is right in the outskirts of Kyoto city. They refuse to surrender, so we're gonna burn the goddamn thing down. Fry up the women, the children, the old men. Burn the goddamn temples, the old palaces, every goddamn thing that'll spark up. One massive firebombing, modern-like, whole city at once. You hear the planes?"

"Can't miss them, sir. But we've been firebombing Japanese cities for months, haven't we, sir?" I said.

"Jesus, you sound like you got an old girlfriend in town or something. Since Kyoto hasn't been bombed this whole war, there's a lot of virgin city left. And it's all wood. The damn thing is gonna go up like every Fourth of July you ever saw back in, where was it, Ohio, right?"

"Yes, sir, Reeve, Ohio. May I ask a question, sir?" I said. "Why are we bombing the whole of Kyoto? Wouldn't it make more sense to just bomb the enemy part?"

"Hooper." He said my name like he was chewing on a cold sore. "Who the hell do you think grows the food and runs the trains and works in the factories? Jap civilians. Their women make baby Japs that grow into soldiers. They're all in on it. We can shave weeks off this war by killing them." He ticked off those sentences like throwing stones into a steel pail. "We're saving lives here, mister." Bang.

"You said I have some duty connected with all this, Captain?" We were almost shouting at each other over the sound of the planes now.

"Tomorrow, as our hero, you'll lead a patrol into Kyoto city center, first light. We'll send reporters from Stars and Stripes, probably Chaplain Savage to get him the hell out of my way. Kind of a plum assignment, Lieutenant, so smile, you get to take the victory lap on this one for Uncle Sam. OK, now beat it and get yourself something hot to eat."

As I turned toward the tent flap a soldier pushed past me, carrying some scrap of a message form. Captain Christiansen signed for it and without looking up, snapped at the soldier to straighten his helmet.

"It is straight, sir," the soldier said.

"If I say your helmet isn't on square, it isn't on square," Captain Christiansen said.

"But Captain..."

"I said straighten the helmet and you will straighten the goddamn helmet."

I was afraid for the young soldier, but as Captain Christiansen rose from his seat with his fists balled the soldier fixed his helmet and backed out of the tent. I could feel the sound of the planes pressing on my ear drums. It was inside me.

"Captain, there's something I need to say. I'm not sure I'm the right guy for the victory lap and all. See, there's more you gotta know about—"

"Save it for someone who cares, Lieutenant Hooper. We're all just doing our job here and sometimes it isn't what we wanted, sometimes it feeds someone else's appetite." He'd snapped in, no more joking, deep into the real war now. Then just as fast his body went brittle, the air let out, and he sat back down. It isn't often that a guy like Christiansen won't meet your eyes. "You'd think I'd get tired of having to explain that to kids like you." Not aggressive or sarcastic, an assertion.

There was a lot of whiskey-hurt in it, but it fell into one of those cracks because I was too caught up in my own mess with Naoko and Sergeant Nakagawa to feel much about someone else's. I didn't know whether it was a confession coming from Captain Christiansen and if it was, if it was the first one or the last one. He started twisting the ring on his left hand.

"Hooper, you really want to know why I don't give a rat's ass about what we do? Because I want to go back to Arkansas and drink until this all can't ever catch me sober again. I divorced once into Army life, didn't care, juice wasn't worth the squeeze back then, so what's another one. You know, when I was last home, I slept at the kitchen table plenty of nights because I still thought then my first wife'd come back late and I wanted to hear the door open. But no matter. I already know the second wife won't be in bed when I come in at 3 a.m. One day I'll cap it off, but I'll be at home when I do. You'll learn, Lieutenant. This shit doesn't end when the war does, it only ends when we do."

OUTSIDE THE TENT AN overture of weather and reconnaissance aircraft in pairs flew over, and the noise cracked the sky itself. The moonlight caught on the polished aluminum skins of the B-29s, and soon everything in the world was replaced by planes. An explosion lit up the undersides of the next row of bombers, turning them from silver to orange, until the rising smoke got so thick I couldn't see the planes anymore. Every flash silhouetted another bit of Kyoto, teasing the planes to go get it. Maybe someday, I thought, they'd make bombs smart enough to have nightmares, but for now those would be ours.

I heard something new, growing in volume until it was louder than the planes themselves: The soldiers around me were cheering.

Lieutenant Nathaniel Hooper: Japan, Hilltop Outside Kyoto, After Midnight, 1946

"LIEUTENANT HOOPER? I'M DOCTOR Klein, Division Assistant Medical Officer. They sent me all the way up this damn hill to meet you because of your patrol into Kyoto tomorrow."

Doctor Klein was an ugly man, the kind you look at, then turn away from, then look back at, even though you feel wrong doing it, something like the way people behave around toupees. He was every puggy bastard that ever made someone else's life more difficult. And now he was standing there, chewing on a Hershey bar, talking to me.

"You want a bite? Captain Christiansen said Major Moreland ordered me to prepare you and your men for what you may encounter tomorrow in Kyoto. Hey, you heard what happened, right? Christiansen took a full swig of tobacco juice from his spit cup the other day at the staff briefing, never even flinched, just gutted it like a champ," Doctor Klein said. "The pool on that had been up to $50. I think Chaplain Savage won. You sure you don't want a bite of this chocolate? Now about Kyoto, ever seen the aftermath of a firebombing before? I haven't. Made it damn hard to figure out how to prepare you for it. The best I could find in the manual is to issue your men were these yellow atabrine malaria pills."

"Leave 'em, Doc, and I'll take care of it," I said.

"Normally that'd be SOP, but since Major Moreland is taking such a personal interest in your mission I need to report to him how much I helped you. I'm trying to get promoted you see, and frankly, with this war going so well for us, there's not much time. I'd hoped you would be a sport about this."

"Look, I'll tell everyone you did a good job," I said.

"No, that would be dishonest, and I'm a moral man," Doctor Klein said, raising his voice over the sound. "Here, the pills, take them, for me. Please." He said that last word as if he had to squeeze it out past a hemorrhoid.

"Please, Lieutenant, we've all got our jobs to do. Be sure the men take three pills a day. Have them report to me immediately if their urine turns purple. See how easy that was? Didn't hurt a bit, eh? Hey, you feel that? What the hell is that?"

A hot breeze blew back my hair. That was where I was headed at first light. That was Kyoto, burning.

Chapter 3: Oh, the Night Does Not End in Kyoto

Lieutenant Nathaniel Hooper: Japan, Kyoto, 1946

KYOTO AS WE TOOK her was the opposite of impregnable. For all the Japanese fears we'd rape their women, they thought too small.

We were in a couple of Jeeps heading toward the city the morning after the firebombing. Ahead of us, smoke rose from inside piles of wood. The ground was uncomfortably warm for winter when we stopped to take a piss. The sky was the shade of old jeans, with the sun a chalky dime. We saw a few houses with the side toward Kyoto city charred black and blue. The trees looked like something alien that'd been replanted by the fires, branches twisted into skinny arms, smoke still reaching off them. It would've looked like cotton candy, except cotton candy wasn't black and stabbed into the sky and didn't smell and wasn't liquid and thick like this. Everything was covered in a fine gray ash, the devil's snow, one of the guys called it. It was a fitting way to say it, because this looked like what I'd imagined back in Ohio when the preacher wound up to describe hell to us on Sundays. At first I thought the only thing missing was demons walking around.

WE THOUGHT WE COULD drive into Kyoto by dead-reckoning, as it was a big enough target. Instead, the narrow, unmarked roads brought us to a place where the straight way in was lost. We had no detailed maps, and even my compass was of little use when every road took us through three directions just to travel half a mile. We were lost, in no way sure what was the right thing to do, so we blundered in the way we thought was correct. There was no one to ask for directions, and our new Jap translator had been to Kyoto as many times as I had. Without knowing what we were doing, we finally entered the outskirts of the city.

A JAPANESE WOMAN, THE first live person we saw, waved us over. She had streaks on her face where her tears had run, scarring the soot like mascara. She pointed to her mouth and then her belly, universal signs for hunger. She made an obscene gesture and held out four fingers, asking I guess for four dollars, or four yen, or four more days to live, in payment. She opened her top to reveal her breasts, trying then to cup them seductively. The fire had flash-burned the pattern of her kimono on to her skin.

"Hope you brought some flowers, Lieutenant," one of the men said, laughing. "I think the bitch's gonna be your Jap girlfriend."

"A harlot right out of Sodom and Gomorrah," Chaplain Savage said. "No wonder God struck this wicked place. I pity the men He chose to act through. Imagine how they felt having had to do this."

The woman whispered something to us through the translator.

"Kill me," she said.

"Nah," one of the troops said back. "It won't be that easy, girlie."

THE NEXT PEOPLE WE encountered described through the translator how at first the firebombing was beautiful. They had no experience with such things in Kyoto, the city never having been bombed before, and many people stepped outside to watch. The live ones we were talking to were those who did not stay long. They lived near the river and ran into a kind of tunnel they'd dug in the embankment. They said it was like looking out through a child's toy.

"I do not know the exact word for it," the translator said. "The kind where you peer down a tube and turn it to see different colors and shapes."

"A Kaleidoscope," I said.

"Yes, that is it, a kaleidoscope," the translator continued. "They saw red, then black, then it became orange, then red again, and then black again. They say it sparkled. At first the airplanes frightened them but soon enough they could not even hear the planes as the sound of the wind became as loud as during a typhoon."

The translator pointed out one woman who said she had crept outside for a moment to look up at her home. She thought it had not been hit. Then the windows glowed like what she said was a summer paper lantern. The flames soon shot long lines of sparks into the sky, and the next clutch of bombs with their streamers caught the light and looked like falling stars as they got pulled into the fire. When her home collapsed, she returned to the tunnel. She said she looked away from the opening after that, back into the darkness, but she could still see the imprint of the light from the fires and nothing else. She said now the night never ends in Kyoto.

"Do they want food?" I said.

"They are asking for kerosene to make fires," the translator said. "Also matches. Or a cigarette lighter."

"I got a lighter, sir," a solider named Garner said.

"Shut up. Translator, ask them what they need that stuff for? We just set the whole damn city on fire," I said.

"They want to cremate their dead."

"They're already cremated," I said.

"Not the right way," the translator said. "They say everything else here is burnt already and they cannot start proper fires without gasoline."

The Chaplain pushed his way through our little group.

"Now translator, ask them a question for me. Are any of them Christians?" the Chaplain said.

"They say they are all Buddhists."

"Oh, never mind. I was going to ask if they needed me to pray for any of their dead. Let me know if we find any Christians. I don't want to feel like my whole goddamn day here is being wasted," the Chaplain said.

"LIEUTENANT, WHAT ARE THOSE little black piles?" one of the men said.

"Burned stuff."

"People?"

"I guess, people."

"Like the enemy, right?"

"WHAT THE HELL'S THAT sound?" one of the soldiers said. "Too loud for cats, unless there's thousands and there isn't because the Nippers would've eaten them already. You know they eat cats, right?"

"More like it's the Japs, but I don't think even Japs are supposed to make sounds like that, to tell ya' the whole truth," another said.

"I heard it before, back home, when we herded the cows together. After you slaughtered the first one the others would know."

"I think it's burned Japs that ain't dead yet. What should we do, kill them?"

"To hell with them, they're already dead, they won't admit it yet. Let 'em burn."

"Amen to that, brother. They started this shit."

I couldn't say a word. I thought then we were at the bottom of the swamp but I was stupid.

AS WE WALKED, WE left a trail of silver chewing gum wrappers behind us. The gum helped cover some of the smells, because if hell smelled it smelled like this, and it felt better to be doing something, even if it was just chewing. No mind the clouds, the wrappers glittered against the darker ashes. As we encountered live children, they scurried to collect up the silver paper, a distraction I guess, felt better to be doing something, certainly nobody's trail of breadcrumbs home. They quickly figured out about the gum part.

"Throw those kids some more. Look at 'em smile, least a little," one of the troops said.

"But their mama-sans ain't smiling. Why ain't they smiling?" another said.

"How would you feel if the Indians handed out chocolate to Custer's kids after Little Big Horn?" I said.

"Aw, LT, lighten up, we're just tryin' to get them to like us more."

"How much chocolate you gonna need?" I said.

SHE LOOKED CRAZY AT first, seeming to pull out her hair in clumps. It took another glance for me to realize she wasn't pulling it out. It had burned all crispy, so every time she touched it it crumbled apart in her hands. Same for her eyebrows; she smudged them off with her fingers.

"She is looking for her children," the translator said. "But she ran through the smoke and she is blind now. She is asking if we know where her children are. She says they're named Mei and Satsuki, if we spot them."

"Hey, translator," one of the men said, laughing. "Tell her I found one of her kids."

On the woman's back was a burned lump, the one she must have been carrying in a sling.

"The woman," the translator said, "she says thank you, and when we find the other child, tell her mommy said come home and not be so naughty."

"THIS MAN WANTS TO know why we did this," the translator said.

"I don't know," I said.

"He says he does not know either, so he asked," the translator said.

"Ask him why he's still alive."

"He says he does not know."

"I mean, how come he didn't die?"

"He says he does not know that either."

"How come the firebombing didn't kill him? Was he in some kind of shelter?" I said.

"He says he does not know," the translator said.

"To hell with it. Just tell him I'm sorry," I said.

"He wants to apologize, too. He says he is actually dead, and you are talking to his ghost."

"Excuse me, translator," said one of the newspapermen with us. "Ask the 'ghost' if I can take his picture for *Stars and Stripes*. Tell him he'll be in newspapers all over America, maybe that'll cheer him up. I gotta get this shot, he's the first of these that still looks like a whole person. And what a joker. A ghost, sure thing, pal. Smile for Uncle Sam." The Japanese man jumped at the camera flash.

"So, *Stars and Stripes*, you gonna write about who's responsible for all these things we're seeing? You going to let the world know that?" I said.

"Oh, that's a sensitive subject, Lieutenant," the reporter said. "You see, I heard back at HQ the old man's trying to take all the credit, which is getting Division's back up since they cut the actual orders. Sort of like a rooster taking credit for the sunrise, amiright? Meanwhile, Major Moreland has his nose so far up the old man's butt looking for some pat on the back he might be Pinocchio. They act like there's only one more medal left to issue in all of the Pacific Theater. Oh, hey sir, sorry, I just noticed. Nice Purple Heart you got there."

"Lieutenant, excuse me. I'm Warrant Officer Rand, 20th Army Air Force, strategic bomb damage assessment branch, acting deputy chief assistant assessor. I might be able to help explain all this. I'm also filling in for the Office of the Army Air Force Historian. They're quite busy."

"I can imagine," I said.

"Oh, you don't know the half of it, sir. We've bombed 60 Jap cities down to the dust, but then we keep bombing them over and over, our pilots don't have much else to do and the brass figures idle hands are the devil's workshop and all. Every time we destroy one city again, well, that means more history. Once you get behind, it's damned hard to tell the new damage from the old damage, and then the records get skewed."

"You want people to remember this?" I said.

"The good Lord willing, yes, sir," Rand said. "Now about these civilians being alive, frankly, we don't know why, that's another big part of why I'm here. No matter what we try, a few always squeak through. Fire's a funny thing, sir. It can skip around with the wind and all. But we're working on getting some 100 percent spreads in these death events, if only the war'll last long enough for us to finish the calculations. Hate to have to wait until the next war to pick that up again, lose our rhythm and all."

"What do you make of that guy over there?" I said.

"Not uncommon, sir, no, not at all, in my experience. Usually what happens is they try and push open a metal door that got real hot, and their arms kinda melt, right to the elbows. Bad ones are when they lean their whole body against something hot, and stick. Sometimes there's enough left to tell what happened, so we can record it properly in the stats. Easy on us when we have to collect samples, because with the water and fat all boiled off you can get several of 'em into one sack. Other kinds of melting out there, too."

"Melting?" I said.

"Oh sure," Rand said. "Saw this one head sticking out of the road, looked like a Halloween pumpkin left outside too many days. We all got a little chuckle out of that. What we figure happened is the asphalt melted, the guy got stuck, and sunk in up to his chin. Like those dinosaurs in the La Brea tar pits outside L.A. Ever see those, sir? Quite a sight if you get the chance after the war."

"I'll see if I can get there, Rand."

"Lieutenant, a word of advice? You really need to stop thinking so much about the Japs that got killed and start thinking about the Americans who didn't. You don't seem to be enjoying this at all, but everything you see here means we're winning. C'mon, let's lighten things up, Lieutenant, it's gonna be a long day otherwise. Here, I got a joke for you. How do you explain a Jap with both legs, one arm and his head shot off, you know, just the other arm left?"

"God help me, I don't know, Rand."

"Somebody ran out of ammo! Pretty funny, huh, Lieutenant? See, 'cause he only had one arm, and we should have shot that one off, too, right? C'mon, you gotta laugh or you're gonna cry."

"What'd you do before the war, Rand, back home?" I said.

"Small town, sir, Nebraska. Taught high school. Math, so I'm good with numbers. That's how I got this job."

"Isn't it gonna be hard to go back to that school, after this?" I said.

"You could say so, sir. Sometimes back in the office I start imaging what kids I see would look like burned dead, you know, fat ones and skinny ones," Rand said. "Guess you could say I'll take my work home with me. Another joke there, sir."

"These things don't bother you Rand? These..."

"Not really, sir, kind of my job. Maybe another guy would lose perspective on all this and see it as something it's not. But atrocities aren't organized like this. Lieutenant, see, this war is really underrated. Maybe you should talk to the Chaplain about it."

"So, Rand, you're saying this all is good?"

"No sir, not good," Rand said. "I'd have to score it pretty close to perfect to be honest about it. Almost nothing left standing. That's an achievement."

"If you're so smart Rand, tell me, why are there so many logs blocking up the river? What caused that?" I said.

"Oh, those aren't logs, Lieutenant."

Chapter 4: The Children of Kyoto

Lieutenant Nathaniel Hooper: Japan, Kyoto, 1946

"I SPEAK ENGLISH. DO not shoot, please. I am a professor."

"Identify yourself. And why the hell are you wearing a top hat and a vest?" I said. With his odd clothing and small, impeccably groomed mustache, he looked like some character out of one of the old British books I didn't finish in high school.

"I am Professor Shinichiro Kanazawa, Department of Western Philosophy, Kyoto University. My card. I am here as a vicambulist, someone who pleasantly strolls around cities for recreation, though like you I prefer the vernacular 'to ramble.' As to the why, I typically wear a top hat and vest when I go out for a walk. It is splendid English wool, this vest, from when I studied abroad. Oxford, you know. I think that covers your queries. Oh, yes, manners. My regards to your President Harry S. Truman. Quite a little experiment he has succeeded with here. I read a funny thing about him, though perhaps you already know. The 'S' in his name does not stand for any name, it is just an S, though followed always by a period. Now, how else may I assist you?"

"Hey Professor, Warrant Officer Rand, 20th Army Air Force, strategic bomb damage assessment branch. Filling in for the historian, too. One of our goals here is for intellectuals like yourself to spread the word about what happened in Kyoto, to compel your government to surrender. We really don't have any way to communicate other than via these dead bodies, you know, to send a message. Would you agree to do that for us, sir?"

"Oh, absolutely," the Professor said. "Delighted to assist. The bombing has been quite helpful, you know. Once this city was all windy paths and twisty dead end streets, quite inconvenient for walking. With everything burnt down, I can get between any two points now in a straight line. Saves so much time. The only minor concern, and I am so hesitant to even bring it up, is the rats. I suppose it is really a Japanese problem, us dying hither and yon and such."

"Professor, you have no pants on," I said.

"True, sir, true. A keen eye. You see, there was no time to dress fully, as I just watched my wife die. No time even to cremate her before my walk, but I did not think she would really mind. She was always a good egg."

"I'm sorry, that must have been horrible, Professor," I said.

"Indeed, indeed, for her. She watched me fetch the things for the cremation while I waited for her to die. Cheers!"

KYOTO HAD BEEN A city of one million souls. They didn't open their mouths to answer the silence. They weren't hiding, they just... weren't. Everywhere else on earth there was always something. Here there was nothing, and nothing made its own sound.

In many parts of the city we traveled through you could see for miles, as thousands of tons of incendiary bombs can clear quite a path. Behind the emptiness, the haze and smoke covered the rest. For the most part, even the roads we walked on were uncluttered, as there was little stone or concrete rubble to have collapsed into them like we saw in the pictures from Germany or the London Blitz. Just soft ash. You almost could've walked barefoot. It had all been made of wood, paper, and cloth, and it had all burned. Well, maybe not all of it. Everywhere were charred ceramics, glazed chinaware that survived the heat. Forget the rats and roaches; the only thing certain to survive the end of the world will be dinner settings.

I saw three bodies in the street, a little vignette. Came down to this:

The black stick of a woman was fused by the heat hunched over a small child—there was no he or she—probably trying to shield the kid from the fire. The little ones like that, the soldiers took to calling them roasted peanuts, not because they didn't want to care, more because they couldn't care any more about dead seven-year-olds as a military objective. Beyond the beast was the body of another sexless child, the arms extended. Must have reached out to the mother at the last moment. If mother had been looking back, and the devil would have forced her to do so, that's the last thing she saw. Flakes of char were blowing off them. If there was any solace, it was the wind was gentle, nature saying maybe, "Here's one small thing I can do to help."

"PRIVATE, ARREST THAT MAN for looting," I said. "Corporal, make a note: I observed the subject pulling a wagon around, around whatever the hell part of Kyoto this is, stripping fragments of clothing off the dead. Looting. Got that? We don't need to add looting to everything else that happened to this city." I felt better helping, doing something at least halfway good.

"He denies it, Lieutenant," the translator said. "He says he was collecting clothing for children who need it. The children are not far from here, in a basement."

THE BASEMENT WAS DARK, though some light came through the small windows set at ground level, catching the dust and creating yellow fingers. Moving among the children was a single woman, dressed in what must have once been a nurse's uniform, still looking somewhat white against the background. She was using chopsticks to pick bits of burned flesh off a child's back. She was gentle and slow, staring ahead into the darkness as much as watching her work. Dozens of children lined up behind her in a ghost parade, snaking off into some corner we could not see into. There was moaning that lasted way longer than the sound.

"Translator, ask her, how many children has she helped so far?" I said.

"She says just the one. Because it's only been 20 hours since she started, she says, and the child keeps falling asleep."

I saw one of the reporters write that down.

Most of the children had no clothes. Either the clothes had been burned off, or the kids had torn them off because of the pain from their burns. There was skin peeling off their backs like paint chips flaking. They weren't even human, as alien as if they glowed in the dark. To me the children were more horrifying than all the corpses because I knew our weapons would not be finished with them for some time, as the burns healed but only over a period of years. That was real revenge for Pearl, something beyond an Old Testament God's imagination.

I saw handwritten signs on the walls. The translator said they were the names of relatives who'd come looking for their children. They posted their names in hopes their child might find his way here, and know auntie was alive somewhere. One sign had a picture, an unsmiling adult who must have belonged to someone in this city. How the picture survived, and how it got to this place, was just another shrewd invention of the devil. Was anyone ever reunited, I asked the nurse. No, she said, the children are mostly too young to read, and there was only the one photo every child stopped to look at many times, as if the person in it might change.

I felt huge and terrible. "Ah, Christ, here, here's my sweater for one of them if they're cold. Tell them the American Army will bring them lots of sweaters, soon."

"Is that true, Lieutenant?" the translator said. "Because this boy wants to know if the American sweaters are going to fall from the sky. He says can we please bring them by train instead."

"Lieutenant? I'd like to give the children this if I may. Maybe they could sell it and raise some money," the Chaplain said. "It's a samurai dagger. I took it from one of the houses we visited earlier."

"That's looting, Chaplain, for Christ's sake."

"Looting's what they do. For me it's a war souvenir, you know, a trophy," Chaplain Savage said.

"Chaplain, time for you to shut the hell up," I said.

"Same to you, Lieutenant. You're starting to really piss me off, son."

"It is very possible I feel the same way about you," I said. "Now goddammit, translator, ask the man what he really needs."

"He says he would like a bigger wagon, please."

THE TRANSLATOR EXPLAINED during the 1923 Tokyo earthquake, people dove into rivers to escape the fires in the aftermath, but since they could not swim, most drowned. Learning to swim was then made part of the standard school curriculum, and the government built pools outside most public schools. He said it would make sense for children to have gone to such places for safety, and suggested we have a look.

"HEY SIR, THAT POOL, the one the translator guy told us was here?" the Corporal said. "I checked it out like you said to. It looks like a bunch o' kids were in it, but they got, well, boiled, sir. The bodies alongside the pool are black like everywhere, but inside the pool they're more kinda pink. Look like department store mannequins, 'cause most of them was all still kind of standing. It was so crowded, I think they ended up leaning against each other."

As I turned away, the Corporal followed me.

"Hey, sir, um, Lieutenant Hooper?" the Corporal said. "You got a second? I'm sort of wondering, maybe what we've seen is sort of the bad parts, you know, the worst. There's not stuff like this everywhere, right?"

"I don't know, Corporal. This was a big city, maybe a million people. Probably a lot more around like we've seen," I said.

"You mean there might be hundreds of more kids who look like that?"

"Thousands."

"See, I'm not sure anymore," the Corporal said. "When the Japs were shooting at us, it was pretty clear, you know, sir? I guess I just thought it'd be different, that's all."

"So what do you think, are we good guys or bad guys?" I said.

"We're just soldiers, sir, following orders," the Corporal said. "Don't let us off too easy."

I LOOKED AT THESE people, the Japanese. They weren't fighting over food, they weren't looting, they hadn't gone feral like you'd have expected. We were not going to break these people with bombs. We could kill them or force them to do what we wanted, but we were never going to really win. They owned their own hearts and minds and some free food wasn't gonna change that.

Before Kyoto, I'd been told we had killed 110,000 people, made a million more homeless and burnt down a quarter of a city in one night of firebombing over Tokyo, the greatest death toll in a single act in the history of human warfare. *Stars and Stripes* did a couple of pictorial stories on it.

I realized standing there we had no strategy for victory other than simply to keep fighting. Our mission was not to take terrain or seize positions. There was nothing in Kyoto we wanted to capture, no fortress, no strategic hill. It was just killing.

"LET'S TAKE FIVE," I said. "You, Private Garner, what the hell are you doing?"

"Throwing away the crap I don't like from these K-rations. I hate the crackers, sir, too dry without a lot of water and then I just gotta pee," Private Garner said.

"Did you see that? Some little kid just ran out and grabbed them crackers. Throw him something else, see what he does," one of the men said.

"There ya' go, kiddo. Hey, Garner, you got a light?"

"Here you go. And hey, careful where you throw the butt. Don't wanna start another fire around here," Private Garner said.

"Them jokes ain't so funny no more, Garner."

"Hey, Jap kid, look here, you know what this is? It's chocolate. Cho-co-late. Tell him, translator."

"I do not think he can speak," the translator said. "I have asked him several questions earlier but he does not answer."

"Tell him to nod his head if he wants the chocolate," another soldier said. "Ah ha, see, now that worked. Little bastard wants it. Here ya go, kid, a whole Hershey bar, courtesy of your Uncle Sammy."

"See if he'll talk now. Ask him where his parents are," a soldier said.

"Hey, stop it. The little bastard grabbed my lighter," Garner said.

"Let him have it. Ask him again, about what happened to his parents."

"Oh Jesus, he's holding the lighter to his own hand, that's his goddamn skin burning, stop him," Garner said.

"He is speaking now. He says 'My parents, that is what happened to them,'" the translator said.

AS THE PHOTOGRAPHERS WERE packing their gear, a thick kind of rain started, a real Noah, dropping in long, heavy needles, coating us and everything around us with some kind of black goo. The bomb damage assessment fella, Rand, said following a big firebombing, hot ashes rose, cooled, mixed with rain, and fell. Black rain, he called it, even though it turned the pavement silver in the light.

Private Garner, the one who hated crackers and lost the lighter to the little boy, began screaming, saying over and over again "Get it off me, get it off me. It's people, get it off me."

Garner was the sanest person left in our party.

Chapter 5: The Battle for Private Garner

Lieutenant Nathaniel Hooper: Japan, Outside Kyoto, Behind American Lines, 1946

"LIEUTENANT? LIEUTENANT HOOPER? HEY, sir, I'm Private First Class Wintergreen. Major Moreland wants to congratulate you and your men on your damn fine heroic mission into Kyoto after the firebombing, so Captain Christiansen said you gotta be at the command tent in 30 minutes."

I tried to wipe away the soot from around my eyes, and spat out some of the filth that had gunked up in my mouth. It was hard not to think what Private Garner had said: they were inside me now.

"Captain Christiansen said you'd need the 30 minutes to wash up first. Captain Christiansen said you'd be all covered in crap after your mission and the Major wouldn't care for that shit. Captain Christiansen himself told me to say that to you."

I muttered something obscene.

"Captain Christiansen said the same thing, sir. You know, we got the General coming up tomorrow and Major Moreland heard from Captain Christiansen that the General's orderly said he likes hard-boiled eggs. He made Captain Christiansen send half the battalion out to buy up any eggs the Jap farmers have been hoarding. Word travels fast and we've already run up the price of eggs like 200 percent so the Japs are hungry because they can't afford to buy eggs only we can. Every farmer that's got a live hen left is tickling her cootie trying to pull out one more egg for us. I already told Captain Christiansen that. Then Captain Christiansen said 'nuts.'"

Lieutenant Nathaniel Hooper: Japan, Outside Kyoto, Behind American Lines, Major Moreland's Command Tent, 1946

"LIEUTENANT HOOPER, PLEASE COME in, bring your men in. Get out of this horrible rain. Who ever knew rain to feel greasy? You know it also rained on the battlefield at Agincourt," Major Moreland said like that was somewhere near us. He had the first pictures *Stars and Stripes* published out of the wreckage of Kyoto tacked up all around this tent. Had a couple *Stripes* had given him privately, ones they thought might be too much for the folks at home. He'd tacked those up, too. Chaplain Savage's stolen samurai dagger was on the desk. Major Moreland made a point of telling us the Chaplain had presented it to him.

"Begging the Major's pardon and all, but we'd just as soon get back to the medical tent and see to Private Garner, sir," one of the soldiers said. "He's still over there screaming. Sir."

"Wounded man, Lieutenant?" Major Moreland said.

"He had a tough day in Kyoto. We all did, sir." I turned toward the men. "Hey, everybody, sit the hell down. Major's gonna address us. Garner'll still be screaming after we're done here."

"Thank you, Lieutenant, I'm sure he will. I have great confidence in your men," Major Moreland said. "Lieutenant, I want to commend you again for your personal bravery. I've put you in for a commendation. I've got Captain Christiansen writing it up myself. You may never do anything this important again in your entire life. You should be proud."

There was a lot of stir starting among the men behind me.

"May we get over to the hospital if we're all done here?" I said.

"Now, I've spoken to the bomb damage assessment man, nice fella named Rand, and the reporters from *Stars and Stripes*, and they all were pleased, damn pleased, with what they saw inside what's left of the city. And no looting. Outstanding. Chaplain was a bit shaken up, but he'll be okay, probably the Spam from the chow hall disagreeing with him again. *C'est la guerre*, eh? Speaking of food, I've ordered ice cream sent up from Division HQ just for you gentlemen, as a small token of my thanks. Chocolate, vanilla and I think they even found some strawberry. It'll be waiting for you as soon as we're done here." Major Moreland looked pleased with his decision on the ice cream. "I guess we really whooped them in Kyoto, eh?"

"Yes, sir, they got really whooped. You could certainly say that, sir," I said.

"You know, it was one of our own great leaders, General George C. Marshall, I believe, who said, 'War should not be prolonged an hour longer than is absolutely necessary,' but I think he'd make an exception in Kyoto's case. How about that, fellas?" the Major said.

"Any chance the goddamn Major could finish this some other goddamn time?" one of the men said from the back of the tent.

"Oh, I understand, all full of vim and vigor, eh? Had I ever been in combat, I imagine I'd feel the same way. I am reminded of what an ancient wrote: 'Go tell the Spartans, thou who passest by, that here, obedient to their laws, we lie.' That's a quote from the monument to the 300 Spartans who died at Thermopylae. Name means gates of hell or something like that. You are now in their fraternity."

"Hey Major, I don't feel like a Spartan, I feel like a ghoul," one of the soldiers said.

"Son, I understand. Heraclitus believed strife in war was man's dominant and creative force. You're in good company, young man," Major Moreland said.

"You know, that's just swell. But, Major, I got a question," one of the men said. "Major, why the fuck is your uniform clean?"

"Son?"

"Why didn't you watch a fucking kid set himself on fucking fire today? Why the fuck aren't you in the goddamn fucking medical tent screaming like Garner?" a soldier said.

"Well, I'll be damned," the Major said.

"Won't we all," the soldier said.

I dismissed the whole group before a riot started, and they ran for the door, as glad to leave as I was to see them go.

"Lieutenant, thank you for clearing that up. I guess our men, well, maybe they're still a bit keyed up," Major Moreland said. We were alone. "Say, Hooper, a quick word, between us old troopers, eh?" He walked me out of the tent, hand on my arm. "I understand you may have seen a few things in Kyoto, shall we say, out of context. Let's let the press handle that properly, and let the rest be our little secret."

"Sure, Major. Our secret. But don't the Japs already know?" I said. The city covered 300 square miles.

"Oh, it isn't that kind of secret. I mean secret from, you know, well, maybe more of a concealment than a real secret. Morale and all," Moreland said. He let go of my arm. "And be sure to get some ice cream. I went through a lot of trouble to get it for you."

"I gotta see Private Garner," I said.

"Oh right, the wounded fellow. Maybe the Chaplain could help. Should I send him over after he gets out of the latrine?"

Lieutenant Nathaniel Hooper: Japan, Outside Kyoto, Behind American Lines, Medical Tent, 1946

AFTER FAILING JONES AT NISHINOMIYA, I was here in the medical tent for Garner.

"Doctor Klein, I'm Lieutenant Hooper. We met before I went into Kyoto? The malaria pills? The Private over there, he's one of mine."

"The one bleeding to death or the one screaming?"

"Private Garner, Doc," I said. Klein's face didn't change; mine did. "The one screaming."

"Lieutenant, if you're upset, I can call Chaplain Savage for you," Doctor Klein said.

"I'm worried about Private Garner," I said. No sign of recognition from the Doc. "The screaming one."

"Oh, right. Lucky for him. Because the other one's going to die soon from internal bleeding. Garner is likely to just be insane for the rest of his life, mind torn apart and all that. His body's in terrific shape, not a scratch. But the question isn't so much why Private Garner is screaming. It's why we aren't, Lieutenant," Doctor Klein said. He fumbled with some medical instruments on the table between us. "If he had a bullet in him, I could pull it out. I could issue him more malaria pills, for Christ's sake; see, I do remember you. But I can't do much about the war now, can I? Really gets its teeth into you."

"Doc, what are you going to do?" I said.

"I think we'll keep him here for a few days, see if he somehow recovers. Who knows, maybe he'll be hit by lightning, too. If not, we'll have to ship him to the rear with all the other stuff we can't use anymore."

We were interrupted by someone needing something signed by Doc Klein. He seemed to have to do a lot of that as part of saving lives. I shifted my weight a bit, more to hide my impatience than to stretch my muscles. It was then I realized the floor was sticky. The Japs had made a lot of holes in boys.

"Can't you give Garner something, I don't know, like morphine, to quiet him down?" I said.

"Morphine is for wounded men. Garner is just insane."

"Isn't that wounded?" I said.

"Indeed, it used to be, indeed it did," Doctor Klein said. "Then there were too many wounded men, so we had to change the definition to statistically reduce the suffering. Besides, Garner went insane because of what he saw in Kyoto. Curing him means I'd have to convince him seeing the burned children he's shouting about was not a reason to be insane."

"But Garner is still wounded under the old rules, you admitted it. Like that man next to him bleeding to death internally," I said.

"But that is a clear case. He is definitely wounded. There are tests," Doctor Klein said.

"Okay, Doc. How about when the man dying from internal bleeding dies, can Garner have his morphine?" I said.

"Lieutenant, I want to help, I really do. How about when the bleeding man dies, in the gap before the next real wounded man arrives, I give his unused morphine to Garner? That seems fair."

"Doctor, excuse me," a nurse interrupted. "The one they brought in yesterday, the chest wound? I'm afraid he's passed on, sir. Sign here."

"So Doc, can Garner have that man's morphine?" I said.

"Sorry Lieutenant, that wasn't our deal. Garner waits for the internally bleeding man to die. No special treatment."

"Does it bother you to be so casual about seeing men die?" I said.

"Let me ask you a question, Lieutenant, since you have this all down," Doctor Klein said. "Is the morphine for Garner so he stops screaming, or is the morphine for you so that you don't have to hear him screaming? He probably feels better screaming."

"Doc, what are you doing here?" I said.

"Just my job. Following orders." Doctor Klein said. "Lieutenant, do you think Garner is frightened of dying any more?"

"No, Doc, I think he's probably more frightened of living at this point," I said.

"Wait a moment, would you please? Yes, can I help you? Who are you, son?"

"Sorry to interrupt, Doc. I'm Major Moreland's orderly, Private First Class Wintergreen. Can you tell me which one's Garner?"

"He's the one screaming. We were just wrapping that up. Why do you ask?" Doctor Klein said.

"Major Moreland sent me over with his strawberry ice cream. Can I leave it here? It's starting to melt."

Chapter 6: For Her

Lieutenant Nathaniel Hooper: Japan, Kyoto, 1946

AFTER THE FIREBOMBING, WORD came down we'd be relocating north of what was left of Kyoto, mopping up as MacArthur made the final push into Tokyo. Intelligence reported a few remnants of the Japanese Army around us. Their resistance wasn't coordinated; they maybe just didn't know what else to do, so they kept fighting.

After burning an entire city of people to ash, two days later we were now to become the good guys, all with an eye toward "winning the peace." A new order came down on minimizing civilian casualties, and even on trying to talk the Japanese soldiers into surrendering if we could. Swell. I wondered if the Japanese could remake their image of us as fast as we expected them to, but orders were orders.

I was learning it is harder to finish wars than to start them. This all was more stubborn than I was, and was not going to let me quit. Getting through what seemed like the last days alive, without having to kill anyone, and without getting any more of my men killed, was exactly the strategy I wished I'd been pursuing from the moment I got my feet wet at Ashiya Beach. I wondered where the last man to die in this war was right now.

Though there was still a grubby blanket of white left, and it was too early to declare spring, you could believe it was out there on an afternoon like this, the peace like an acorn under the snow. We'd been ordered to an old temple north of Kyoto the firebombing had somehow missed. Americans had been killed in the area, sniper fire. We were supposed to clear the temple, killing, capturing, cheering up or resettling as refugees whoever was inside, depending on how things worked out. It'd become a helluva war.

"I don't see why we don't just call down some arty and get it done. I'm hungry," said one soldier.

"We're trying to win over what the brass are now calling 'hearts and minds,'" I said.

"Well and good, sir, but I say grab 'em by the balls and their hearts and minds will follow."

"Somebody needs to tell the Japs about our new strategy. They're still playing by the old rules," a second soldier said. "The scouts reported a guy with a rifle in there, maybe a second Jap, too."

"Yeah, this war sure is all over. It's all over this goddamn temple."

"Translator, over here, with your megaphone," I said. "Convey this: 'I am Lieutenant Hooper of the United States Army. Come out of the temple with your hands up.'"

Nothing.

"Okay, let's try it again. Tell 'em this, translator: 'Lay down your weapons. Your war is over. You have fought well and suffer no disgrace.'"

"You really want me to say that last part, Lieutenant? I mean, I had a buddy killed on Iwo. It isn't right to kiss up to the Jappers," the translator said. He was a new guy, an American soldier who spoke some of the language, anxious along with the rest of them to get this over. They were horses all smelling the barn now, and had no interest in racing.

There was a single shot, way high over our heads.

"Aw, dammit, sir, they just shot at us. That enough of a not disgraceful response for you?" the translator said.

There was movement at the temple; someone without a uniform, no weapon, emerging from a side door. I knew this kind of thing was gonna happen and I dreaded it. Civilians again. Then, we all saw it clearly enough. There was a white cloth, held by a mouse of a Japanese woman.

I wouldn't need the translator. I went forward myself.

SHE HADN'T CHANGED MUCH, and she had changed.

"I heard your voice," Naoko said.

"Good Christ, why are you here?" I said. "It's Sergeant Nakagawa inside shooting, isn't it?"

"Eichi does not want to kill you. He wants you to kill him," Naoko said. "He cremated his parents the same night the Americans burned Kyoto. He said the small fire would be overlooked. He said they were not supposed to die before he did. He was prepared to kill himself, then stopped and said he would first claim as many Americans as he could. He shot seven these past two days."

"Jesus God. Why here?" I said.

"If listen, you can hear voices in the stone and wood of this place. It has withstood every earthquake, every typhoon, and every bomb. The people see it as a symbol and, well, he and I had also been here before..." Naoko paused and looked at the photo she had with her. She held it tightly by the edges, turning her finger tips white.

"Hooper-san, he shot only to provoke you. You know the bullet came nowhere near hitting anyone. When Eichi understood it was you, he convinced himself if he could die by a soldier I respected, that would be a proper way to conclude his life. He does not think you would be killing him; he thinks you will be saving him. I am not sure if he knows what he is doing anymore, but I told him I would convey his request for you to destroy him."

"Naoko, tell Sergeant Eichi Nakagawa he must give me one minute to speak with him. If he won't do that, I'll leave him in there alive to suffer until hell freezes over."

"Hooper-san, why are you doing this for him?" Naoko said.

"I'm doing it for you."

Lieutenant Nathaniel Hooper: Japan, Kyoto, Inside the Temple, 1946

"ARE YOU HERE, LIEUTENANT Hooper, to offer me an American chocolate bar? Some nylons, perhaps?" Nakagawa said. As she had done days ago at the house, Naoko stood between us, translating every word. They all were important now.

"Come out with me, Nakagawa. Your war is over. You don't have any obligation to kill yourself, and neither do I."

"I, I, I, when you say it that word disgusts me. Obligation is not about what we want," Nakagawa said. "Unnatural vices are forced on us, are they not, as Naoko always said."

"Sergeant Nakagawa, How can we stop this?" I said. I looked at Naoko.

"We can't. What you believe is fanaticism, Lieutenant Hooper, is instead what matters most. If I was in the winning army I would get a medal for believing that."

Nakagawa's eyes met Naoko's. A decision had wordlessly been made. He turned toward her, and closed his eyes. "I see the drops of water on your skin from that day we swam in the river. I saw an old man burned to death for a mistake an American pilot never knew he made. People who should have comforted me instead gave me this rifle. You do not write poetry after such molestation, you molest. Naoko, I am sorry."

"It is my turn to keep the photo, until spring, but I am... unsure... I shall be able to return it to you then," Naoko said. "Here."

"No. Please hand it to me in my next life, and in my life after that, and in the one after that. It will be like the past the way we remember it, not the way we were made to live it."

"Eichi, let us be together," Naoko said.

"We will. It will just take a long time," Nakagawa said.

He shifted his rifle. His hand worked the bolt back and forth, his finger slipping on and off the trigger. It was only me that didn't yet know how this would end.

"Nakagawa, why didn't you kill me back at Naoko's house?" I said.

"For her," Nakagawa said. "Lieutenant Hooper, why didn't you kill me then?"

"For her," I said. "And you could've killed me out there, or in here, but you didn't. Why?"

"For her."

"I must leave, Sergeant Eichi Nakagawa," I said.

"Lieutenant Hooper, you both must leave," Nakagawa said.

He paused.

"For her."

WHEN NAOKO AND I reached American lines a moment later, I sent her off with the Corporal. I looked back, hoping the temple might not still be there.

"Hey Lieutenant, I got battalion artillery on the horn, all cocked and locked. Sergeant back there says we're doing them a favor with this fire mission, says they're overstocked on napalm. Says it's time for a fire sale, Lieutenant, get it, a fire sale? Hey Lieutenant, what should we do? Lieutenant?"

"Have them shoot off a colored smoke round. Verify the target," I said.

"Sir, they already have the precise grid coordinates – "

"Tell 'em to fire a smoke round, goddammit," I said.

"Roger. There it is, sir. Dead on. That's... dead… on."

"Have them fire another smoke," I said.

"Lieutenant, any more spot on and the damn round'll go right through the window."

"One more smoke," I said. "Private, any sign of movement out of the temple?"

"Nope."

"Any white flag?" I said.

"Nope."

"Check again," I said.

"No. Nothing. He ain't gonna surrender, they never do. Bastards act like they own the damn place. So, yes or no, sir? What should we do, Lieutenant Hooper?"

Before Kyoto, The Battle for Naoko's House

Chapter 7: Smoldering

Lieutenant Nathaniel Hooper: Japan, Inside the Destroyed Nishinomiya Train Station, 1946

PRIVATE ALDEN JONES OPENED his eyes.

"Lieutenant? Where are we? Are we dead?"

"Not quite. Still in Japan, Jonesy," I said.

"Where's Smitty? Polanski? Sergeant Laabs?"

"Dead. Jonesy, they're all dead. Just us now. The Japs must have pulled back to Kyoto."

Jones was in bad shape. A bit of poking revealed he couldn't feel much in the one leg, while the other hurt like hell. Wiping a bit of the goo away, I could see the flesh around the wound was blackened. In addition to the leg wound, something was wrong with his knee. It had swelled, and when I put my hand on it, the bone fragments felt like a bunch of marbles moving around, little bits of a disaster going on in there.

"That hurt, Jones?" I said.

"Yes, sir, a lot more now with your hand on it," Jones said. "What kind of blood do you see, Lieutenant Hooper? And don't lie to me, sir, I'll know."

"What do you mean by 'kind of blood?'" I said.

"I grew up around livestock, see, and we'd slaughter the animals," Jones said. "My dad would tell us the pumping kind of blood meant the animal would be dead quick. The oozing kind meant you'd missed the vein with the knife. Which one do I got?" Jones said.

"It's not pumping. There's a helluva a lot of blood, but it's kinda oozing," I said.

"That's the good kind," Jones said. "Lieutenant, down there, between my legs, I didn't lose my..."

"No, Jonesy, nothing vital."

"Pretty much everything down there is kinda vital, sir."

"Jones, those Oklahoma girls still have a lot to look forward to. You keep warm, and I'll have a look around. Think you can handle that?" I said.

"I think so, as long as the blood's the good kind," Jones said.

"I wouldn't lie to you, Jones."

OH, I LIED TO Jones.

His blood blossomed up fresh every time I wiped some away, a blurp that swelled and broke, his heart working now mostly to push more life out of him. I started this war with a disadvantage, coming from a world where blowing chunks out of farm boys' thighs didn't happen. I didn't understand how this all worked. I didn't understand how valves, airplanes or carburetors worked either, but no one had ever asked me to stop one from bleeding out. I worried I was just too soft and ignorant for my real mission: I was going to keep Private Alden Jones alive.

I crept out of the Nishinomiya train station, following the path back in time, past the dead Sergeant Laabs, past the other stiffened men's bodies. Outside was like leaving a matinée, the light sharp as a librarian's chewing out. The sky blinded me, an unfair blue. I thought I heard a shout in Japanese at one point, but then it was quiet again. Nothing moved but the small swirls of wind-blown snow. There were many dead birds, they being especially susceptible to the mortar shells' concussions.

The human dead were on the ground in front of the station, also having been susceptible to the mortar shells. Those boys were now left like things people dropped leaving a ballgame in a hurry, and had never gone back for and now nobody would. The snow only obscenely covered them, leaving hands and legs exposed. Some must have been Japanese, some American, though they were all now the same ivory color. Every muscle hurt on me, and when I walked, the ground moved like I was on a boat. The path straight across the field, the route we took in the night of the battle for Nishinomiya, was direct, but I went the long way to not step on the frozen brown that scabbed the snow. My boots crunched hard on the gravel. The lives of a thousand men were behind me. There was a Japanese house in the near distance. I walked forward.

Chapter 8: Sparks

Lieutenant Nathaniel Hooper: Japan, Nishinomiya, Outside a House, 1946

UNLIKE THE ONES I'D seen destroyed days ago in the village, this house was intact. A bit of smoke coming out of the chimney. I'd gone back for Jones. The walk over had not done anything good for him. I helped him aim his rifle at the house door.

"You ready, Jones? If I run into trouble, fire everything you can at the guy who takes me down. And hang on. This is gonna turn out to be one of those million-dollar wounds for you. It'll be all strawberry ice cream and sweet young nurses for you back in the world."

"Don't know about the million dollar wound thing, sir. Feels more like a buck and a quarter right now."

"You keep the change, Jonesy. Okay, here we go."

I PROPPED JONES UP inside the Jap house after no one challenged our entry.

It took a second for my eyes to adjust to the dim light. The house was fragile, colors only time can give to wood. Sliding screens between the main room and the ones off to the sides, what looked like a kitchen in the back, a rear entrance. Vertical posts holding up the ceiling, one with notches carved into it and what I'd guess were dates and some kid's name. Kind of a big bath in another room. Straw mats on the floor, worn in the centers, but they were clean for something that looked like a pile of sticks.

There was a single kerosene lamp burning; a moth was trapped inside making a moving shadow. Still, I'd have needed a flashlight to see all the way into the far corners of the room. I could see an awkward desk, big for the room. It was piled high with books and a chess set. There were some ghosts of old cooking. It was the kind of house that should have stunk of cat, but instead really smelled of yellowing paper, like in the stacks at the agricultural college library. Back home we'd say the place needed a good airing. The room was otherwise empty, except for the silence.

So neither me nor Jones were ready to hear a rustle of cloth, and see another light deeper inside flare up and then extinguish.

"*Buki wa nai desu. Honto ni nai desu. Korosanaide de. Nan de mo shimasu kara.*"

A mouse of a Jap emerged from the shadows, her hair frayed out in a loose ponytail. She wore a kind of smock over loose pants that were likely blue a lot of washings ago. No shoes, instead, white socks with big toes like mittens. Not any older than me, but even in the dim light I could see lines on her face like the hairline cracks on porcelain.

"You. Speak. English?" I said. I started to lower my rifle, and then stopped.

"Yes, I do. Quite well, in fact. Now, take what you want, but do not hurt me," the Japanese woman said. "And please, put that rifle down."

"Just you here?" I said.

"Now. My father and mother were killed the other night in your attack on the Nishinomiya train station. You will find their bodies wrapped outside. Check if you wish, but please remove your boots. They are soiling my *tatami* mats."

"Boots? No way," I said, "You might make a move. Now, understand there's a wounded man here. Make a place for him to lay down, and boil some water. Tear something up we can use for bandages. He's gonna bleed on your quilts but there's nothing I can do about that, some Jap coward shot him. Clean out his wounds, and we'll take things from there."

"Sir, you gonna let the Jap touch me?" Jones said.

"Soldier –" interrupted the woman.

"I am Lieutenant Nathaniel Hooper, United States Army. You will address me as Lieutenant Hooper, or sir."

"And I am Private Alden Jones, United States Army. Address me, as, um, Alden."

"Jones, shut the hell up," I said.

"And I am Naoko Matsumoto. And I will help, but I am not one of your men and I am certainly not a 'Jap.' I will call you Hooper-san and Jones-san."

"Enough with the cultural lessons, Mama-san, and tend to Jones, what you'd say your name was, Neko? Damn names are hard to say."

"Hey sir, let's call her Jenny, OK?" Jones said.

"No, no, you will call me Naoko. You may shoot me, but you must call me Naoko as you do." Naoko, frowning, fetched up a wet rag, rung it out, and leaned over Jones. "Jones-san, this may hurt. No, my English is bad. This will hurt."

"YOUR JONES-SAN HAS FALLEN asleep. His wounds have gotten worse," Naoko said.

"I can smell them. Is there anywhere around here he can get more help?"

"Your planes bombed the Nishinomiya hospital. I am sure by accident," Naoko said.

"Of course it was by accident. Americans don't do things like that on purpose."

"Hmm. The large red crosses on the roof must have been hard to see," Naoko said.

"Naoko, why won't your people stop trying to kill us and let this war end, so accidents like that don't have to happen?" I said.

"Because you are trying to kill us," Naoko said. "And our hospitals."

"That's only because you started killing us first. Pearl Harbor," I said.

"Eye for an eye, yes, then everyone ends this war blind."

"Why are you people fighting, Naoko?"

"For the Emperor, we are told."

"That's caused you to do terrible things. You beheaded prisoners who couldn't defend themselves," I said.

"Like firebombing people who could not defend themselves?" Naoko said.

"That's different. It's part of war, allowed under the rules, the law even," I said. "You know, justified."

"Hmm. Rules. You come from a land where bombs never fall and then you make such rules and laws about what you can do to others."

"Look, Naoko, once this killing is over, we'll do a lot of good things for you. You'll be safe for once. Japan will become more like America. You'll get some pretty nylons for yourself, we'll build schools, hospitals, and roads, and hand out chocolate to the kids."

"Ah, yes, your chocolate. We are eating roots and dirty rice to survive, and you are carrying candy here all the way from the United States and think nothing of it. Would you prefer that I beg for something to eat, or will you just hand it out to make yourself feel like you are doing good after destroying our country? You Americans, you really do not understand what you are, do you? Clumsy giants. And take your boots off inside this house, Hooper-san."

"Why are you so worried about these straw mats, anyway? Just get some new ones. You'll see here in Japan how things'll work out with us in charge, Naoko."

"Such as with your internment camps? Will you have those for us here in Japan as well, same as for your so-called Japanese-Americans?" Naoko said.

"I don't know much about that, but it was to protect Americans from the Japs, I guess."

"And there won't be Americans to protect here from 'Japs' once you occupy us? Don't stay and pretend to do what you think are good things. Go home," Naoko said.

"Spare me. I'm just the mailman, I deliver the letters. I'm not responsible for what's inside," I said.

"Is that why you fight, Hooper-san? You're a mailman?"

"No. Well, maybe, I'm not so sure, but at least I don't fight for an Emperor."

"So do you fight for your President Harry S. Truman?"

"Of course not," I said. Maybe I was less sure than I wanted to sound. "Maybe I fight for our flag."

"For a piece of cloth?"

"No, not a piece of cloth. Haven't you seen pictures of the Marines raising the flag on Iwo Jima, Naoko? That flag is a symbol," I said.

"And the Emperor is not?" Naoko said.

"Naoko, this whole thing is to bring you democracy, to free you from tyranny. We're here fighting for your freedom."

"That is funny, Hooper-san, because we are fighting now against you for our freedom."

"YOU CHANGE JONES' BANDAGES?" I said.

"Yes. He did not cry out. He is weak," Naoko said. She told me to give him some water, and when I wasn't sure what to do, showed me how to wring a wet cloth, drop by drop, onto his lips.

"Naoko?"

"Yes? More bandages?"

"No, thanks. I mean, Jones-san, damn it, Jones, he'd say thank you if he could," I said.

MY DREAM OF A faraway warm bed ended with the wood-on-wood clunk as the sliding screen door hit the cedar frame. Naoko's shadow falling across me tore away the last bits of sleep.

"You have been noisy snoring and I am afraid someone outside will hear. Will you see Jones stays comfortable while I make tea?"

Small-town Ohio was not a big place for tea drinking. Tea was at best something tolerated when old ladies served it after church with little cookies. You added milk and sugar so it'd taste like something. Naoko instead filled two bowls with boiling water. She then took a tiny wooden spoon and added a small amount of bright green powder from a ceramic jar. Didn't stir it at all. No milk. No sugar. Just tea that smelled like damp leaves.

The first sip was a surprise; the stuff was bitter as hell and twice as hot. When I could feel my tongue again, I realized this was the kind of situation my mother would have said called for polite conversation, so I tried.

"How is it you speak English so good?" I said.

"It is 'how is it you speak English so well.' My father taught me from childhood. I may have been speaking English longer than you have, Hooper-san. He was a professor at Kobe University. A civilized man. It was so different, we were so unprepared for what followed. Back then mother played piano and I sang while my father hid behind his newspaper trying to watch me without me seeing him do it. He taught English, real English, poetry and plays."

"Those his books on the desk?" I said.

"The dusty ones. The others are mine. It is a kind of diversion for me, thinking about beautiful words. Do you know Walt Whitman? He was an American poet who wrote about your Civil War. He was very enthusiastic about at first, but was changed by the horrors he saw in the field hospitals. Whitman was a favorite of my father."

"What happened, I mean, before your dad was killed?" I said.

"As the war became all we knew in Japan, there was little need for western poetry, and most of the students were called to join the military anyway. Father and I were then conscripted ourselves. Can you imagine someone risking their life to deliver a newspaper? But our spies in the U.S. would do that, to pass

American newspapers through a long chain of hands back to Japan, to my father and me to translate. The military believed by understanding your politics, they could anticipate your war strategy. I translated article after article about debates in Congress over how many men to draft, about budgets, arguments among lawmakers over whether to favor the European or the Pacific War. Sitting in that small office with my father, we joked we were the best informed people in Japan."

Naoko paused. More tea.

"The only good of it all was that our work was seen as important, so we qualified for the best food. We would smuggle out bits of meat to share with the neighbors. Mother loved her books, father his poetry and his chess. They were better people then than we have become."

"Did you say chess? American chess?" I said.

"Well, the western version of chess, yes. I think it is still one of the few things you Americans have not claimed to have given to the world," Naoko said. There was the set, the pawns and knights on the board, black, and white, the paint worn off the tops of each piece.

"At first I did not realize father let me win and that mother was pretending when she would make fun of his 'losses.' I miss them both now, very much. No matter, anyway, it will be light soon. I must wash my hands and make the rice for breakfast."

"You haven't really said how they died."

"They were killed by a stray mortar round." Naoko brushed aside a tear before her face hardened. "Like every child, I always feared losing my parents. Now they are gone, killed by someone unforgiven. I do not even know who did it or why. I doubt he knows he killed them or why. Hooper-san, look at my hands. They are stained only with your Jones-san's blood. I can make them clean. Your soldiers killed my family. You cannot wash that away, ever. This whole terrible war, all I have done is translate old newspaper articles."

"You translated the sports pages? The funny papers? How's Orphan Annie doing?" I said.

"Do not mock me. I could not refuse orders. My superiors wanted those stories so they could better defend Japan," Naoko said.

"Defend Japan," I said.

"So my father deserved to die, is that what you are saying, Hooper-san? Are your parents wrapped in quilts in the back garden? If they are not, quiet yourself, Lieutenant Hooper of the United States Army. Or go outside, and tell your tales to the dead until you feel better about what you have done. But fine. We are practical people. If you want me to cook for you, here, cut the rotten bits out of these potatoes. We will have them with the rice."

"You cut up the potatoes. That's woman's work," I said.

"It is only woman's work if you can get a woman to do it," Naoko said. "We all need to do different things now. As you say in English, 'don't you know there is a war on?'"

She had the taste of a smile for the first time. I removed my boots for the first time. And picked up a potato.

Lieutenant Nathaniel Hooper: Japan, Naoko's House, 1946

I COULD SEE IT now, like the fireflies we used to catch when I was a boy in Ohio. They'd go into a jar, the air would get used up and their lights would go out. I knew what was coming, even if they didn't. It wasn't really blood draining out of him anymore, it was time.

"Lieutenant? Am I gonna die?"

"Nah, I don't think so, Jones. Hey, I even saw you looking at Naoko. Jeez boy, leave some clothes on her," I said.

"I wasn't tryin' to be rude, I just wanted to... to remember what a girl looked like," Jones said. "Besides, sir, I seen you looking the same way at her. Hey, you wanna see a picture I carry with me?"

With much difficulty Jones put his left hand in his pocket and brought out a little leather wallet. It had thick stitches around the edges, and was embossed with some Western scene. You could buy them anywhere back home, cheap as spit.

"See sir, I don't have a girl. I sorta pretended about 'Jenny' around the fellas so they didn't make fun of me. Look, sir, it's me, in the picture. See, that's me when I was eight, wearing a cowboy hat. And that's a real pony. But it's a toy gun."

"Can't be you, Jones, cute kid like that," I said.

"It is, honest. See, my mom wrote the date on the back and everything," Jones said, smiling with his eyes. "Um, Lieutenant, I'm feeling really dizzy."

"What should I do?" I said.

"Can you call me Alden for a while, sir?"

"Okay, Alden. You're from Oklahoma, right?"

"Tulsa. Well, near there. Sir, I'm getting cold."

He was hard to hear, whispering now, but not because he wanted to. I don't think I'd ever been that close to a man's face before. I saw soft hairs above his lip, the kind you have for a few years before you need to shave.

"You much for praying, Alden?"

"Sometimes, sir. Not sure God always listens," Jones said.

"He'll hear you," I said. I looked to Naoko.

"If God listened, I don't think I'd be like this now," Jones said. He looked away. "I wanna be older. I got a dog at home older than me."

Former Lieutenant Nathaniel Hooper: Retirement Home, Kailua, Hawaii, 2017

I SQUEEZED HIS HAND 70 years ago.

We each owe God one death, somebody wrote, and Jones paid his tab. I did not cry. There would be other deaths. I was made solemn by this.

Naoko touched my hand, and her fingers guided me to close Jones' eyes. I lifted him, leaving his indentation on the quilt. It is Japanese custom, Naoko said, to wash the body, so Jones would go to whatever afterlife he was destined for clean, the way he came in to the world; we cry at both ends of life, she said. She tried to undo the buttons of his uniform, but it was difficult, so I used my jackknife to cut off the layers of GI-issue wool. I pressed too hard at one point, and nicked his skin, which still drew blood; Jones had not yet turned that drained gray they do. Without thinking, I said, "Sorry, Jones."

It was then I cried. I cried for Jones, I cried for Marino, I cried for Polanski, I cried for Laabs, I cried for goddamn all of them.

Something that started deep and only found its way out as a sound I never knew was there, rage, not sorrow. At one point it had gotten easier to watch men die, but now it had gotten harder. I should've been crying for them when they were still alive but I thought time would always be there.

There had been so many futures and none of them would ever happen now. That was what I was responsible for. Time ended for the dead, but stretched out all to hell for those unfinished lives, the place where a father sits with his cigar poking an orange hole in the dark, where a wife wearing a man's t-shirt cries dreams of slow dancing with her husband again in the kitchen.

They're not necessarily people I'd have chosen to know, and I didn't cry because I missed them. I had no idea whether they were good people back in real life. I didn't want to make them all into something other than whatever they were, and then weep for that. I cried because I was there and they were dead and I was less sure than I was a day earlier why that happened.

Naoko was gentle. She directed me to wrap Jones in the quilt he'd lain on. It was still warm. We placed his body outside, with her parents, and Jones would be cremated alongside her own. The town held the bodies until the skies looked overcast enough that they could risk a fire without the American planes zeroing in. The pilots wouldn't know they were bombing people already dead.

The fire will do away with their bodies, Naoko said, and give their souls to the wind.

Chapter 9: Smoke

Lieutenant Nathaniel Hooper: Japan, Naoko's House, 1946

THE COLD AIR RUSHED in from the dark ahead of Naoko. I watched the last bits of snow melt against her hair as she returned from seeing the cremation fire take her parents, and my soldier.

"We believe 'Although the form of a flower has scattered, its scent lingers on,'" Naoko said, as much to the house itself as me. "Your Jones-san is at peace. No one knew he was not Japanese; the dead belong to no one. The ceremony was quick, not what we normally do, but this is war, and as a poet my father enjoyed wrote, unnatural vices are forced on us. Still, it was almost beautiful, the orange embers rising into the night sky. They reminded me of the fireflies I saw as a child over the rice paddies those summers ago."

NAOKO CAME BACK FROM the kitchen with a ceramic flask of *sake* she had warmed in a hot water bath. She was almost embarrassed to be seen drinking, she said, but explained the rice wine had belonged to her father, and it seemed good something of his was comforting her now. The cups were small, smooth on the inside and rough and unglazed on the outside. The *sake* tasted sweet to me, not like any of the liquor I'd had before. It was warm all the way into my belly, and even more so as it filled my head.

"What will you do after the war, Naoko?" I said. There was something deep in the back of my mind I was trying to find against the pull of the sake.

"What after? Your war ends when go home. Your mother has kept your room tidy for you, has she not? You will just walk through the door and throw your war pay on the bed. Your dog is there, safe in his own small house, yes? This is not even real for you, Hooper-san," Naoko said.

"But you'll be at peace."

"There will be no more bombs, yes. But our men will become black marketeers living off your discarded cans of food, and our women will sell themselves to survive. Already in the marketplace we are hearing a new word, *pansuke*, a terrible name for the women who are willing to go with the American soldiers; even among prostitutes there will be a new depth of disgrace. This all will leave scars that need much time to heal, long after you are eating meatloaf and your awful mashed potatoes and gravy again. I hope I have the strength to survive the peace alone."

"Alone? You won't get married once this is all over?" I said.

"Hooper-san, how much more American could you be, talking about that at a time like this?" Naoko said. She set her cup down in a way that made the question into an exclamation.

The *sake* fumes in my head cleared. I knew now what that thought was I'd been trying to catch. Someone can get used to mashed potatoes and gravy, can't she?

Her voice sounded different too, as if she had found something sweet tucked in her cheek by surprise. "You have been in love, Hooper-san?"

"Maybe," I said. "Yes."

"Living in fear, it was easier to forget a past ever existed. But having sent my parents on, perhaps I can make myself feel better by talking. So what is the girl's name, the one you 'maybe' love, Hooper-san? Is she a chubby girl from Ohio?"

"Her name is... not important now. And it doesn't take that much time to fall in love, right, when you know you're in love?" I said.

In the pause she refilled both of our cups. As I sipped from the edge of mine, Naoko drunk deep from the center of hers.

"This war, Hooper-san, it does not allow a broken heart to mend, only tire."

We were seated on the floor, using small cushions pushed close together on the straw mats, my weight now entirely in her world. I had grown comfortable without chairs. Naoko shifted, sitting up, before tucking her hands under her. She was no longer looking at me. It was as if she could see something no one else could inside the cup.

Lieutenant Nathaniel Hooper: Japan, Naoko's House, After Midnight, 1946

"HOOPER-SAN, THIS DAY... it is late, but I must relax. Perhaps a bath. Do you know what a luxury that is? I have not had a hot bath for, well, for I do not remember. It felt selfish earlier to be comfortable. It will mean a lot now. And whenever you last bathed, it was also a long time ago, and we have spent too much time dirtying our hands in the worst of things," she said. "Do you know how our Japanese bath is done? The water will be mercilessly hot, and you slide down until it is up to your chin. When you leave to sleep, you will take the heat with you. Who knows, you may even dream of that girl you are in love with. It is required in Japan for the guest to bathe first. The water is hottest for you, Nathaniel Hooper. Did I ever call you that before? Your first name, Nathaniel? Strange it would come out now. Perhaps it is the *sake*."

My name sounded like she was experimenting with how it felt in her mouth. She wanted then to know why I was named Nathaniel. I explained it was after my father, and that opened the gates for me to tell her what I'd kept to myself. My dad had been a soldier, wounded in World War I, and no matter how much he discouraged me from joining up, I wanted to be him, injuries and all if necessary. When he stood straight, even in his farm clothes, it was as if he was still in uniform. I wanted to look into a mirror and see just that, instead of having to deny the reflection. I wasn't drafted; I entered this war because I wanted to.

It made little sense to her; soldiers in Japan had no choice. She brushed off my confession, saying, "We have a task ahead of us and it is already late. It will take time to heat up enough water. Nathaniel."

AS I PEELED OFF my uniform, sand from the Ashiya Beachhead trickled out from inside pockets. I tried to gather it up and stuff it back in, but it scattered all over the floor. I hadn't been out of my clothes since I'd landed in Japan. My naked body felt unfamiliar to me.

In Japan, you washed outside the tub, sitting on a small stool and dipping a wooden bucket into the hot water to rinse off. There was a drain in the floor. One bit of soap, or one bit of dirt, in the bath ruined the water for the next person. When I was sure I had washed away enough, I slipped in to soak.

With the bathroom's sliding door closed, I could feel the darkness, deep. The cold air brought up towers of steam. The tub was cedar and gave off a scent. The warmth crawled up me, like ivy on a building, pins and needles in my legs, my chest, arms and neck. I knew every drop of water as they wrapped around me, and tasted the air. As my eyes adjusted, the moonlight through the window made the surface of the water black, so I could see only the mountains of my own knees rising out of the sea. The water could keep secrets.

There was a shush of the door as Naoko entered the room. She put a finger to her lips, quieting me before I could draw breath to speak. My chest contracted as if the bath water had turned frigid. She slid the small metal clasp home like a gasp, locking the door against something in the empty house.

Naoko stood still, her face puffy from crying, watching me, waiting for something I couldn't begin to understand. The darkness protected her as she moved deeper into the room. Without a sound, she peeled off the layers she wore against the cold, and sat on the small wooden stool to wash herself. I could make out the curve of her shoulders, the stubborn roundness her buttocks retained despite the lack of food. But as she stood, her ribs betrayed her, standing out in relief. Her skin was translucent without the vitamins her body needed, and her neck showed itself thin as she lifted her hair. She did not speak; we were here together, but we were not.

I had never seen a woman naked, and burned to learn the shape and feel of her. I was perhaps the only serviceman in the history of warfare who was frightened enough by the hygiene lectures to sit out the paid treats of Honolulu. Naoko put down her washcloth, and abandoning the moment's pause, entered the tub. Her legs breaking the surface of the water made ripples, like when a stone is thrown, that crossed the gap between us. The water spilled over the side, looking thick as honey. I felt the sound as it touched the floor and watched it mix with the sand I'd left behind. Hunger had sunken Naoko's breasts and hollowed her belly. She was utterly beautiful.

"*Mo nani mo kamo wakaranaku natte shimattan desu. Tada sabishikute, sabishikute. Watashi wa do yatte ikite ikeba ii no. Tsurakute mune ga harisake soo nan desu.*"

"Hooper-san, I do not know how to say these things in English. Perhaps it is not for us to understand together," Naoko said.

The sound as I lifted my hand out of the water to touch her was unwelcome in the silence. You can't choose what you want, only what you do.

"I felt so many terrible things in this war, I cannot feel any more tonight. I want to cry but I cannot let myself. I want to be alone but I cannot. The rest, I do not know how to say it, we say *ishin denshin*. It too does not translate."

"Try."

"As best I can say is that it means 'what the heart knows' but I think a better way to understand it is that there is much said in silence," Naoko said. "Or maybe it describes a kind of sadness, like you feel as summer is ending, and you want it to last just one more day."

Naoko's sobs were sharp against the frost etched on the outside of the window. The wind was finding a way in, pressing us, something unseeable but very real.

"I think it's snowing outside," I said.

"I cannot see the snow. I could not feel wet even in the rain," Naoko said. She paused. "Shhh now. No more words."

Chapter 10: Fire

Lieutenant Nathaniel Hooper: Japan, Naoko's House, Early Morning, the next to last day, 1946

SOMEONE CONTINUED TO POUND on the door, even as Naoko slid it open. I watched from the kitchen as he shook off the snow. He set his rifle down only long enough to remove his boots. He spoke to Naoko in Japanese.

"Sergeant, I am sorry, but I was only a moment ago asleep," Naoko said. "May I ask, are you from north of Kyoto?"

"Do you mock my stupid country boy's accent? Wait... My God, Naoko? Answer me, or I will know I am still unconscious."

"Yes, yes, yes, Eichi. I never saw you again, I never heard from you. I could not know what happened to you," Naoko said.

"I was sent to the countryside for my safety not long after you moved away, and the war came for all of us," Nakagawa said. "I opened my eyes only an hour ago inside the Nishinomiya train station. I saw Corporal Takagi's dead body stuck to mine. I have no idea how long I had been out, but glancing at Takagi's frog-belly white face it had been some time. I could feel pain, so knew I was alive, very much so. I needed to find better shelter en route back to Japanese Army lines, and saw this house... and you. But wait, I believe I have something I am obligated to return. I have carried it a long way."

"It is my turn, is it not, Eichi? You kept the photo of us much longer than our arrangement said you should," Naoko said.

"I have no excuse. But, my manners. Your parents, are they well? The Professor? Your dear mother?" Nakagawa said.

"This war, as you said, came for all of us. But now, Eichi, there is a small amount of tea left, and today is a day one saves things for. We have much to talk about."

It grew quiet. I stayed hidden. The screech whistle of the tea kettle scared the hell out of me.

"Naoko, when we last saw one another, I was not sure of my feelings. Yet in each difficult moment since I have looked at our photo, and gained the strength to know I have lived this long to be here. Wait. Naoko, why is there an American rifle by the desk there? Is everything…"

Hearing the man's voice in Japanese change to one of alarm, I knew I had to move, for my safety, and for hers.

"Hooper-san, put that pistol down. It is okay," Naoko said.

"Tell him, Naoko, tell him hands up or I'll shoot him," I said. "Dammit, Naoko, you're in danger here."

"Hooper, he is not the one pointing a gun," Naoko said.

"Naoko, who is this American? Get behind me for your safety," Nakagawa said.

"Naoko, get behind me so you don't get hurt. I'm gonna kill the bastard," I said, finger on the trigger.

"Naoko, tell the barbarian not to harm you. He can kill me but he has to let you go," Nakagawa said.

"Naoko, what do you want me to do?" I said.

"Naoko, what do you want me to do?" Nakagawa said. He reached for his pistol.

"Enough. *Eichi, yamete.* Hooper-san, stop, now. *Anatachi no aida ni watashi wa tatsu wa.* If you kill one another, you will kill me. *Hikigane o hikeba watashi o korosu koto ni naru.* On the count of three, both of you lower your guns. One—*Ichi*—Two—*Ni*—Three—*San.*"

"Okay, Naoko, who the hell is this yellow bastard?" I said. We each lowered our weapon.

"Naoko, who is this white devil?" Nakagawa said.

"Quiet, both of you. I will translate, and I will explain. Put those... damn guns away. There will be no war in my house," Naoko said.

"Nan de aitsu ga koko ni irun da?" Nakagawa said.

"Eichi, this American officer came here on his own with a wounded soldier, seeking help, as you have."

"Wait, Naoko," Nakagawa said. "This white man seated across from me is a soldier? Why for God's sake is he dressed in a Japanese man's clothing? Has he harmed you? Your father would never rest if he learned you were no longer as he knew you, especially at the hands of this animal."

"No, he did not... touch me, Eichi. I am still the girl as you knew her back home. He has been kind to me. He needed fresh clothes."

"I will not raise my weapon, but I will keep it close. If I see even a glance I do not like, I will kill him in that second. I have not found you to lose you again," Nakagawa said.

"*Hai, hai, wakarimasu, Eichi. Wakarimasu yo,*" Naoko said. She turned to me. "Hooper-san, please, listen. You must leave. I cannot have you both in this house. What if more Japanese soldiers come?"

There I was, once a soldier, now dressed in Japanese clothing taken from a dead man. I must have stood a foot taller than Naoko's father, something I only now came to see, with his sleeves coming to my elbows, and his pant legs ending below my knees. I realized I still had on my olive green GI socks. I might as well have been wearing a dress.

"Hooper-san, you do not understand," Naoko said. "I did not invite you into this house, and no one asked you to come to my country. You invaded both places. I helped care for your wounded man Jones-san. But now I have no obligation left to you."

"Naoko, please—"

"Hooper-san, no. I cannot hear that, it is not fair now. You are a butterfly. How long have you even been in Japan, less than a month? Are you planning to marry me, meet my neighbors, stand in line with me at the market?"

"No, no, Naoko. Come with me. Once we reach American lines, there must be some refugee program or something we can get you into," I said.

"Is that what I am to you, Hooper-san, something to save, a lost dog to take in? Perhaps as with a dog you can call me whatever new name you like. How about Jenny?" Naoko said. Where I expected her voice to rise, it thinned. "There are so many things you do not understand."

Chapter 11: Ashes

Former Lieutenant Nathaniel Hooper: Retirement Home, Kailua, Hawaii, 2017

I COULDN'T STAY WITH Naoko like I was Anne Frank; the Battle for Nishinomiya and what happened to Jones that had put me in her house were long gone, Kyoto was yet to come, and I knew I had to leave, find my way back to American lines.

But none of the three of us in Naoko's house anticipated the American air strikes when the weather broke, or the equally fierce snow that followed. Steel or snow: I was pushed into the impossible situation of staying in that house with Sergeant Nakagawa and Naoko until something cleared up.

Naoko was caught not just between Nakagawa's and my intentions, but translating between us. We remained wary, but were curious to come face-to-face with our enemy. Naoko realized a diversion was necessary. It would be chess; she would teach us the game she learned from her father and we would play, two soldiers under her orders. The damn board had been staring at us from the corner since we each arrived anyway. We would be occupied in enough of a competition, and her need to translate would be minimized to chess taunts. Or so she thought.

No doubt like her father, Naoko proved to be a good teacher. I had some sense of the fundamentals from back at school. Nakagawa played *shogi*, a Japanese chess-like game. Both pitted pieces of various strengths against one another. Both demanded a winner and a loser. Nakagawa and I took to the game with grim determination.

This was war.

Lieutenant Nathaniel Hooper: Japan, Naoko's House, 1946

"LIEUTENANT HOOPER, THOSE ARE two more of your pawns," Nakagawa said.

"That's what they're for, Sergeant Nakagawa. They go to war knowing they'll be taken for no real point," I said.

"No, their sacrifice will have purpose. They just may not understand it until after their death," Nakagawa said.

"Nah, they're just dead. Like you, Nakagawa. Your unit probably thinks you surrendered. Why not walk outside and blow your head off yelling banzai or something? Or you expect me to do it for you?"

"You do not understand, do you, Lieutenant Hooper? Because you stand to one side, when you fall it will have no meaning but to remove you from this earth. If I had two lives I would not care about this one. But since I have only the one, simple death is not enough."

"That matters, Nakagawa, after you're gone?" I said. "Dead is dead."

"You speak as if my life was more important to you, Lieutenant, than it is to me. I value my own life only because I must use it to die properly. You have been taught to kill as the highest expression of patriotism; we have been taught to die for the same end. We say in Japanese that 'Life is one generation, what you leave behind is forever.' Why do you Americans treasure your own small lives anyway, just to use them for nothing? To go home? Watch baseball and purchase a new car? Living is easy; it is dying well that is hard. A soldier's life should be the search for the right place to die," Nakagawa said.

"Like those suicide bombers who threw away their lives under our tanks at Nishinomiya? Why didn't they just fight like your damned samurai?" I said.

"If we had tanks left to kill you with we would certainly do so, Lieutenant," Nakagawa said. "But under the current circumstances, those suicide bombers are our heavy weapons. Our bravery must be earned in close, as men on the very ground, not at 20,000 feet like cowards."

"Every American soldier out there is willing to die for his country, Nakagawa, so cut the crap."

"You claim they are willing to die, but then wait for some battlefield accident, or perhaps a well-aimed shot from one of my men, to kill them," Nakagawa said. "We are not simply willing to die, we step onto the battlefield, or into a Special Attack plane, knowing we will die. Our loved ones cherish that. The cowards are the ones who fight not to die."

"What you think is noble is crazy, Nakagawa."

He was quickly on his feet, the chess board slipping to the edge of the table.

"*Baka yaro!* What you think is noble is crazy, Lieutenant! *Nan de aitsu ga koko ni irun da!*"

"So you wake up every morning with a plan to die?" I said.

"I go to sleep dreaming of a proper death," Nakagawa said.

"And that goes for your whole country? That why Japan won't surrender? Do we have to kill every goddamn one of you?"

"The leaders of Japan have been entrusted with the salvation and not the destruction of our nation," Nakagawa said as he retook his seat. "We may all need to die for that."

"And so why are you still alive, Nakagawa, here at Naoko's side, talking about your future and some damn old photo?"

Nakagawa said nothing. He reached to shift a chess piece, but his shaking hand knocked it over instead.

"You two boys must stop," Naoko said, alternating between our two languages. "Do not turn my father's beloved chess into something else. I will not translate any more of your nonsense. And Eichi, what has happened to you? You are no longer the sweet boy I knew back home." She switched to me, in English. "Hooper-san, talk with him. Please, explain how you feel about this war now. I... I... do not know if I want him... to go away."

She could not find a comfortable place to look in the room. I knew I had no choice but to talk with Nakagawa, for her. I tried to lighten my own thoughts first, so I secretly renamed the bishop on the board Chaplain Savage.

"Um, Sergeant Nakagawa, before me, had you ever met an American?" I said.

"I killed fourteen. Does that count?" Nakagawa said.

"Nakagawa, tell me, honestly. Do you really think Japan can win somehow? We have more men, more tanks, hell, even more food," I said.

"Yes, but Japan has never been conquered by an outside enemy. We speak of the *kamikaze*, the divine wind, actually a great storm that blew the invading Mongol fleet out to sea in what you call the 13th century. Twice. Look at the blizzard outside. It is no coincidence."

"America won't be stopped by a little snow, Nakagawa," I said.

"You presently are, Lieutenant Hooper," Nakagawa said. He returned his attention to the board. "Check."

"To hell with the weather, why do you really think you can win this war?" I said. I moved my queen out of harm's way.

"Because this country is ours, and you are just playing a game here," Nakagawa said. He slammed down his next move, the sound more a rifle shot than wood striking wood. "My knight puts you in check, Lieutenant. The knights are the key to winning. Oh, not check. I was mistaken. Checkmate."

"Dammit. Set 'em up again. Tell me, Nakagawa, do you want to kill me?" I said.

"When I first entered this home, you were prepared to kill me," Nakagawa said. "Bishop takes pawn."

"I'd kill you, but only if I had to, for Naoko's sake," I said. "Your move."

"I didn't kill you, for Naoko's sake. Move."

"So yesterday we'd kill each other. Maybe tomorrow a politician who calls the shots far away from the shooting will tell us to cease fire, and we'll stop. You don't see it, do you, Sergeant Nakagawa? This war tricks us into thinking we have to do what we're told is necessary, some kind of obligation. Half the evil in the world is done with those words."

Air raid sirens; American planes were coming.

"It appears your own knights are after you now, Lieutenant," Nakagawa said. "If they strike us the game is over. Mmm, a last move; my knight takes your queen."

Lieutenant Nathaniel Hooper: Japan, Naoko's House, 1946

I WOKE TO THE smell of cold. The air felt undisturbed, and there was no earthy scent from the tea Naoko usually prepared, none of the hisses and clinks that were her in the morning. On the low table across from me were two notes, one in Japanese and one in English.

Sergeant Nakagawa entered the room, in uniform, armed. He swept the note in English aside, and read the other. I saw his hand slide down the length of his rifle. He slapped in a full magazine, five rounds if he needed them all. He took the safety off. Our eyes met.

"*Kedo, ore wa Naoko no tame ni, koko de ima omae o korosanai ga, oretachi wa izure jigoku ni ochiru daro yo,*" Nakagawa said.

I couldn't understand him without Naoko, but when he spat on the floor his meaning was clear enough. I braced myself. Nakagawa then surprised me by stepping out the front door. He didn't bother shutting it behind him, and as it swung in the wind I stepped forward, seeing him walk off into the distance. I picked up the note in English:

I WATCHED THE CLOUDS chase each other many times, covering great distances with ease, and wished I could be like them. I will return to my parents' old house outside Kyoto. Perhaps one day I will see you again, Lieutenant Nathaniel Hooper. Sometimes tears are sad, and sometimes they are needed to wash away things so one may see clearly. Naoko.

THE DOOR WAS STILL open, as Nakagawa had left it. My old uniform, stiff with Jones' blood, lay in the backyard. It did not belong to me anymore. I wore Naoko's father's clothing, with one of his hats low on my head, a disguise of sorts.

Before Naoko's House, The Battle for the Nishinomiya Rail Junction

Chapter 12: Because That's the Way It Works

Lieutenant Nathaniel Hooper: Japan, Large American Encampment, Near Nishinomiya Train Station, 1946

ON THE WAY INTO Nishinomiya, ahead of massing for the battle planned for there, we walked through the place where we'd heard that American soldier had assaulted a local. There was not just the one house we'd been told had been torched to hide the crime, but several, burned to the ground. Everyone said that can't be us, we're the good guys, but there was that smell, that goddamn smell that was becoming too familiar to a kid from rural Ohio. I saw a couple of scraggly farm animals lying shot in the street, the birds having picked them over when the locals refused to. It takes a lot of hate to stay that hungry.

Maybe that's why as we moved through this village there were no old men who bowed to us, no kids curious enough to want to play soldier. They'd seen what soldiers do. I'd heard from buddies who fought in Europe about the crowds there, welcoming them as they walked through liberated small villages like this. The kids, they said, played that age-old game, soldier versus street rat, them begging for candy, us for fun teaching the little brats to cuss in English, then maybe asking playfully after their older sisters. "Hey Joe, you okay, Joe."

There was a U.S. Army field jacket and one boot off to the side of the road. Who'd take off their jacket in this weather? Japanese eyes walked us through. If we could talk to each, they'd confess how easily they moved from being afraid of us to wanting revenge against us.

"WE'RE BACK IN THE U.S. of A. now, at least close enough," Polanski said. "Base camp, with all the trimmings. Beats living in the field any day."

Base camp also meant it was time for me to do something every infantry leader since the Roman Legions had had to do: inspect feet. This had been drummed into me in training, held to be nearly as important as map reading, how to make a bed so a quarter will bounce off it, and how to lay out your gear properly on a GI blanket for inspection. These were strange things for someone like myself, only months out of Mom and Dad's house, to have learned.

Infantry lived on their feet, so it was a practical thing, but it was also a ritual that showed an officer cared about his men. So, with a lot of joking I was duty-bound to absorb, the men all found places to sit and took off, for the first time in how many days, their boots. I poked at tender blisters on a few, causing one to shout out "Mom!" I told another to go see the doc over a cut that was festering, and I slapped at the soles of the others, their toes all wrinkled and damn near fermented from sweat inside their green wool socks. Dry socks, people said, were worth more in the field than any quantity of brains or balls. I asked Sergeant

Laabs to settle the men in. I had to go see Captain Christiansen again. I'd rather have stuck with the feet.

Lieutenant Nathaniel Hooper: Captain Christiansen's Command Area, 1946

CAPTAIN CHRISTIANSEN HAD TAKEN over what was left of a Japanese house as his office. Something had blown out the windows, and the endless rounds of soldiers walking past had ground up what looked like it had once been a small garden.

Unlike at the Ashiya Beachhead which we were building up into a small town, this place was not treated as much more than a rough camp site, occupied with the hope only that it'd be useful for the day or two we intended to duke it out at Nishinomiya. The heavy lifting of logistics for the battle was mostly over, and only needed the tightening of a few screws here and there.

I met Captain Christiansen outside the house. There were a couple of the Captain's aides there with him, smarmy bastards I remembered from Day One. They tried to look busy while all the time leaning in in hopes of seeing me get chewed out again. With a jerk of his head, Captain Christiansen sent them on their way. He looked at me like a horse he was still unsure about betting on.

"A couple of days ago you were ready to cry like a schoolgirl. Better now, Hooper?" Captain Christiansen said. "I forgot your first name or I'd call you by it and make you feel all warm and cozy."

"Nathaniel sir, people at home call me Nate."

"Hooper, take this cigarette off me, and listen up. Things have changed 'cause of the weather turning bad. The chance of air cover now is zero point shit. And we've been seeing more suicide attacks, Japs filling backpacks with explosives and running into our lines. The ones that crawl under our tanks strapped with explosives call themselves 'Sherman Carpets.' There's a shooting war on up here."

"I noticed, sir."

"Now word is the entire Jap 16th Area Army is going to make a rush into Kyoto before the weather clears. If we can take Nishinomiya rail junction in a few hours and prevent that, Kyoto will be mostly empty when we get there, and we'll have nothing to do but run search-and-destroy missions on *geisha* houses. But if we fail to take this rail junction, we will face tested and rested Imperial Army regulars."

Captain Christiansen steered me into the house.

There were straw mats on the floor, all torn to shit by the boots that'd been walking on them. I'd never seen the inside of a Japanese house before, sliding paper walls, a big bath half full of snow from the hole some weapon had opened in the roof, old wood beams, and busted ceramics in the kitchen. Most of the windows were either what looked like oiled paper, or now-broken glass, the shards criss-cross taped together in what had been an effort to keep them from flying across the room when the bombs fell. Who'd lived here? Were they inside then, eating, or sleeping, maybe praying with the guns talking around them? Do Japs pray? They must, but it didn't work. There was a broken crock, rice spilled across the floor. I picked up a tea cup and mindlessly put it back on what was left of a shelf.

In making the house his, not theirs, Captain Christiansen had pushed aside some Japanese-style, low-to-the-floor tables and seat cushions, and set up a field expedient desk, a couple of crates laid on their sides like an altar, more crates for chairs, a coffee pot on its last legs puffing against the cold, some maps, and not much else, except letters, a lot of letters, with envelopes and stamps, all over that desk. Looking at the letters upside down, I could see most ended lonely, midway on the page, no signature. The Captain took a chair, setting it down next to the desk, not behind it where he'd see the correspondence he must have been working on earlier.

"Sit down, Hooper, we got one more thing. We're trying to get all the ducks in a row ahead of this assault in case some of the ducks don't make it home to quack." The ritual of tapping the end of a cigarette and lighting a match seemed to give him a moment he needed. "You write your letters to the next of kin for those men you saw killed yet?"

"No, sir," I said. "I don't know how."

"Aw, jeez, you probably want me to hold your hand when you're jerking off, too, Hooper. Look, most of those soldiers already wrote their own death letter in case they got killed. Look in their stuff. And if you don't know something, make it up."

I remembered Steiner's letters to his girl back home.

"Look, Hooper, every letter is the same. You say he was a good guy and everyone liked him and he died quick and for a noble cause. That's the way it works in the Army," Captain Christiansen said. Unlike his usual near-instinctive blend of grump and gruff, his voice dropped off a bit during his last sentence. I never would have believed he could talk to anyone quietly, but there it was.

"I think that's all just us doing what we think we have to, Captain," I said. I'd manned up a bit, gotten angry a bit, was confused some.

"So fine, Lieutenant, you don't want to write bullshit, don't write it. I'm proud of you for taking a stand." His eyes bit me, fixing me in place same as if his hands were pushing down on my shoulders.

"And here's what your goddamn principled stand accomplishes. Some pudding-faced old ma who did nothing more than spend 18 years raising a son gets to spend the rest of her life thinking what it looked like when that kid decided the way to thank her for all those skinned knees and happy Christmases was to have the Japs turn his face into hamburger. Maybe you could tell her about the gray and red and pink goop, too. That sound about right?"

"I'm sorry, Captain. Every time I think I'm doing the right thing, it's the wrong thing," I said. "I should've shot the damn puppy back on Day One and fed the village."

"I'm regular Army, a retread," Captain Christiansen said. "I've been looking down the wrong end of somebody else's weapon since before you got rid of your baby teeth. And I don't know anything about puppies, Lieutenant, but I do know you better hold it together."

Grandma used to say we look into the mirror with fool's eyes. So many of us, maybe even me at first, wanted to go to war and have the experience we thought we'd have, the one we'd read about in boy's books. But to see the reality of it all and then want to do it all over again in a new war like the Captain—knowing—was different. In front of me was a man who was no longer bothered by what he'd done, a guy who'd had his affair, got caught, and had nothing left to say to his wife.

I waited for the Captain to tell me to scram, but he didn't. I started on my own out of the house, then paused at the door. I turned to face him.

"Those men of mine who died, I didn't know most of their names," I said.

"Go see the Corporal. He's got them on some goddamn list," Captain Christiansen said. He looked away, a dismissal of me, and sat down at his desk, those letters of his own still there, now facing him.

Lieutenant Nathaniel Hooper: Retirement Home, Kailua, Hawaii, 2017

THERE WAS ALWAYS THAT question of why Christiansen was still a Captain, a fairly low rank given his years of service, combat experience on Okinawa, and apparent war daddy enthusiasm. You'd expect a guy like him to have been at least a Major, more likely a Colonel. It wasn't until many beers later at several unit reunions that I heard the straight dope on Christiansen, doled out as puzzle pieces I finally put together.

On Okinawa, Christiansen'd got into some sort of trouble that dogged him, they said.

On Okinawa, Christiansen'd really pissed off some Colonel and got busted down in rank, they said.

On Okinawa, Christiansen'd been told to frontally assault a hill in broad daylight. He instead waited until dark to take it, they said.

On Okinawa, then-Major Christiansen'd been told to frontally assault a hill in broad daylight, a near-suicide move ordered mostly so the newspapermen could some get good pictures. The fight hadn't been going well and the folks at home needed the morale boost action shots would provide. Christiansen meanwhile had his own morale problems, having grown tired of carrying around a crowded cemetery inside of him and crying on dead kids draped over clumps of mud. He told the Colonel that ordered the attack over an open radio net to go to hell and take his mother with him. Christiansen then, fully against orders, waited until dark, flanked the hill, and tore it from the Japanese. He saved who knows how many American lives. We use the word hero too goddamn loosely today.

The few men Christiansen lost were wounded in the initial movement, then suffocated to death under the mass of Jap bodies killed after their desperate counterattack. Christiansen got a Silver Star, then was busted down from rising Major-Enroute-to-Colonel to Captain-Stuck-for-Life for insubordination. He survived, and so did most of his men, but survival alone confers no rank.

All the sand on the beach was once rock. My ending was already known—if I stayed at this war long enough I'd become him. That was Captain Christiansen's real story.

Lieutenant Nathaniel Hooper: Chaplain's Tent, 1946

I HAD ONE MORE stop to make before briefing the men and then settling myself in to wait for the order to attack. I felt stupid going to see Chaplain Savage again, knowing he'd be no help, but was short on other places to go. The other battles had been spontaneous, but this one at Nishinomiya was planned. Gave me too much to think about and too much time to think.

"I'm sorry to bother you, Chaplain Savage. There really isn't anyone else I can talk to about this kind of thing, especially before battle, so I came here."

"I understand, son. Ask me anything." I think he wanted to frown but ended up offering a little smile that didn't reach his eyes.

"What did you do at home, Chaps, you know, before the war?" I said.

"I was a minister, same as now," the Chaplain said. "My wife and I had a nice house, lots of invites to covered-dish suppers. People'd come to me with problems getting along with their husbands, kids who wouldn't behave, that sort of thing." The Chaplain reached for where his necktie back home would have been. "Anyway, I miss it."

"I used to be a farmer, after my dad got hurt. I can't be a farmer here," I said.

"Yes, that's the way it works."

The tent was empty enough. The Chaplain, like Captain Christiansen, did not expect to be here long, and so brought along few amenities, and only limited tools of his trade in the form of a couple of olive green-covered Bibles.

"To be honest, Chaplain, I'm scared. I never knew kids could die. Why do the Japs want to kill us anyway?" I said. I wasn't trying to sound naive, I really couldn't figure it out in a big picture way. I knew it all started with Pearl Harbor, but since then became an ice cream cone that licked itself.

"Because we're trying to kill them," the Chaplain said. "Eye for an eye. It's in the Bible, you know."

"So if we stopped, they would stop?" I said. "We can just stop killing and the war is over, right?"

"Now I remember you. Lieutenant Hooper, we met at the Ashiya Beachhead, right? Son, God does not like smartasses. Get out. And God bless."

Japan, Large American Encampment, Near Nishinomiya Train Station, 1946

"MARINO, WHAT'D YOU FEEL when you pulled the trigger on that first Jap?" Smitty said.

"I mostly felt the rifle kick back," Marino said.

"But like when you whacked that first Jap, the wounded one. Later I wasn't sure that was the, you know, the right thing," Jones said.

"And Jonesy, what'd you do about it, huh?" Marino said. "Hell, the Lieutenant told me I did a good job, you heard him. Did you tell him he was wrong? Huh? Hell, five minutes before I greased him he was shooting at us, in case you forgot. Eye for an eye. If your conscience is bothering you, go see the goddamn Chaplain."

"I'm just saying it don't feel right, even if we gotta do it," Jones said.

"I killed one old guy that was dying anyway. In that paddy we killed a bunch more. When we bombed Tokyo we killed four or five Brooklyn's worth of them. Bayonets, bullets, napalm. Same church, different pew, that's all it is," Marino said.

"Back home—" Jones said.

"We ain't back home, Jones. You can't be no house cat out here," Marino said. "The brass knows what we're doing, and they keep sending us to do it. That makes it official."

"I ain't saying we shouldn't kill Japs. It just is different when they aren't shooting back is all," Jones said. "Like me and you back at that farmhouse, with the Jap and the knife and all, Marino."

"You keep your freaking mouth shut about that, Jones," Marino said.

"Wait, what happened at the farmhouse, Marino?" Smitty said. He'd nodded off, and but woke up as the argument got heated.

"You shut the hell up too, Smitty," Marino said.

"So what happens when we get home? We just forget about everything over here?" Jones said.

"Nothing else you can do," Smitty said.

"We're going home more soldier than person. You think you'll get there, kiss your mom like you've just gone out for cigarettes?" Marino said. "You got shit all over your boots, Jones, and you can't even smell it. Me, I don't care. But you, Jones, hell, you haven't figured out how things work yet, have you?"

Sergeant Eichi Nakagawa: Japanese Lines, Nishinomiya, 1946

"WELCOME SERGEANT NAKAGAWA," THE Major said, "to Nishinomiya. And no need to report. I already heard what happened."

"The *sake* warehouse, Major? I can explain. We will pay for it all," I said.

"*Sake*? No, nothing like that. I am referring to your action against the Americans recently in the paddy fight. I understand you and your men harvested your share. With bayonets no less! Save the bullets for later, eh?"

"Yes, sir. Takagi and Otokita are all that are left, but we are here now to defend Nishinomiya."

"That is good, Sergeant Nakagawa, because the importance of our job has grown. With the American aircraft grounded by this weather, higher headquarters decided the 16th Area Army can move by train. We must hold the Nishinomiya junction for them. After we succeed, we will make for the Kyoto *geisha* houses as heroes. We will have extended the war by weeks, if not longer."

"I know my men and I had hoped for that, sir."

"Well, your ambitions will be realized, right out there. Go into battle light. Take nothing with you but your rifle and your soul; you'll need one at first, and the other after you are killed. And, oh yes, get something to eat—there is cold *nabe* stew with vegetables we have been hoarding—but please do not ask where the meat came from. The only assurance I have been offered is it is at least from a four-legged animal."

"A last meal, sir?"

"Ha, for some I suppose, but we cannot all be the lucky ones, can we?" the Major said. "Nakagawa, are you afraid?"

"No sir, of course not... I am, sorry, yes, yes I am. As I wait for the attack, I want to grab the clock, I want to tear off its hands."

"Nakagawa, fear is not the problem. Overcoming it is. 'Sweet and proper it is to die for your country. But Death would just as soon come after him who runs away. Death gets him by the backs of his fleeing knees.' Please memorize that before tonight."

"And then, sir?" I said.

"Kill Americans. Kill many Americans."

Lieutenant Nathaniel Hooper: Japan, Large American Encampment, Near Nishinomiya Train Station, 1946

I FOUND THE MEN resting after I left the Chaplain. Marino and Jones had settled with their backs to one another, Laabs was on one knee, and the others had arranged themselves into a kind of half circle, seated on ammo crates. It was my turn to tell them what was to come, aping Captain Christiansen's brief to me, because that's the way it works in the Army. I'd since also picked up some talk that we'd have a couple of Sherman tanks supporting us, good news, but also had heard I'd been stuck with a new guy.

"Sergeant, how's everyone look?" I said.

"They're all a little jumpy. It'll go away at the first shot. Like jumping off the high board. No time to be scared once you're falling," Laabs said. He blew into his cupped hands to warm them. "Hey, Lieutenant, you think they're gonna pull another *banzai* charge on us?"

"They're fanatics," Polanski said. "Every one of them happy to die. Good thing we don't do that kind of thing."

"We sorta do, Polanski," I said.

"Aw, c'mon, Lieutenant, Americans don't fight that way, running men into machine gun fire." It was Laabs jumping in, poking his finger into my chest. "Hell, we don't even need to. One of us is worth two of them in a fight any day."

"Yeah, but there's always that third Jap bastard around, isn't there? And how the hell, Sergeant, do you think we took all those islands across the Pacific? Or when we came ashore at Ashiya?" I said.

"Bullshit, Lieutenant, that's different," Laabs said. "No disrespect. Sir."

"Aw, bullshit yourself, Sergeant," I said. "I heard about you on Okinawa, when you believed in something enough to risk dying for it. What's the difference between that and fanaticism, other than who tells the story?"

"What do you know anyway, Lieutenant Hooper?" Laabs said. "You haven't been in uniform long enough to need a second shave."

"Sure, you're probably right, Sergeant," I said. I lowered my voice so the others couldn't hear. "Sergeant Laabs, over here, please? Take a knee." I knelt down across from him, the classic Army position when you need to get to the real talk.

"Yeah, Lieutenant? Am I in the shithouse with you?" Laabs said. Maybe a question, maybe a challenge.

"No, no beef, Sergeant. Not sure how to ask this, but are you okay?" I said.

"I'm sorry, sir. Won't happen again," Laabs said. "Sometimes I just got a big mouth."

"No, that isn't it, Sergeant. Look, you sure you're good to go? We got a fight ahead of us," I said. "I just never heard you talk like that before."

"Yes, sir, sorry, kind of a special night. You remember, I told you on the beach back on Day One my birthday was coming up? It's tomorrow."

I'm not sure I'd seen Laabs smile before. I know I'd never seen anyone smile like he did there, starting at his lips, working past the corners of his mouth, right into his eyes.

"We'll try to arrange some cake and ice cream for you in Kyoto," I said. "So, Sergeant, let's get it copacetic between us, okay? Um, what're you gonna do after the war?"

Laabs stared back at me like that was the dumbest question he'd ever heard. The pause stuck around, so instead of waiting any longer for an answer I stood, reaching out to clasp his hand and pull him up.

"Hey, sir, you seen this picture? Got it in the mail drop today," Laabs said.

"Girlfriend back home, Laabs? What about that Nisei broad in Waikiki whose heart you broke?"

"It wasn't what you think it was in Hawaii, sir." Laabs turned the photo over in his hand, hiding whoever's face it was. "I'd lie in bed with her, smelling bleach and sweat on the sheets, didn't even know her real name. She had bruises on her thighs the color of eggplant from the last guy. The whole goddamn thing was about as sexy as soap in your eyes; even when she'd drop her nightgown like a puddle on the floor it'd mean nothing to me. Yeah, sometimes I did what I did, appetite, and I was embarrassed to be hungry. But most of the time I'd quiet her down with a few bucks and fall asleep with her, me like I was shielding her from shrapnel more than anything romantic. I just wanted to wake up next to someone and think it wouldn't be the last time."

Laabs wasn't a very good storyteller, but like the best stories, the words themselves weren't what mattered. He handed the picture he'd been holding to me. Nobody keeps a picture of a whore; it showed him and a girl back home, standing in front of some lake. Made me want to live forever.

All 18-year-old girls are beautiful, but this one was even more so, with a roundness to her, pear bottomed, pretty as young Ohio sweet corn. The photo was gentle, the line of a summer dress, the light showing through the thin fabric, the shape of her body, Laabs' hand on the small of her back. If the good Lord ever had made anything more beautiful, He'd kept it to Himself. I looked for a long time until I saw it all. The photo insisted.

Chapter 13: The Battle for Nishinomiya

Former Lieutenant Nathaniel Hooper: Retirement Home, Kailua, Hawaii, 2017

IN MY BED AT home it always starts with a thunk.

In Nishinomiya in 1946 that night fell hard enough to dent a car hood. Just before the fight started I watched some of the men splayed outside their holes, some slumped over inside snoring, some curled up, some so relaxed they looked like a thrown rope. It was a horrific image if you knew what came next.

After you've heard that thunk, you always know it.

Your chest goes trapped tight, like childhood asthma. It's not around you, or in you, it is you. Once you know that sound, being mortared is like a sneeze coming on. It's going to happen and there is nothing you can do about it but wonder if the shell is marked with your name or only To Whom It May Concern. The angle of the mortar tube and how much kick is behind the detonation says how far the shell goes. High school math: a

Japanese soldier has a four-pound shell, with the tube at 56 degrees elevation. How many men will he kill?

Thunk. That's fear.

Lieutenant Nathaniel Hooper: Japan, American Lines, Nishinomiya, 1946

MEN WERE DYING ALL around me in Nishinomiya. Each mortar shell exploded into light so I could see who was being killed, the explosions walking across the battlefield like giants. I was just a spectator to the deaths, because there was no one to shoot back at. About the only thing I could do was roll into a hole and pull my knees up to my chin and try and dig out the dirt and snow blown up my nose. The pressure on my eardrums first emptied the world of sound and then pinched out tears. So much gunpowder residue was in the air it was like I was breathing paint. I wanted to pull the ground over me and hide. My mouth dried to a whisper. There was nowhere to hide; I was inside it.

The Japanese were using impact and air burst shells on me.

The impact ones exploded only after they hit the ground, sending white-hot shards of themselves flying upward and outward in an inverted cone. The shell casings were etched to make the breaking into shards part work well, the engineers who designed them knowing the madness was in the details. But because I wasn't standing, and didn't have my head up above the rim of my hole, and hadn't been too lazy to dig my hole deep—shallow hole, deep grave—these kinds of shells only killed others, and usually only if they landed on or near a soldier. Some did, luck on the Japanese part, but if you fire off enough of them, you make your own luck.

The impact concussion was violent enough to crush and splatter, and the shards sliced and shredded, tearing the breath out of lungs, sucking out a last scream, with much of the body disintegrating into tiny fragments that returned to the earth as fleshy snow. The sound, the moving air, the concussive effect, punched and squeezed your lungs.

But for the men who dug their holes deep, stayed in them with their heads down and had not yet used up all their luck (I knew one officer who wouldn't play poker, believing he was born with only so much luck and he didn't want to waste it winning money), these impact shells did not kill them. If they didn't know better, it seemed the craters appeared by magic around them, the beginning of Judgment Day.

We had been taught that scientists studied the problem of impact shells being so inefficient at killing, and came up with a solution to those lives. The new air burst shells sensed when they were still a few yards off the ground and blew themselves up in the air.

Because the concussion was less, men screamed, louder and louder, because they were made deaf by the explosion, and needed to hear themselves dying. And because the shards spread out more, death was less complete. Soldiers' limbs were severed, and they saw their arms lying separate from their body as their last pulpy vision. I listened, waiting for someone, please God, someone, to crawl over and shove morphine sticker after morphine sticker in until the torso was sedated or dead and it was quiet again. The morphine wasn't for him, it was for me.

Until the next thunk. Then I screamed my own screams. Nobody but the dead were safe from the hollow demands of shouted prayer.

There was another sound. Sharper, closer, our mortars replying. We had the same kinds of shells, and I knew they were creating the same hellscape among the Japanese. But I truly did not care. I wanted them to all die in as horrible and painful a way as I was watching happen to us. I was on my knees in my hole now like every other man, thanking a no doubt horrified Baby Jesus for the American mortars.

Only as my vision and hearing movie-faded back in after a new explosion, so much louder and brighter than the mortars, did I see Sergeant Laabs in my hole, an inch from my face, shouting that Japanese suicide teams with explosives strapped to their bodies had crawled under the two Shermans that had moved up to support our assault, and blown themselves up with the tanks.

The battle became a living thing that ate men. We had no air cover because of the weather. We had no tanks left. We had no element of surprise. We had already lost maybe, I didn't really know, half of our men, and the living were scar tissue. It had become harvest time in our field. Then we heard whistles and shouts. Whoever was still alive on our side ordered the final assault on the Nishinomiya rail junction to begin.

People who have not experienced this level of madness cannot understand why men like us left our holes and advanced. People will say "Why didn't you refuse?" or "Why didn't you surrender, or quit, or run away, or hide?" Any man who tells you he did not consider each and every one of those choices is a coward for not telling the truth.

But if you can't understand how guys who spent all of a few weeks together 70 years ago can greet each other like brothers today, then you can't understand why we ran forward. The best I can do for you is say time out there is dog years, a place where we gained and lost significant things, our one minute of combat together worth seven of your suburban existence. We were 18-year-olds facing things even most 90-year-olds don't understand.

You learn what's private and secret about a man whose first name you don't know, because out there you don't talk about honor or duty, you talk like goober poets about girlfriends and baseball games you screwed up in high school and dads, and sometimes about the dark.

And so if love at first sight is possible at home, then love after a week in war is also possible, because the opposite of fear out there isn't safety, it's love. And you do insane things for those you love, including die for them. The brotherhood you hear about isn't friendship. It's about knowing what happens to you depends fully on what happens to all of you. It works that way, and always has, and the people who start wars depend on it. So do the soldiers in those wars.

I did not refuse or surrender or run away or quit or hide because I saw Sergeant Laabs move forward like dying wasn't a possibility. There are no medals for things like that, Laabs just acting like sergeants leading men in combat have done since Julius Caesar's time. I don't know why he did that just then, maybe he saw someone else advance, but once I saw him move I knew I had to move. Then someone saw me and stepped out, and someone saw that man, and we advanced, all that were left in our group—Smitty, Polanski, Marino, the new guy Hermann, and Jones. I was no longer a man but one finger on a hand.

Star shells from our mortars, illumination rounds, big firecrackers really, whooshed up and then trailed a spiral of smoke on the way down, casting all the world in a dancing green light before they hissed and burned out. In the space of their dark we stumbled over arms and legs trying to advance. Then the next star shell would came up and we looked around for each other, shouting, "over here Polanski, this way Marino, move Jones, somebody find the new guy, shit, where the hell are you," and thus regroup and move ahead until the next blackout. Smitty had the idea of grabbing his white handkerchief and stuffing it into the back of his trousers like a signal flag so we could follow him easier through the dark, and then Hermann pulled out his flashlight and cupped his hand over the end to make a weird red glow through his palm. We ended up holding each other's belts and making a long chain that stretched and contracted to stay together.

Tracer rounds from Japanese machine guns tore blue-white streaks, while our mounted weapons' tracers cut bright orange lines. A mortar shell crayoned the snow red with someone's blood. One side fired off yellow smoke to hide something.

It was more like the blurry photos from Antietam or Gettysburg than anything I imagined belonged in a modern war. Years later, when I saw the first pictures of craters on the moon, the views were familiar. The battle had been handed to us on the ground. Men would pay for yards with their lives.

WE REACHED A CLUMP of trees.

"Lieutenant," Sergeant Laabs said, "We are in the asshole of the world. If we wait for a gap between the flares, we might be able to run and get right up alongside the station wall, outta the Jap fire, we'll be too close, and they won't see us. Smitty, try to raise someone on that radio and see if they'll hold off on the goddamn star shells for a few minutes."

It was suicide to stand up, but we were certainly going to die lying down. Me, Laabs, Smitty, Polanski, Marino, Hermann, and Jones.

Sergeant Eichi Nakagawa: Japanese Lines, Nishinomiya, 1946

THE THUNK OF OUR mortars was a comforting sound, because it meant our side was going after the Americans with aggressiveness. It soon became apparent that the struggle for Nishinomiya station was going well. We ate cold stew while our scouts spotted the Americans early on by their cooking fires, and our mortars had already chewed through their ranks, a magnificent display. A cheer went up when we heard the big explosions, and word was passed the American tanks were now gone. Without their airplanes and tanks, the Americans were just men again. Men die easily.

Our officers positioned us correctly. Several on our side grew up in this area, giving us a tactical advantage. It was our chessboard. The Americans only thought they would be here forever. We will.

As the fight continued, we did as we were told and assembled inside the station, behind cover and thus invisible to the Americans. We were situated perfectly to destroy them from the flank.

"Nakagawa, take your men and set up fire across the field, low and steady," the Major said. "The Americans are remembering they are soldiers and coming out of their holes. Our mortars will drive the sons of whores past you. Take lives."

Then like the leader said they would, all at once there came the Americans, running from their holes first in ones and twos, then in great numbers, a suicide charge, weak as it was, we all recognized. Sometimes their own flares would fall on the other side of the charge, and the Americans would silhouette themselves for us.

"Over there, Otokita, several bunched up," Takagi said.

"Hey, Takagi, watch me kill one, that one, the one with the big radio. He has got a white handkerchief sticking out of his pants. It looks like a rabbit tail."

Lieutenant Nathaniel Hooper: Japan, Inside Nishinomiya Rail Station, 1946

MARINO RAN RIGHT INTO the station wall, bouncing off it. Laabs dropped and rolled the last few feet, moving like he was a piece of the night. I was close behind. I counted off the men as they grouped around us, Polanski, Hermann and Jones. Smitty was still trying to run as the next star shell burst overhead, spotlighting him. He'd been weighed down by the engineers who designed his SRC-300 radio, the damn thing now killing him with its thirty pounds and its two ten-pound spare batteries. That radio was the deadliest weapon the Japs had to use against Smitty.

Smitty obediently began the process of disintegrating.

He didn't say "I'm hit, Sarge," or get shot and belly crawl to safety, or strike a heroic pose. He twisted in pain and rage in impossible ways and screamed in pantomime amid the noise as he bled out. Smitty fell apart in front of us like cardboard in the rain.

As the rounds stopped his forward progress, other Jap gunners swiveled to the stationary target. What was left of Smitty's body was held vertical for some part of a second by the force of the bullets, before he gave in and fell forward with the greatest possible violence and the least possible grace. Polanski demanded someone save Smitty, but Laabs shook his head enough to show he'd heard the question so Polanski wouldn't ask it a second time.

Watching Smitty die, my brain squeezed down to a lump that pushed everything aside I thought only moments before. We'd gotten this far, proven ourselves; why did we have to go forward again? Couldn't some other outfit do that, men I didn't know? What if we stopped shooting at the Japanese, wouldn't they figure it out and stop shooting at us? Two male pitbulls snarling at each other, who in the end back away, deciding the bitch wasn't worth it?

I unbuckled my web belt and was ready to throw away my weapon. It was only Sergeant Laabs, again, who pulled me back into his landscape, deciding for all of us.

I was a coward because I didn't quit.

Sergeant Laabs led us—me, Polanski, Marino, Hermann, and Jones—crawling, pressed as tightly as we could against the foundation of the building, away from the Japs, their weapons still picking at Smitty's corpse, or aiming at other soldiers trapped like light looking to hide in the sanctuary of shadow. The wall near me had whole constellations of bullet holes violated into it.

As we neared a door, Laabs shouted, "They're in there, I can smell the bastards. We'll break through and scare the shit out of them, catch them by surprise. Follow me."

How the man could think clearly, I can never know. He could squeeze away everything else and what was left was not what was desirable or nice, but what was necessary. That's what makes war such a terrible thing for an otherwise decent society, because you don't want monsters like that teaching in your schools or working in your hospitals, but you need them for a time here before you want them to go away until the next war. You're looking for a man mad enough to commit murder, with enough conscience to come home feeling a little guilty.

Laabs.

The group of us burst through the door, screaming prayers and curses, and hid behind a busted slab of office wall. I heard men scuttling across the floor. The Japs had moved to the other side of the office, our two groups separated only by that wall. We heard the clink of metal against metal. They were loading a heavy machine gun, like the Nambu we faced on Day One on the beach.

"You two, Marino and Jones, job opportunity for you, around that side, throw your grenades and make as much clatter as you can pulling back to distract the yellow scum," Laabs said. "Polanski and Hermann, you shoot any Japs that come around after them. I'm going alone around this other side. Lieutenant, watch it, because I don't intend to let any of 'em past me and if you shoot me by accident running back I will return from the grave and kill you myself. If this works, I'll get most of them, and the four of you will take apart any of the others."

"American, you dung man." The Japs were calling at us in broken English from the other side of the wall. "You surrender, you no die tonight, GI."

"Gentlemen, I'll see you all on the other side," Laabs moved up to his corner. "Marino, Jones, on my count."

"American, you die tonight."

Laabs, loud: "One."

Jones mouthed the word alongside Laabs.

"You no never see your mama home."

Laabs, louder: "Two."

Jones made a low sound.

"You die here, American."

Laabs, a whisper: "Three."

Marino and Jones turned their corner. Laabs stepped forward, me leaning to watch him.

The Jap Nambu opened up, spraying bullets perpendicular to the corner. Laabs would run right into them. Marino came back first, screaming, followed by Jones. Those two flopped on their bellies on our side of the wall, with Polanski and Hermann crouched above them. They rolled another grenade around the corner just far enough to miss Laabs on the other side.

Marino fired around his corner, and a Jap went down, shot in the face just below his right eye. Marino rose and fired again, into the now prone target, all eight rounds his M-1 held. As the magazine emptied with that metallic sound the spring inside made, a second Japanese soldier rounded the corner and shot Marino twice in the chest. The bullets blew out the whole of his back. I heard Marino's skull connect with the concrete floor with a soft crack, a sound people who'd never a heard a rifle shot or a skull break think sounds like a rifle shot. Jones shot the man who shot Marino who earlier had grenaded the first Jap to die.

Me, Laabs, Polanski, Hermann, and Jones left.

Sergeant Laabs stepped tight around his corner, between the wall and the stream of rounds coming out of the Nambu. He grabbed the red-hot barrel of the machine gun, screaming as it hissed against his bare hand, and swung it aside.

His hand had fused to the hot metal. He tore it off, leaving a mitten of flesh on the weapon, and fell on the one Jap left. With bloody fingers he stabbed at the man's eyes, spitting and snarling as he slammed the head over and over against the concrete.

Laabs could not stop, the head now in both hands, the blood in the cold air. We—me, Polanski, Hermann, and Jones—had come around the other corner. Laabs had, in the most violent way possible, beheaded the man.

Sergeant Laabs stood up, using his boot to nudge at the disembodied head in front of him, as if there could be any doubt the man was dead. Panting, he glanced at me, and then looked to Polanski, Hermann, and Jones.

"Jones," Laabs said. "You, Polanski, and take the Lieutenant, get into position on the right, find something to get behind. Hermann, cover my left. Keep low. Standing around here can get a man killed."

The war was now between Laabs and the Japanese.

I knew hundreds of other American soldiers were fighting somewhere around us, opposed by hundreds of Japanese. I heard distant mortaring. I heard far off screams.

I saw only Laabs.

"Oh hey, Lieutenant, you wanna hear a story?" Laabs said.

"Laabs, what the hell are you talking about?" I barely recognized his voice.

"On Okinawa. We're clearing caves with flamethrowers, a day before that bullshit I did saving those kids. I never talked to anyone before now about this other cave I ran into, where all I found alongside the smoked up bodies were pencil boxes and schoolbooks. Two minutes later the Doc was giving first aid to one school kid that somehow was still alive. Two minutes between one thing and the other. Go figure. And you know the worst part? It didn't even bother me until now."

"Laabs, I'm sorry. I don't know what else to say."

"Nothing more to say. That was the whole story. Now get into position with Jones," Laabs said. He smiled. "Got something I need to do."

I scrambled to join Jones and Polanski. Gunfire flashed from deep inside the station, as if the Japs were taking photos at a wedding. I watched Hermann get shot through the head. Two minutes between one thing and the other.

And there stood Laabs. What was left of Hermann's body lay nearby. There is a lot of blood inside a man, and it looked as if some naughty boy had spilled two full cans of red paint on the garage floor while his father stood there scolding him, "You've just wasted perfectly good things for no reason. I have a mind to make you clean this up all by yourself right now."

Everyone who'd been in the field long enough heard of a guy who one day under enemy fire just stood up and took off his helmet. Laabs left it up to us to figure out the difference between self-sacrifice and self-destruction.

I actually think he was dead before he stood up, the Jap bullets unnecessary even as they tore him apart. That's how Jones, Polanski, and I watched Sergeant Jason Laabs die inside the Nishinomiya train station the day before his 18th birthday in 1946.

JUST ME, POLANSKI, AND Jones left.

How the next wave of incoming rounds did not hit me is one of those decisions God, or nature, or fate or physics just makes. Jones and Polanski crawled forward like the rodents we'd now had to become to survive. They were both hit more or less at the same time.

"Lieutenant," Polanski said as he bled onto the concrete.

"Lieutenant?" Jones said as he bled onto the concrete.

I had three choices, but not having the guts to run away, belly crawled forward to try and save the other two. The floor was slippery. It wasn't oil.

"Lieutenant?" Polanski said. But I grabbed Jones, closer to me by a yard.

I watched Polanski's head come apart even as I heard a Jap who must have shot him laughing at, I don't know, God, or nature, or fate or physics or me. I saw the white bone pieces, and the gray, and the pink. I wanted to believe it hadn't hurt because it was so quick, but why pain even mattered with death as the end I couldn't answer. He could've been killed a year earlier at home in a car accident, or fifty years later by cancer, but Polanski died instead just beyond arm's reach.

"Lieutenant, we gonna die?" Jones said. His legs were bloody.

Deep breath. Calm, waiting for my turn. An explosion, and a bright flash.

Sergeant Eichi Nakagawa: Inside Nishinomiya Rail Station, 1946

I SAW THE CRAZY American stand up and throw off his helmet so I killed him. I did not see the American bullet hit Otokita at almost the same moment. His helmet clattering across the floor happened in slow motion. His blood seeped out from under him. I crawled over, bloodying my own uniform. Otokita was dead.

Takagi had also been shot. I reached him, his last strength devoted to curling up inside my arms. His eyes were open, but not clear, and the gurgling from his lungs at every breath was plain. Amid the dust and noise he said *okaachan*, mother. Was he hallucinating, thinking somehow he was with her? Was he calling out, hoping she would come to him?

Takagi's eyes closed. He was sucking at the air, drowning in his own fluids. A large explosion rocked us, and he reacted to the sound; he was still alive. With blood following it out of his mouth, he said the word again, *okaachan*. I knew what my obligation was, and I said "This is mommy. I am here with you." He smiled.

I am not sure of the precise moment Takagi died, but I spoke gently to him anyway.

"Do you hear that sound, Takagi? The trains are passing through this junction. The Americans failed. The trains with our men are moving past us to Kyoto. We won."

There was an explosion, and a bright flash.

Before The Battle for the Nishinomiya Rail Junction

Chapter 14: Who Really Deserves It?

Former Lieutenant Nathaniel Hooper: Retirement Home, Kailua, Hawaii, 2017

I'M LUCKY ENOUGH TO have a friend with a boat. Sitting at the stern, I watch the boat create its wake, then as we speed away the wake fades just as quick. Thinking about the war doesn't work that way. About the best I can hope for in real life is to be able to put what happened in a box. The box stays closed most of the time.

Some guys try and keep it shut by making life meaningless—liquor for the old ones, drugs for the young ones, a little of both for the handlestache Vietnam vets in the middle. The Friday nights drinking with the boys become Wednesday mornings drinking alone in the bathroom with the door shut. Some let that run its course and just tap out.

But absent a few orange plastic containers next to the bathroom sink, for me, I took my neighbor's grandson out to the zoo, made dinner, went to work, all the time the curator of some secret museum. The memories don't go away like the people do.

If the box pops open, some people try to push such thoughts away, stopping with just their toes in the water, thinking they've gone swimming. But after a while I knew I had to go into the deep end, because only there could I confront the real monster: the essence of war is not men dying, as Eichi Nakagawa did that day in 1946 at the temple north of Kyoto. The essence of war is killing, as I did that day at the temple when I called down artillery on him. War isn't a place that makes men better. Flawed men turn bad, then bad men turn evil. So the darkest secret of my war wasn't the visceral knowledge that people can be filthy and horrible. It was the visceral knowledge that I could be filthy and horrible.

MY PART OF HAWAII is very peaceful. Some tourists, but not too many, little of the tawdry spank of Waikiki. Sometimes I get lonely for some noise though, and find myself over there, enjoying a little ice cream and a walk.

For me the war is like a shirt I always know is there in my closet but don't wear often. I'll be absently out and step onto an unfamiliar path and it'll be just the right crunch of gravel under my feet. My eyes will involuntarily lose focus for a second, and if I'm with someone they might ask, "Nate, everything okay?" and I'll lie and smile, "Oh you know, just a senior moment." But memory slaps me just the same way stirring up the ashes of barbecue coals turns them red. I've failed many times to remember a time when I had nothing particular on my mind.

The Honolulu end of Waikiki beach is anchored by a Department of Defense hotel, run on taxpayer money as a low-cost vacation destination just for service people. The military is comical about telling them to "keep a low profile," supposedly so they don't become targets of the terrorists presumed to haunt these beautiful beaches. But of course you can tell. The buff bodies stand out against the fleshy look of the regular tourists. The odd-patterned tans—all dark brown faces with pale white everywhere else—betray a recent trip to the Middle East.

I'll sometimes nod to them, mostly out of politeness. I generally keep to myself the fact that we know a lot about each other. A few will nod back, maybe say a few words and leave you to fill in the silence, but I find the ones who talk too easily are generally part of what I call professional veterans, guys with little dirt under their nails who get a lot of free drinks and airline upgrades in a September 12 world. Some of these are the same assholes who quote Whitman poems they've never really read, or write horrid warrior-poet memoirs about the clash of truth and the beauty of brotherhood in a supply depot. Jesus. They're immune to the guilt of action, or bad luck, or accident that settles into others. I'm grateful after meeting them for those portions of my stroll when there's less time for my thoughts.

Once in a while someone who fought some of the same kind of war I did is obvious—a missing hand on a 20-year-old, some thick pink scars, a face that looks like bacon. It could've been a car wreck or a factory fire, I guess, but I know that wasn't what it was. I wonder what his friends thought the first time they saw him, or what his ex-girlfriend said, or what he thought being as scared to come home as he was scared to go to war. This is the guy who, after Wolf Blitzer moves on to the next story, cries trying to touch his daughter's hair, and knows just because he changed from cammies to beach shorts that's not a shortcut back into normal life. If you see these guys on TV, you always see them young and still strong, showing courage learning to use their new robo-prosthetics. You never see anything that shows what their life is like ten or forty years down the road. Alive, sure, but not living.

Out on the beach, some people won't stop looking, like a 10-year-old's focus on a a pile of Legos, and some won't look at all, but either way this is all happening, like the wars did, simultaneously while other people are eating at Applebee's and going shopping. It gets hard to keep it all in the same world. And you, sure, go ahead, you go on and use the term "unbearable pain" the next time you hit your thumb with a hammer.

Of course, there are also those you don't see, the boys and girls who bought the long zipper, the one that closes a body bag. Yes, Mrs. Mom, we took your son, but look, we gave you back a neatly folded flag. See, it's in a triangle shape, representing the hats of American Revolutionary War soldiers, isn't that interesting. And if you have a second child, and you call now, we'll double your order.

Me, we, they, you, I don't know the right word to ever use, because it wasn't just our side. I'd seen something on PBS saying that during the 1950s and early 1960s you could still see a few Japanese soldiers around the train stations, wearing bits of their old uniforms, some with crude prosthetics, begging, failed in the end by disregard. Young people, dressed in the latest western styles, passed by, eyes on the ground, embarrassed about men humiliating themselves in the midst of the post-war economic miracle. What if a visiting foreigner saw them, what would he think of Japan? Older people would slip the soldiers small bills, hoping if they had some money to buy rot gut or food they would go away.

A few guys like Private Garner ended worse off than the physically wounded, spending the weekends with their regular companions Samuel Adams, Johnnie Walker, and the cops. Get some sleep and have a drink, they were told, only don't let it turn into too much of either one, or it'll be suicide on the installment plan. Each bad thought seemed like a page that needed a twelve-ounce can of paperweight to hold it down. All we ever thought about was coming home; "If the army doesn't kill me, I've got it made for life," we said. We were naive; too many of us survived the war only to come back wanting to die every day.

You learn to be alone in crowded places, deep in your own head. Imagine being on this beautiful beach and not caring to even look up and watch a father try to make his way across the hot sand balancing four dripping ice cream cones.

They'd lost things whose importance they only recognized when they weren't there. They've come to think today means nothing, tomorrow means nothing, and develop a sense that only things that already happened matter. Nothing has taste or color. Regrets swell when it takes all night for the mercy of dawn to come, but luckily, for me at least, not always on these beautiful Pacific days.

Me and Private Garner might find we often see the same face in the mirror. My generation had no counselors, no clinics, no support groups. In my Ohio hometown, before the wife and I retired to Hawaii, every Memorial Day there'd be little flags first made in Iowa, then Hong Kong, then Japan, then Korea and now China and Vietnam—Vietnam, for Christ's sake—on every porch. Half the people my age watching the parade then were vets in wheelchairs. I had a nice welcome home party when I came back, and plenty of good Veteran's Days to try and use to subtract things from the parts of the fight I dragged along with me. But the underlying message was the same as in every war, whether delivered nicely or crudely: deal with the real stuff in private, we don't want to know. You pack out your own gear, trooper.

Drinking hurt, but for some it hurt less. Everyone learns it just sends your pain off to wait for you, but still it was something to look forward to, the first fizzy beer of the day tickling your nose, or the throat-burning shot of something stronger biting into an ulcer. Drinking wiped away hours when someone had too many of them, all the way back to 1946 sometimes. Pain can be patient, waiting for that one guy who had a little too much wine at a wedding and started talking about blood and brains in some alcoholic dialect until a couple of other vets walked him outside where he told stories from his knees for an hour which they alone could understand. A lot of this festers not out of what you saw and did, but the realization that what you saw and did really didn't matter in any bigger picture and you had to make up some smaller picture to justify whatever. It should've had a reason, and go to hell ahead of us if you want to pretend burning down cities or blowing up wedding parties by remote control is patriotism, or protecting freedom, or defeating some tyrant we used to support. People say, "whatever you have to tell yourself," but they forget you can't lie to yourself alone at night. Imagine what it's like to be my age and scared of the dark.

I came to think of it like taking apart a jigsaw puzzle. You couldn't say exactly when, but at some point you couldn't see the picture anymore. It's the last drop of water hanging swollen on the end of a faucet.

Well-meaning people would say, "open the wound, let it out." The problem was those wounds had never closed in the first place. Other people get it a little better, knowing it's not about overcoming as much as coping. They tell us, "You've got to fight as hard at home to beat this as you did over there to get home," except we're not sure what we're fighting for. Our lives? Uh huh. That's a big part of what caused all this in the first place. You want to know what it's like to have a breakdown in the meat aisle at Safeway, buying steak? We can tell you. Even so, we don't want to be called victims and disabled out, and we're not seeking some third party's moral redemption. We just want to get this shit out of our heads.

IN ADDITION TO THE beach side strolls, I've found myself at Pearl Harbor a few times, just curious, you know. It's fashionable to talk about forgiving one's enemies if everyone is old enough, and here in Hawaii the reunions between old men from Japan and old men from the U.S. who once fought each other are set-pieces. As you'd suppose, everybody says the right things to the 26-year-old third generation Japanese-American newscaster who comes out for an easy feel-good story on a slow day.

In private, however, I hear the old vets say the Japs deserved it. That kind of thinking bothers me, especially when it starts to thicken like a callous in my own head. We feel our side's barbarism is occasional and mistaken, or individual and deviant, while their side's was part of some evil culture. Nobody personally knew more than a handful of people killed, but we all wanted to see as many on the other side die as possible. Somehow war can be both personally vengeful and impersonal at the same time. Emotions like that make complete sense to a scared young man who thanks God for saving his personal sad ass by burning down a whole city. The thing of course is, after the smoke clears, we should hope important decisions about war are not being made by scared young men.

We were told mine was the last war where right and wrong were clear. I've seen a history book that makes quite a point of being shocked that when the Japanese captured shot-down B-29 crewmen from firebombing missions, the fliers were often burned alive by civilians on the ground. Another book described how elsewhere bodies on fire sizzled and smoke came out of the eye sockets, making hissing noises. Did that description of the sizzling and hissing come from the firebombing of Japanese civilians, or from the burning alive of American prisoners? It was one of the two, though it describes both.

People talk a lot about moral ambiguities, the tough calls policymakers face in the middle of the night, what historians have insight into only from the safe black and white of home. But evil isn't an opinion, and you can't squint hard enough to make it gray. Everything else is just backstory created to allow us to feel better about what was done. If what happened in my war wasn't wrong, then nothing can be wrong. And if after knowing that, you still insist this was the Good War and we were the Greatest Generation, well, only people who are moving their lips reading this think things like that.

Chapter 15: Teach a Man to Fish

Sergeant Eichi Nakagawa: En Route to Nishinomiya Train Station, 1946

"WHY IS THERE NO more food?" Otokita said.

"Because it was only a small dog, you idiot," I said. "And what the hell are you laughing about, Takagi?"

"One of my chores back home was to feed the dogs our kitchen scraps out," Takagi said.

"And now they are repaying you," Otokita said.

We were crossing a frozen area, and I noticed the ground under the snow was a regular pattern, small mounds separated by low troughs: farmland. The people in this area, we knew, traditionally grew yams and other root vegetables. Those things not only kept well through the cold weather, but could also be raised in the troughs, hidden from foragers, human or animal. We would need to break the ice over the low areas, then dig into the frozen ground using our mess kits as scoops. We were not doing much else with them. It was as I was giving the order that an old man came running out of the nearby village, shouting at us to stop.

"The Army did not order you to steal my village's yams," the old man said.

"Yes it did. We are soldiers."

"No, you are not. You are just skinny boys."

"What do you know, old man?" I said.

"See my hand? Only two fingers. I left the others in Korea when I was one of the Emperor's soldiers myself 35 years ago."

The old man beat me with a stick he had with him, without much strength but with some enthusiasm.

"You should show me respect, you fool, I am older than you," he said. "You know how long this killing has been going on?"

"I know, old man," Otokita said. "We were taught in our training the Empire secured many valuable resources from Korea via your generation's efforts. We thank you for your service. We have used the bastard garlic eaters' iron, for example, to construct a powerful navy."

"Do you know where that powerful navy is now? Sunk by the Americans," the old man said.

"Sir, respectfully, my training was that additional resources were gained from Korea. I may list phosphorus, magnesium, coal..." Otokita said.

"...and human beings, you dolt. My unit's task in Korea was to gather up women to ship back here. We said *kyoseirenko*, forced transportation, but others called them 'comfort women.' We would reassure the girls they were going to factory jobs, but in fact it was the Army's brothels that needed to be kept well-stocked. At first we stole the beautiful ones, but we were soon told to look at endurance instead. Sometimes when we saw a sturdy one we would grab her right out of a field, mud still between her toes. Even so, their health would fade after being used twelve hours a day and we would need to often replenish the supply. So do not tell me about resources from Korea."

"*Zegen*," Takagi whispered to me. "Pimp."

"To hell with you," the old man said. "I was a soldier. I followed orders. We were trained in logistics school to calculate the allotted time for officers and regular troops to know how many to take, because officers were allowed more time between their legs. And the official term for harvesting women was *choben*, an old quartermaster word, 'gathering food for the horses,' not *zegen*."

The old man spat on my boots. I raised my hand, but, after meeting his eyes, lowered it just as quickly.

"I had absolute control over human beings. I could do anything I wanted to them," the old man said. "Want to know what happened? Hah, exactly what you think happened. You can imagine the kind of men attracted to such work, eh?"

"Did you..." Otokita said.

"Take a little taste for myself now and then? Of course. But the others did to, everyone did. That was not so bad in itself. But using them ourselves was against military waste regulations, so we had to destroy the evidence."

He moved some dirt around with his foot. "They tried to still be human, but there were too many of us that took our real pleasure in making them less. You know, there was often no bedding, underneath them was just earth most times when we put them... to work. They cried 'Mummy, it hurts.'"

"I—" Otokita said.

"Otokita, just be quiet. Can you not see every time you say something you just encourage this old buzzard?" I said. I wanted

Otokita to think he was a liar, instead of helping him see the lie. There had been rumors of these things.

"Look at yourselves. You are stealing rotten yams from the elderly," the old man said. "That is the way of it now."

"We are here to save you from the Americans and need our strength," I said.

"What are you protecting me from? The Americans passed through here a day ago, and they did not want my yams."

"The Americans were here?" I said.

"Yes, hairy white beasts, but they gave us some food. It was horrible, a type of canned pink meat. It smelled like feet, but we ate it. You can only die once, right? And it was better than monkey meat," the old man said.

"There are no monkeys here. Have you gone insane, old fellow?" I said.

"You will soon learn some of your tastiest meals arrive on two feet, young soldier. Just be sure not to die before those other two."

"Enough of this. My rifle says you must give us food now," I said.

"Ah, so you boys are in a hurry for your first taste of monkey meat then, eh? Anyway, you do not want us. We are rotten, all suffering from dysentery. If we live long enough, the Americans may be back with something to eat, and medicine for us. Maybe you should wait for them. I will put in a good word for you."

"Why are you not prepared to fight the Americans instead of taking what scraps they'll give you, like whores? Every one of us Japanese are expected to defend the nation, with pitchforks, kitchen knives and strong hearts," I said.

"Look at us—do we look like an army? Do you?" the old man said.

"That is not important. What is important is to die with honor," I said. I looked to Otokita and Takagi for support.

"We will die here with honorable dysentery," the old man said.

"Why do you not support the troops?" Otokita said.

"Yes, I suppose I should," the old man said. "Look at how much we in this village have benefited from this war. You are lucky we do not clear you lot out ourselves. Perhaps with pitchforks and kitchen knives."

"Look, old man, can we be reasonable?" I said.

"Perhaps. Will you stop stealing our yams?"

"Perhaps. Will you give us some food?"

"Perhaps. Do you have any grenades?" the old man said. "There is a frozen river not far from here, and we cannot break through the ice. Underneath may be fish. If you have grenades, you can blow a hole in the ice. The shock will kill any fish down there and they will float to the top. We will all eat tonight, and there will be enough for your men in the hospital as well," the old man said.

"What men? What hospital?" I said.

"Grenade first, then I will tell you."

"No, you go first," I said.

"No, you hand over the grenade first," the old man said.

"Send for another man from the village. He and Private Otokita will take a grenade down to the river. If Otokita does not come back with fish, I will shoot you down where you stand," I said.

"And for dinner eat my heart?"

"We will see, though I suspect you have none," I said. "And after the fish, then you will take us to this hospital you say has Imperial soldiers. We may need them."

"Of course. You can have as many as you like."

"Okay, Otokita, go fetch some dinner," I said. "And you, old man, take us where we can get warm. It is cold out here for hungry men."

TAKAGI AND I FOLLOWED the old man into his village. Maybe not a village; the place looked more like a fistful of little houses washed up from the river. There were no young men. The teenage girls, we were told, were hiding in the hills in case we sought to use the last of our strength on them. They had done the same when the Americans came.

As we turned to enter what was the old man's home, a middle aged woman stood in front of us.

"Kill me. I cannot stop myself taking food from my daughter," she said. "Every time uncle distributes food, I take hers. Please, I do not have the courage to kill myself."

She grabbed my rifle barrel and screwed it against her forehead. The old man pushed her aside.

A grenade exploded in the distance, and soon after Otokita returned with fish. Not enough, but almost enough. I took one and cleaned it in front of the old man. I flicked the guts to the ground with my knife. The old man snatched them up, stuffed them whole into his mouth and swallowed as if he was worried I might pull them out and eat them myself. He closed his eyes, and allowed his tongue to dart out to lap up a bit of fish blood left on his lips.

"Sergeant, forgive my manners." He belched, then smiled at the taste. "Now I have a small test for you to take. You just saw my niece begging you to spare her the shame of knowing she stole food from her own child. Take that fish and follow me. I want to teach you something about war, one old soldier to another."

The old man called over a young boy.

"Sergeant. Give that boy your tasty fish," the old man said.

"You are crazier than I thought, old man. The boy will get his share later," I said.

"There is not enough to go around. Give the boy your fish. He will die without food."

"No, I need it. I have to fight, to kill Americans, for Japan," I said. "And, um, to protect your village."

"I think we have covered that already, Sergeant. Give him the damn fish, you coward. Bah, you have no more balls than my niece."

"I can do terrible things now," I said.

"Congratulations, Sergeant, you have learned something about how war works. One old soldier to another."

THE OLD MAN WAS not done with me. As he claimed, the village had been caring for a handful of soldiers laid out in one of the homes, the so-called "hospital" he had spoken of. The cold did not mask the sweet fog of decay.

"A week ago about 40 Imperial soldiers passed through our village," the old man said. "They were in a hurry, with their officers beating them, driving them forward, and so did not even stop to steal our food. An American airplane came screaming into this valley, firing its machine guns. All of the soldiers dove for the ground. When the plane did not return, several of the soldiers appeared to rise from the dead, standing up unhurt. They collected these few wounded. They told us to care for them, and someone would return to help. Half of the wounded begged us to kill them so they were not later taken prisoner, and half begged us to hand them over alive to the Americans in hopes they would be fed and receive medicine. We have no new bandages left, and the women will not wash the pus out of the old ones anymore so we can reuse them."

"What now?" I watched a fly explore one of the faces, lingering near an eye before settling at the corner of the man's mouth.

"The ones with beriberi swell. We lay them on one side, then we roll them over to drain back the other way when the fluids build up. On their backs they drown. The ones who got tetanus from the soil they laid on while wounded just die. See that fellow? Today his skin turned the color of young leaves. The two you smell are the worst. Dysentery. We have no choice but to leave their trousers off and stuff their backsides with leaves. We thought the one by the window there with the glasses had died, even covered him with a straw mat, but then the next morning he moved the mat aside and mumbled 'I am breathing again.' We give something to eat to those who appear able to survive on their own, and withhold the food from those who seem destined to die soonest."

"And who must decide who to feed and who to allow to die?" I said.

"The previous man to take on the task ran off into the mountains. Have you seen him, by chance? Listen to them, Sergeant. They all want their mothers. I always think, well, where was your mother when you were called out to war? Probably at the rail station waving a paper flag and cheering."

"So what do you want me to do, old man?" I said.

"What can any of us do? The dragon has been unleashed and will not go back into his cage until he has had his fill. Sergeant, leave here. You cannot help us. We cannot help you. Move on if you must. Perhaps they can feed you there, though given your upcoming task that does seem a waste of good food."

"Despite your insolence, I appreciate what you tried to teach me, old man," I said.

"Yes, yes, you are welcome, but if you insist on continuing, you have learned nothing," the old man said.

"Maybe, old man, maybe. I hate the Americans, but I now also hate something of what we have become. And I will die because of it. I even look forward to it," I said.

"Death? Oh, yes, so do I, Sergeant. Maybe we are not so different after all."

Chapter 16: Hungry For It

Former Lieutenant Nathaniel Hooper: Retirement Home, Kailua, Hawaii, 2017

"DON'T WORRY ABOUT THE soldiers who complain," Sergeant Laabs once said to me. "Worry about the ones who don't."

The near-constant complaining we did was a way of getting rid of gloom without denying it existed; the only forbidden thing was self-pity. Privates bitched about corporals, who complained about sergeants, who grumbled about officers, who bad-mouthed MacArthur, who groused about Truman. The buck stopped there.

There were a few, mostly the real backwoods country boys like Burke, who made the best of it, with a cheerful contempt for the hardships—"Oh, been colda' 'an this," or "Nope, this ain't nothing compared to a real winter, no suh." As for the rest of us, we complained, usually about that same cold, the one that pressed on us, the one flowing into our foxholes. To fight back, we cut down pine boughs and filled the bottom of our holes with them, giving us something better to stand on than the frozen earth. We wriggled our toes to keep warm, and to keep from nodding out on watch. We would've killed for a snort.

The only thing worse than the cold was if you were moving enough to start sweating. We had nothing but body heat to dry our things out, and it got cold again faster than that would work. Back home, dry underpants were just something our mothers handed us on wash day, but out there they could save a life.

I wish there was a better way to tell this, maybe a box full of dirt, damp web gear, cigarette butts, and rags soaked in rifle oil I could drop off at your place. And food, because about the only nod at pleasure we had was our K-rations—K-Rats—canned food and other things packed into waxed boxes. K-rations were an improvement over the older kind of field food, C-rations, which came in cans the size and shape of dog food. K's came in a smaller can, about the size and shape of cat food.

Other than the Fruit, Peach, Canned, Syrup-Type, it was the instant coffee—it was called soluble coffee then—that was the real prize with your K-rats. Most times you just poured the crystals right on your tongue, or kept them in your cheek like dip, and let them dissolve. Other times we made little stoves out of a metal tin and a block of paraffin wax to heat up the coffee, right in a canteen cup. The taste wasn't so good, a gesture more than a drink, but it was a damn welcome gesture. The metal canteen cups would glow a nice cherry red. They had a rolled metal rim that would grab the heat and not let go; sometimes you'd burn your lips, sometimes you'd thaw them out as your teeth chattered against the metal in Morse code. I heard of a guy who'd never washed his cup, the whole war, so by victory day he just needed to splash hot water in to make coffee.

Another piece of news inside the K-rat box was a tropical Hershey bar, special chocolate with as much of the flavor removed as possible and flour added so it would not melt in the heat. This was of course somewhat less of a concern in midwinter Japan than on Guadalcanal.

The bad news in K-rats was Spam, pink and salty as all hell, and about the texture of snot. More rumor than actual meat, we still ate it, never thinking we'd one day be wrestling with high blood pressure and 300-plus cholesterol counts. Spam took the idea of "food as fuel" about as far as it could go. The stuff was also known not affectionately as bunghole cement because it didn't exactly promote what Grandpa called "healthy digestion," but that was sort of okay, given that the alternative was to expose your backside to freezing temperatures and enemy snipers. That's also why we pissed in our helmets and threw the pee out over the sides of the foxhole.

About the only good thing to say was that the K-rats made me remember back at home every Friday there'd be a fish fry at the fire house. I hated that stuff then but out in the field I'd have killed for something so hot and wonderfully greasy. I wanted to go home and eat what I wanted when I got hungry, sleep with my hand tucked under a real pillow when I was tired, and go to the toilet anytime I had to go without worrying about getting shot. People who have never been in the service or prison undervalue things like being free to walk away from something. For a kid who not too long ago wished for a catcher's mitt, hoping just for a hot meal while not dying was a change.

Every K-rat box also had a few cigarettes inside, usually Luckies. It might just be an exaggeration to say some guys chewed the cigarettes to get the nicotine into their bodies faster, but just. Lighting a match at night invited death, but we cupped our hands to hide it, forcing scary shadows on our faces, deciding, back then without irony, that smoking was worth risking dying for. The pony packs of four smokes fit snug inside the magazine pouches on our web belts, and we carried them that way. Everyone joked that free cigarettes were the only good thing about being in the service. Cold coffee and a pack of Luckies for breakfast, didn't get any better than that.

But what we really wanted more than free smokes was to think we were closer to home, though the more you forced it, the more it just felt worse out there. Like when they made a big deal out of serving us a traditional turkey dinner for Thanksgiving when we were on Kyushu. I ate it all, but to tell the truth, I really just wanted it to be Friday. "I'm glad that's over" is what most guys said after the pumpkin pie.

Out in the field at night, I set up watch rotations, so someone would be awake to tell us we were about to die when the Japs came. The Japs couldn't pronounce L and R sounds right, so I picked challenge passwords like "red lollipop" and "lazy river," and thought I was clever. As close as I got to any real leadership those nights was showing up. I'd slide into a hole, tell the men there to keep an eye out and move on. I was younger than some of them and not much older than the rest, but I called them son those nights because they wanted me to. I knew it was fake, and so did they, feeling like that last Christmas when I knew Santa wasn't real but pretended anyway. It was, literally, the least I could do. They did not respect me or look up to me, and I'd have worried if they had.

In the end there were only three ways to spend a night in a foxhole: cold, scared, or cold and scared. Sometimes it took all night for the sun to come up, leaving me so exhausted I was wide awake, demanded to know why God made night. Four a.m. was a place, not a time. Every hour was a week, every night was a month, all in a weird state of sleeping but not sleeping. The hole was about as comfortable as a front-row church pew. Sleep, when it came, came without warning and hit like a heavyweight. Some nights the moon tried to hide behind the trees and there was not a crack of light, dark as the inside of a cow's ass, some nights it was bright. Some nights the stars were sharp and I listened for the Japanese. Some nights it was cloudy and peaceful and I listened for Ohio.

I knew the other soldiers were out there, in their holes, but we could not see each other. We were close enough to touch but could not. Night was a room, and morning wasn't inevitable. By a certain hour, any fear was real. I could feel the darkness and taste metal even as my tongue was stuck to the roof of my mouth.

Just before when I knew dawn was coming to forgive me, time slowed down even more, like it did back in geometry class, when it took forever to get from 11:12 to 11:14. It's a helluva thing to wake up pushed into a day where you might be crippled, or blinded, or worse, have your balls blown off.

It was a primitive way to live, putting us in the dirt, moving us to a new hole like mole nomads every night. In those holes we all experienced the most common emotions of war: loneliness, littleness and boredom, puckered with seconds of fear. You'd hear a leaf brush against a tree branch and it became a tack in your heel and you'd hold on to your rifle just that much tighter.

I thanked God back then for my M-1 Garand rifle. It was heavy at nine pounds, though I think the thick wood stock made it seem even heavier. It was definitely heavier at the end of the day. But the damn thing could fight. It was easy to clean and nearly indestructible. You could fire .30-06 rounds off as fast as you could pull the trigger, eight shots in a row, then a metallic spring would eject the empty magazine and you could shove in another. Had to watch that ejection spring, though; if the enemy was smart enough, that twang would announce to any and all you were out of rounds for the moment.

People collect M-1s now. Some old soldiers have one mounted over the fireplace at home. I loved that rifle. I never want to see another one ever again.

Chapter 17: Please Sir, More Sake

Sergeant Eichi Nakagawa: Inside an Abandoned Warehouse, 1946

I WAS GIVEN COMMAND of Japanese soldiers, real soldiers, to lead into the fight against the American invaders. I was proud of this, even though my command consisted of only two men, Corporal Takagi and Private Otokita. I did not yet know them well. Nonetheless, we set off. Because our army's resources were scarce, we were largely left on our own to procure, find, or in a pinch, take, what food and shelter we could. It was war and normal rules did not apply.

We quickly ran across the bodies of several dead Americans. Each had been overburdened with enough food to feed several men, and we gathered as much as we could. Our next bit of luck was to stumble on a warehouse just as dusk was closing in. It was a fine place for us to rest overnight, having thick walls and clear fields of fire. In the morning we could move out towards Nishinomiya.

"Sergeant Nakagawa, this is a *sake* warehouse," Takagi said. Had he had access to more food, he probably would have been the heavy boy we teased in high school. "It is full of large barrels."

"Of *sake*," Otokita said. He was lean, but not tough. The uniform may have weighed him down.

"You see, it is just that Private Otokita and I were wondering, given the calamities of the day..." Takagi said.

"...That perhaps it would be best for all of us to have a drink. Against the cold," Otokita said. "Just a sip, for the war effort, as if it were medicine. Sir."

"HAS IT BEEN JUST a sip since you, no, I, then we, started, my good, old friends?" I said.

"I am also not certain, my dear Sergeant-san. Alcohol does not know time, my father would always say," Takagi said.

"My father would always say the fastest way to become drunk was to open the bottle," Otokita said. He belched heartily. "Or the barrel."

"I think our fathers knew each other," Takagi said.

"Should we be drinking so much?" I said.

"Why not, this is a warehouse, they have more."

We were in a room heavy with vats of the drink, big barrels upended, made from oak. I would be wrong to say you could not bathe inside one if you wished. Diving perhaps would not have worked, but indeed it was for the best that no one suggested it.

We were filling and refilling our cups from a small spigot at the bottom of the nearest barrel. There was plenty to drink inside even one, and so no need to move around to any other station. Our tidiness with the spigot grew less cautious by the cup, and soon we were sitting in cold puddles of *sake*. But not small puddles. No, these began that way, but soon grew, refill by refill, aided by spills, into small lakes. Our clothing grew sticky. The rich smell from creeping whiffs of the *sake* soon was inside of each of us. The smell cleared our heads in rhythm with the alcohol dulling them.

"I am certainly sure the *sake* has sneaked through my belly and into my legs. I cannot stand up, Sergeant," Otokita said.

"When did we last eat?" Takagi said.

"We had something, I think," Otokita said. "That old man's goddamn yams. Was that yesterday already?"

"Let us see what that American food is we took from the dead ones. Open it," I said. "The canned thing. Try your knife on it."

"Here you go. First bite to the boss," Takagi said.

"What is this? It might taste like pork under all that salt. And it seems to be similar to the right color." Takagi and Otokita took slices off the knife for themselves.

"It tastes more like the can than food we know. I think I am licking a coin," Takagi said.

"It is just pink mush. And it smells terrible. Perhaps the letters S-P-A-M mean 'shit' in their language," Otokita said.

"You are funny. And drunk. And also funny. But even the Americans do not eat shit. Do they? Still, I have never known meat to be this way," I said. "It may just be they have different animals in America."

"Yes, but my God, it is surely meat of some sort. It has been a long time," Takagi said.

"And this? Brown hard candy crumbs?" I said. "Eat it, Otokita. See."

"It tastes like coffee," Otokita said.

"How do you even know? You never had coffee before," I said.

"No, no, once my father took me to Kyoto, before the war. He bought coffee at one of the new shops. It came in a cup, like for tea, but bigger and with a curved handle. He said I should know the modern world better, and let me taste it. Like this, it was so bitter. I remember it..." Otokita said, and then passed out.

"WAKE UP, MAGGOT BOY, and talk when spoken about. Do you even remember where we are?" I said to Otokita.

"The last thing I remember was being awake. Maybe I just had too much to dream, um, to drink," Otokita said. He wiped his mouth after every other word and burped more than I could count.

"What did she look like? In your dream?" Takagi said.

"She had beautiful shoulders, pale, soft skin. I was kissing the back of her neck. That is as far as I got before you two bastards woke me," Otokita said.

"That is as far as you will ever get. Not even a girlfriend to hold hands with at home, right? Are you wearing a *senninbari*, a thousand-stitch belt, under your shirt, Otokita?" Takagi said.

"Of course. It brings luck."

"Did you have a girlfriend to make it for you?" Takagi said.

"My mother made it," Otokita said.

"So did mine," Takagi said.

"So did mine," I said. "But I had, well, I thought about having, a girlfriend. Naoko. Her name was Naoko Matsumoto. I have a photo of us from the temple festival here with me, but I will not show you two. You will only think impure thoughts. Get your own girls for that."

"Did you ever kiss her, Sergeant?" Takagi said.

"Did you ever kiss anyone?" I said.

"No," Takagi said.

"No, not ever," Otokita said.

"Well, not me either," I said.

"Oops, what was that, Takagi, you little piggy," Otokita said.

"I let off some gas, I think from the American meat," Takagi said.

"Do you not know poison gas is outlawed in this war?" I said. "Give me more to drink."

"Yes, more to drink, and let us have a toast now, to winning the war," Takagi said. "But I worry if I will have a hangover once I sober up."

"My grandfather always said 'If you cannot drink all night, do not start so early,'" Otokita said.

"Bah, drunk is fine at first, but then I get bitter, I can see that now," I said. "I will be in the loft, keeping watch and nursing my anger. We will still leave for Nishinomiya train station or rail junction or wherever the hell we are going before sun up. Dawn. We must kill them. Do you know what they call us? Japs. Nips. Slopes. Bastards."

I stood, towering over the two boys on the floor. The room was moving under me a bit, but my anger helped steady me.

"Did you know two months ago I was living with Auntie and Uncle? I had not ever had more than a sip of alcohol then, and now as our senior member I have achieved drunkenness. What the hell kind of soldiers are we anyway? This is all no longer a joke, is it? What do you say to that, Takagi, you, um, Jap bastard?"

"May we have some more sake please?"

First Shots in the Battle for Nowhere

Chapter 18: A Fine Day for Everyone to Meet

Sergeant Eichi Nakagawa: In a Foxhole, 1946

"I AM CERTAIN MY testicles are frozen. I want to be in a warm futon far from here," Otokita said

"Well, you are not. We are in this damn foxhole, waiting for the Americans to come kill us," Takagi said. "Why is night so dark here? Wait—I just heard a branch snap."

"Me too. I mean, I think so. After you said it, I mean. Should we shoot at them? They have to be over that way. We should shoot," Otokita said.

I heard my two men from the other side of the small cope of trees we were set up in. Indeed, their voices might have been heard as far away as Kyoto. Had there been any Americans within a kilometer of us we would certainly already be under attack.

"Takagi? Otokita? What the hell are you doing?" I said, crawling over from my own hole. My two soldiers then let loose dozens of rounds in nearly a dozen directions. It was clear no one was shooting back. I was lucky not to have been hit myself there was so much lead in the air.

"We must have killed them all," Takagi said.

"Yes, yes, you two, I am sure you did. The war is over. Or maybe your have given away our position. Now, one of you get some rest and the other keep watch before you really kill someone. Do not worry, you will soon get a chance to shoot at real Americans instead of shadows, I promise."

Lieutenant Nathaniel Hooper: Japan, Later the Same Day, 1946

WE'D BEEN WALKING ALL day without seeing much but different forms of sameness and accomplishing nothing but walking all day. I had heard some random shooting, sounded like about a dozen quick shots, around dawn, maybe some loud Japanese voices, but nothing came of it and we moved out.

There really wasn't a front line. The war was everywhere and nowhere as we walked in a general direction we thought might bring us closer to home in several months. It wasn't like my Dad's war, with enemy lines you could see. Here we sort of wandered around hoping to run into the Japanese and hoping not to run into the Japanese.

I wasn't sure if the quiet parts of war weren't worse on me than the noisy parts. Quiet meant I had time to think, and I didn't like that much. I'd drift back home, wondering what my folks might be doing at that same moment, then I'd wonder how that world and this world could exist at the same time, then I'd wonder if they really did, or whether Ohio got put on hold like in some science fiction story while Japan played on.

To pass the time I tried to imagine what the oddest thing from home would be to have here, to let me fool myself I wasn't homesick. I settled on a tablecloth. Mom always made a little ritual out of folding the tablecloth, so I remembered that. Then my boot would catch on something and I'd realize if I didn't pay more attention it wouldn't matter about Ohio.

It'd been raining and then clearing and then snowing and then sleeting, as if nature too couldn't make up its own mind whether being busy was better than doing nothing. Laabs had some bad news. At our last linkup, he'd heard that one of the guys from B Company had been sent back to base camp for court martial. Rumor was he jumped some farmer's wife or daughter or something, burned down the house to try and hide what he'd done, and set off a shitstorm among the local civilians. It left me wondering whose sins I might end up dying for.

It was at that point that something hard and cold hit me in the back of the neck, that vulnerable space between the bottom of my helmet and the top of my field jacket. I heard Jones shout, then Steiner cry out "Dammit, me too." We were under attack. By snowballs.

There was Polanski and Smitty, hurling one after another at us, packing them tight with the wet snow. Laabs was off closer to the tree line, half in cover, but he was watching with maybe a smile. I packed a tight one of my own, pulling my gloves off so my hands melted the slushy snow a bit more so it'd freeze into an ice ball.

A couple of years on the baseball team had given me a practiced eye, and I threw that ice ball as hard as I could at Smitty, catching him square on the nose. When it started to bleed, everybody stopped and went over to him. Nose bleeds can be a mess, even small ones, and Smitty laughing at how stupid he felt standing there flinging teardrops of blood in a half-circle around him. They melted little holes in the snow.

THE WEATHER HAD FINALLY given up and cleared a bit, and we were only about another day's stroll out of our objective, Nishinomiya. We took a short rest, but the thing to do was to keep us moving as much as possible, out of these open areas. The Japs had snowballs, too.

"Alright, buttercups, pipe down," Laabs said. "Steiner, point. Marino, you and your mouth behind him and Smitty, you and your radio with the Lieutenant, and wipe your goddamn nose. Everybody else, fall in. Jones, lace up your boots and get up. We all good? The plan of the day is mobile, agile, and hostile, gents. I'll have the back door. Heads on swivel, watch your spacing, this doesn't feel right."

"Hey Steiner, you scared up front? Don't lie," Jones said.

"Back home nothing much ever happened, nothing like this," Steiner said. "Kinda exciting, you know?"

"This guy I knew from high school, he got a medal and they sent him home to talk at war bond rallies and he met Betty Grable," Polanski said. "He told us after you kill someone, you don't want to hunt anything with four legs again."

"How much further, Sergeant? I need my beauty sleep," Steiner said.

"Stop dogging it. You can sleep when you're dead," Laabs said.

"And my feet are hurting," Steiner said.

"Yeah, and guess what," Laabs said. "I got a big pain in my ass right now. Move."

Eichi Nakagawa: Japanese Lines, the Same Day, 1946

"TAKAGI, OTOKITA," I SAID. "I have been alerted by our superiors that a farmer whose daughter was defiled by these American animals told us the bastards are patrolling now in our area. We will soon retaliate as part of an L-shaped ambush ahead of Nishinomiya. A full platoon will lead the charge on the long side, and we three will wait on the short side of the L, behind the trees, to begin the crossfire. An excellent day for an attack. A fine day for death."

Lieutenant Nathaniel Hooper: Japan, American Lines, 1946

IT WARMED ME A bit that time had passed without me stumbling someone into their death. It was also less surprising now than even a day ago that a field in Japan looked pretty much like a field in Ohio, at least in the winter when everything was covered with ice covered with snow. We'd been passing through lines of trees grown like fences between each open area. Once clear, I could sort of see to the next tree line. We were exposed, especially with our long shadows, but we also had a good field of vision, a nasty trade off. "Not knowing" was a familiar condition. History books talk about the bigger picture. For an infantryman, it was hard enough to keep 50 yards in focus. We knew as much about what was happening 20 miles away as we did about what was happening on the moon. From my mother's letters I was definitely better informed about the people back home in Ohio.

Ugly dusk was racing for the ground, that time when the horizon is painted the color of a burning cigarette. The men had been doing okay, though they were getting tired. Polanski, with the heavy BAR machine gun, had taken to carrying it across his shoulders, making him look like a Sunday school Jesus.

It was Steiner, up front, who thought he saw something, maybe a little twinge of movement. He hit the ground.

When no shots were fired at us, I ordered Steiner forward to investigate. He got up on one knee, and as he moved to stand, there was the first shot. Then two more. Then another. Had I not seen the rounds slap into him and then the pink mist that hung in the air for just that long, I would have thought he'd just slipped on the ice, the way his legs flew out from under him. His body didn't convulse from the rounds hitting him as much as it looked like it absorbed them.

Steiner went down without grace, clutching his chest and screaming way past his size, trying to shout away the pain. Even from the distance I could see the bald end of his leg bone, the blood coming out around it as the big artery down there pulsed and twisted like a loose garden hose.

It was Jones alone who ran forward, nobody told him to, flopping on the ground next to Steiner. You've been looking at the world one way, then you see a person do something like that. Everyone else, me included, followed Sergeant Laabs' shouts to retreat back into the tree line and lay down suppressing fire against whoever shot at us.

We all carried little first aid pouches called Carlisles on our web belts, really just a field dressing, some sulfur powder and a couple of morphine syrettes. They weren't actual hypo needles, just little tubes like glue or drawing salve about two inches long with a needle at one end and a small loop of wire used to break the seal and release the morphine. You jabbed the thing into a wounded man to dull the pain until either real help arrived, he stopped screaming, or he passed.

The drug made Steiner go from screaming into a low moan, fetal, rocking himself. We could hear something else now; the leg looked bad, but it was an open sucking chest wound that was killing him breath by breath, the bullet caught in his right lung, Steiner now gasping like a fish on the end of a line—in suck, out cough, in suck, out blood, in suck, out spattering air. Jones tried to drag him back toward us, but he was too heavy and Jones' fear of standing to get a better grip was too much, and so after pulling Steiner just a yard or two, Jones belly crawled back alone. I looked out and saw a red arrow on the snow, marking just how far Jones had got him before giving up. Steiner was turning blue, his breathing became a stopped-up drain gurgling, then, finally, just the low hiss of gas escaping an open valve. Only thing warm was the blood, Jones said, as he wiped his hands on his trousers.

Steiner was smoking a Chesterfield when he was hit. The dropped butt was on top of the frozen snow, still letting off a spit of smoke, curling up, before, pffft, it melted into the earth.

Sergeant Eichi Nakagawa: Japanese Lines, 1946

"YOU SEE THE BASTARD bleeding to death out there?" Takagi said.

"One less foreign devil, even though he is soiling our land," I said. "Takagi, over there, in the trees, try and take out that one before our brothers launch their charge. Kill him, he appears to be giving orders to the others. That one, the American wearing glasses."

Lieutenant Nathaniel Hooper: American Lines, 1946

I'D BEEN SHOT AT too many times already since leaving the ship and heading onto the beach, but it never felt all that personal until one went past me now like a fat steel horsefly, hit the tree, and threw some bark down the back of my jacket. Bullets move faster than sound, so the round gets there before the noise. You'll truly never know what hit you unless it doesn't.

This wasn't the Japanese Army shooting at an American Army uniform; it was some Jap shooting at me. Whatever concerns about right and wrong some people lose bit by bit, I lost all at once. I knew what to do, already hearing Sergeant Laabs' voice in my head. You hit harder than you've been hit. Smitty dragged his radio over on my command, and with a few shouted sentences, just as quick, I had a Navy Bearcat inbound from a carrier off shore. The shot at me had to have come from either the tree line to the right, or the one straight ahead, kind of an L-shape. I got to pick; I could make that plane do anything I wanted. I was choosing who would die. I picked... the trees in front.

"Let the Nips come out and fight," Marino said. "My trigger finger's itching for it."

"Well, time to scratch. Here they come, maybe 30 of them," I said. "Fire, fire, contact front. BAR, open up, short bursts, Polanski, now now now."

What was happening fast was happening slow. I was hypnotized watching the BAR exhale the empty brass shell casings out of the ejection port, chunka chunka chunka. This was nowhere; the field had no name. No one would study this at West Point. This would achieve nothing noteworthy for the war effort. It would never be "The Battle of..." so we could tell our kids we were there when they learned about it in school. I knew that, but I pushed it down.

My body was tight, and I could see and hear and smell like I never had before. Cleaning up Steiner'd come later; I'd already thrown a blanket over him in my mind. In this now, I sensed my blood moving. I could taste the air on my tongue. I was goddamn glowing from the thrill of it. Ohio let go and that feral thing inside of me took over.

All that stuff you hear about, guys hesitating when they face their first conscious decision to kill? A pause when they can finally see the face of the enemy? Bullshit. Line up the rifle, shift focus from the sight to the human head, a squeeze on the trigger, the target falls down. It was too easy. It felt like we could have been throwing snowballs and knocking them over. The Japs meanwhile advanced across the field like they were conducting a parade, almost without noticing we were there, running toward our line like Pickett's charge at Gettysburg. As one man fell, and we were killing them easy enough, the others never hesitated. They just kept staring through us into the next tree line as though they hoped to see their mama-sans back there waiting for them with a box lunch. It was like they were more concerned about signaling something to each other than having any impact on us.

The Japs had no mortars, no artillery, no aircraft. There was nothing to keep our heads down, and so we just kept shooting and shooting. It was right out of the Rexall boys' dime books back home. I shouted myself hoarse, I couldn't trust my senses to respond properly, I was God throwing lightning bolts, teasing up some part of me I'd never listened to before. I felt like I'd be eating only dry crackers all my life and somebody just said, "Oh, here's what steak tastes like, eat up, buddy."

Killing was the most powerful thing I'd ever done and made me feel I was living intensively, and that was perfectly addictive. At the same time I knew it was somehow wrong. I tried to think about it as just a way to stay alive, something I had to do, but truth is I liked it.

"You see that? I took the head off one and his damn body just stood there, holding his rifle before he fell. You saw it, right, Polanski? Always better to be the man with the gun," Marino said.

"That one's running away with half his guts in his hands. What should I do?" Jones said.

"Give him a few more yards to suffer then plug him in the back," Sergeant Laabs said. He was laughing. We all were now.

"We're either gonna run out of ammo, or they're gonna run outta men," Polanski said.

I was still worried about the other tree line, the one I didn't pick for the incoming aircraft. I sent three men off to our flank, to have a look.

Sergeant Eichi Nakagawa: Japanese Lines, 1946

"SERGEANT NAKAGAWA, THERE ARE three Americans running this way," Otokita said.

"Let them get closer, right to us. Bayonet them if you can so we do not give ourselves away. Do not embarrass yourselves. And do not be surprised by their blood; it smells like a ten yen copper coin, you know," I said.

"Sergeant Nakagawa, I hear aircraft."

Lieutenant Nathaniel Hooper: Japan, American Lines, 1946

THE PLANE WAS A PINPOINT, became a speck, then a dot, and finally came in low and fast, treetop level, so close I could see the pilot inside smiling. The aircraft held two bombs, 100 pounders. Those tumbled off from under the wings, exploding among the Japanese soldiers as the plane pulled into a near vertical climb, escaping its own fire. Clouds of snow and dirt geysered up where each weapon struck. The bombs did some real work, but while the charging mass of Japs had thinned, it had not gone away. In the confusion, I saw our own three guys make the flank, and go through the trees.

Sergeant Eichi Nakagawa: Japanese Lines, 1946

"QUIET, LET THEM SLIP past the trees. Now, from behind, bayonets, slash, slash," I said.

"I killed one. I killed an American!" Takagi said.

"I butchered one myself, before you did, I was first this time!" Otokita said.

"Look at the blood. They gurgle as they die. Like babies talking."

"Now one has his hands up. Take him Otokita! Slice him in half with your steel," I said.

It was almost too easy, and it was glorious, just like in the war *manga* we boys read at home. To at last use our training to protect our nation, this was what war was really about. I was proud to watch Takagi and Otokita, my two little frightened kittens, take their bayonet-tipped rifles with both hands and move them like plungers. That doubt-free sound was the voice of our victory. I watched Otokita, now off to the side, work his knife through the knuckle of an American's pink little finger, scraping against bone like my fingernails against the blackboard when I was still a schoolboy. Otokita clearly thought the man was dead, and Takagi and I laughed as he jumped back at the American's moan. The sound stopped soon enough, and Otokita pocketed the prize, saying his father told him when he fought in the China campaign years earlier such trophies brought luck.

Lieutenant Nathaniel Hooper: Japan, American Lines, 1946

"THAT LAST JAP OUT front looks like he's putting his hands up. Maybe some of them do surrender after all," Jones said.

"He's falling forward, who the hell shot him from behind?" I said.

"The Jappers shot at him themselves," Polanski said.

"That one on the ground's still moving," I said. "We'll take him prisoner. You two men, go guard him so he doesn't escape."

"I think his legs are blown off, sir. I'm pretty sure he isn't gonna go anywhere," Sergeant Laabs said. Everybody, cease fire. You all okay? Anybody hit? Pumped up? Adrenaline. Happens. Takes a while for it all to slow back down."

I sent Laabs to search the Jap bodies laid out across the field for maps or papers. I allowed myself to focus on Steiner only enough to order Marino and Jones to wrap his body in one of the sleeping bags we'd picked up, so we could take him with us. It was Polanski who I gave the short straw, telling him to go see what happened to the troopers on the flank.

POLANSKI'S REPORT COMING BACK from the tree line was sharp. They're dead. That was the whole story if you knew enough to understand it. But Polanski threw out a few more words in case I didn't get it: gray, crushed, slashed, a soldier's brevity code. Marino and Jones returned from the field with Steiner's remains, the spine twisted like a dirt road in their rough handling.

"What should we do about Steiner's letters, Lieutenant?" Marino said.

"Look, his girlfriend dotted the 'i' in his name with a little heart. Steiner has about a million of them from her like that in his knapsack," Jones said. "Now he ain't gonna get any more."

"Neither will she," Marino said. He tried to smile at his own joke, but even he could only come up with a little twist at the corner of his mouth.

Steiner had those letters, but more than that he had a bunch of unused, pre-addressed envelopes, all going the same place. She'd never hear what Steiner had to say about this shitty day. The thought pulled up that puffy tension behind my eyes, and I tamped it down by biting my lip. You'd think after all the men I'd seen die already, one more wasn't such a big deal, but I looked at the envelopes and there it was—Ethan Samuel Steiner. Ethan Samuel Steiner. I held it together only a few seconds more until I saw the ring on Steiner's finger. I never really knew him. It wasn't just a girlfriend he'd been writing to.

As complex as it would be to anyone who'd never stood in a place like this, it was simple. We'd acted selflessly, reassurances that said we belonged to each other—Jones' crawling out to Steiner, Polanski's taunt requiem, even Marino's crude way of marking Steiner's death. The dead Japs meant nothing.

Black birds circled overhead, calling to each other. Japanese crows are fat as Satan's alley cat, big enough that we could see their yellow eyes from the ground. They were waiting for us to leave and let them get on with their part of the war, while we got on with ours. We were all hungry for more.

Sergeant Eichi Nakagawa: Japanese Lines, 1946

"PRIVATE OTOKITA, CORPORAL TAKAGI, we need to move, now, before the Americans regroup," I said.

"There are so many of our dead. Should we not attack again, Sergeant? Charge those American murderers?" Otokita said.

"I feel life would be easier," Takagi said, "if I was dead."

"No, we have to live for the time being, because there are more we need to kill at Nishinomiya. That is important. It is our primary mission. This was just... for fun. You get to live a little longer. Use that properly as it no longer belongs to you," I said.

Birds had arrived, calling to each other in blue voices, circling overhead where the American plane had been. They knew we would leave soon, and their turn to eat would come. They were anxious to get to the dead. They were hungry for it.

Chapter 19: The Farmhouse

Former Lieutenant Nathaniel Hooper: Retirement Home, Kailua, Hawaii, 2017

JAPS. NO JOKING, THAT'S what we called them, all the time, even in the newspapers and on the radio, if not Nips, slopes, monkeys or just yellow bastards. The Japs must have had similar names they called us, because in every war those words are there—Krauts, Charlie, VC, rag heads and infidels. The Romans must have had some nasty term in Latin for the Gauls.

I would never use such slurs today, and am horrified I ever did, but over there, then, it was different. We heard the Japanese painted American flags on sidewalks just so people could walk on them. Kids in my hometown were taught to squash "Japanese" beetles. The U.S. military had to issue an order stating, "No part of the enemy's body may be used as a souvenir." The rule wasn't followed, by either side, and I saw American troops use their fighting knives to pull gold teeth from dead enemies, or slice off ears, or worse. We all saw dead Americans with their genitals hacked off and stuffed into their mouths. I don't want to think what's hidden in old men's closets around the world for the kids to find. Good Christ it was primitive. There were monsters in the air then.

Lieutenant Nathaniel Hooper: Japan, In the Woods, 1946

"ANYBODY SEEN BURKE?" LAABS said.

The last time I'd seen Burke he was talking about wandering off, mumbling how he was going to shoot a rabbit for dinner, complaining he was sick of eating K-rations, and how back home in North Carolina he'd hunt all the time. Did they even have rabbits in Japan? Burke was always bragging about his heritage down south, some line about having relatives that died in every war back to the one between the states. It got to be like having the radio on in the background, and I paid about as much attention to him as that. I didn't think he'd really go off by himself, something that stupid, that it was just more of his talk, but he must have really slipped away.

A single shot.

Maybe he got his damn rabbit. We had to keep moving, so I sent Marino and Jones off, to pull him back in, rabbit or no rabbit.

We heard Marino shouting first, but it was Jones who came back on the run, saying something about Burke, and how we'd all better come quick.

Burke was laid out on the grass, face down. There was blood on the back of his head, pushing out because there was otherwise no place else useful for it to go anymore. When I got close I saw the single hole and I knew he'd been shot from pretty close. Marino was jabbering about some trail he thought led off into the woods, but before I could pay attention to him, I knew what I had to do. With Polanski's help, I rolled Burke over to make sure.

Bullets enter more or less intact, the nose pointy, and make a small hole going in because they are going pretty fast. But against something as hard as a skull, the tip flattens out and the bullet slows down, meaning when it hits the front of the skull, from the inside, it pushes out a large piece of bone. Blunt force. Burke'd been shot from behind. Execution-style, not like the rules say is right for a soldier.

There was no face except what had stuck to the dirt under the snow. There was not a whole lot of blood splattered, like you'd have nightmared. Instead, it had mostly pooled up in the dent Burke's face made when it hit the ground we'd soon bury the slush that was left of him in.

Marino came back down that trail he'd followed, saying there was a farmhouse. It wasn't far from where we were standing in an angry semi-circle around Burke's body, so I sent Marino and Jones off again, to take a look, just check it out, telling them not to start anything before the rest of us caught up.

Japan, Rear of the Farmhouse, 1946

"JONES, THE BACK DOOR. Holy shit, someone's coming out," Marino said.

"Jap soldier," Jones said. "He's pulling down his pants. I think he's gonna take a poop."

"Let's get him, to hell with the Lieutenant," Marino said. "What if he killed Burke? What if he knows something that'd save our guys' lives? Maybe he knows where the rest of the Japs are hiding. I'll choke him from behind. You go for the rifle."

"GOT THE RIFLE," JONES said. "I'll get the Lieutenant over here."

"Not yet, Jones. Okay, Hirohito-san, who's inside that farmhouse?" Marino said. The Jap soldier was on the ground now, hands tied together with his belt.

"*Tanomu kara korosanaide kure! Onegai da.*"

"What'd the bastard say?"

"How the hell should I know? Ask him again," Jones said.

"WHERE IS E-NE-MY?" Marino said.

"*Eigo ga wakaranai. Korosanaide kure.*"

"He's not gonna talk," Marino said. He swung hard, laying his fist squarely against the bridge of the Japanese soldier's nose. It wasn't the first nose Marino had broken. "See how soft that shit is? The center's just mush."

"*Ore wa nani mo shiranain da. Yamete kure.*"

"See, he knows how to talk, he just won't. Shove something in his mouth so we don't have to listen to him," Marino said. "There ya' go pal. You likee? You speakee English, don't you? PEARL HARBOR? BURKE? Bastard was the one who did Burke. Watch this, Jones. The knife slides right through, see? And not a freaking word out of him; the Oriental don't feel pain like we do. Wonder how many times he used that finger to pull the trigger on our guys, huh? Lemme work on him, then you're gonna shoot him."

"To hell with you, Marino, I ain't gonna shoot him," Jones said.

"You're gonna shoot something Jap, you coward," Marino said.

"Fine, I'll shoot... that goat. That Jap goat over there. Otherwise a Jap soldier will eat it and get stronger and then try to kill us," Jones said.

"Makes sense. But better shoot the goat before the Lieutenant shows up. He didn't want me to shoot the puppy on Day One, so who knows what he'll say about the goat. He let me kill the wounded guy, but Lieutenant Hooper likes animals," Marino said. "You hear the way that knife sounds on bone? Fingernails on a blackboard."

Former Lieutenant Nathaniel Hooper: Retirement Home, Kailua, Hawaii, 2017

WE WENT ON TO storm the farmhouse like real G.I. Joe's, but there was no one inside. We stayed warm that night believing Marino and Jones were heroes. Marino told me the Japanese soldier was sneaking around behind them so he had to kill him in spite of my orders to not take action. I saw the dead man's eyes frozen open, looking like a puppy waiting for its mean owner's slap. I saw the missing fingers, the blood fan spray on Marino, and I saw Jones off to the side, his mouth pressed against the ground to muffle the sound of his vomiting. But I kept my mouth shut, again. It wasn't until much later I learned the whole story.

Jonesy was simple. There might have been paper in his head that hadn't been written on yet, and someday might have been, but at that moment there was no chance he could have figured out just because it wasn't his fault didn't mean it wasn't his responsibility.

And sure, sitting here on the lanai 70 years later, with a glass of sweet tea sweating from all the ice I have in it, I can say it was wrong what Marino did, and what Jones did, standing by while it happened. And it was wrong what I did, saying it was all okay by not saying anything. I thought I'd figured this stuff out back in the village, after Marino killed the wounded Japanese soldier in cold blood, but it turned out it wasn't as easy as I thought.

The first time, at the village, I acted out of what I convinced myself was maybe excusable ignorance of what I'd gotten into. I'd never confronted those kinds of things before and had no idea what was the right thing, so I did the easy thing and congratulated Marino so I'd look tough. The second time, with Marino's tortured prisoner, I was scared, and I acted out of that fear. I knew it was wrong, for Christ's sake we all knew it was wrong. You can kill him, maybe even get a medal for that if you do it by the rules, but carving him up to make his death as horrible as you can, there's no right there. Sometimes the warrior is the war.

I let myself pretend my little war crime was somehow acceptable because I was afraid. And what if the guy Marino tortured really knew something that could have saved American lives? Would I have joined in?

Most times I tell myself no, but sometimes I convince myself yes, and that scares the hell out of me.

Chapter 20: Mama

Lieutenant Nathaniel Hooper: Japan, On Open Ground, 1946

"GET YOUR HEADS DOWN, right now now now." It was Laabs.

The nearest real cover was a clump of trees about as far from us as home plate is from second base. It wouldn't have been safe to try for it under fire even if we ran like it was going to rain.

No one saw whatever it was that Laabs saw, but we all kissed the dirt on his command anyway. I'd heard real combat veterans react somehow even before they hear the rounds snap. Maybe they can taste prey in the air. I'd guess if scientists were to study it, they'd find guys like Laabs were picking up on a smell, a tiny click somewhere caught with the fine hairs of their inner ear and passed on to the lizard brain, the smallest of things in the slightest of ways. But we all heard the shot a breath away from hell a moment later.

"You, Private, move up and shoot at something," I said.

"What should I shoot at, Lieutenant?"

"The goddamn Japs" was the best I could answer.

I could see the village up ahead, same one I'd seen from the frozen rice paddy earlier, where the three men had been pink misted by the mines. We'd made it all the way back closer to where we'd started, at the cost of seven lives. Having failed to do so on the beach, I now fired my weapon, randomly and pointlessly, with the realization that for the first time in my life I wanted to kill other human beings.

"Anybody see where we're getting shot at from?" I said.

"Maybe near those trees? You might wanna get some men out on to the flanks, would be a good start, Lieutenant," Laabs said. I might have heard his eyes roll.

"Um, right, you two, start crawling off to the right and see if you can get into the tall grass alive. Try and get around, you know, dammit what's the word, flank that bunch of trees," I said. The two ran off.

"The Japs stopped shooting. What should we do, Lieutenant?" Burke said.

The worst words in the English language to me had become "What should we do, Lieutenant?"

"Yes, cease fire, stop now. You two on the flank, this is Hooper, shit, Lieutenant Hooper, can you hear me? We're ready to provide covering fire for you to advance," I said, with confidence I didn't own and they weren't buying. They refused to move, at first, then reluctantly rose up.

"Sergeant Laabs, how am I doing with this?"

"A lot of on-the-job training opportunities for you today, Lieutenant. You're handling it like a fish at a swimming lesson, sir."

WE WERE DOING WHAT the Army calls a "movement to contact," something that sounded fine in training back at Fort Polk when we were only attacking a swamp. That hadn't prepared me for this any more than looking at a cake would've prepared me to be a baker. Out here we were bait for the

Japanese to find and thus expose themselves. It was a lot like hide and seek, except the losers died.

I'd wet myself as those first rounds came in, and hoped it would freeze on my pants before I had to stand up. The two men I'd asked to run out to the flank emerged from cover there. I'd no idea what to do if they hadn't moved out. I couldn't figure out how to sound like an officer, talking so that it leaves no way to disagree. The soldiers wiggled forward maybe an inch, then another, then a foot. One shouted he saw a foxhole. Like the inexperienced soldiers they were, the two stood up, took a few steps in the open and leaned over the hole.

The rest of us, minus Laabs, who stayed stapled to the ground, then also stood up and walked over to the hole as if we'd been called to look under the hood of a stalled car and give our opinions on the next step. Could be the carburetor, you know.

"Jap soldier here, sir. He's real dead," Marino said. "Like they said in training, shallow foxhole, deep grave."

"He looks old. And he stinks. Maybe like cow drop," Jones said. "See, I grew up on a farm, and—"

"Shut up, Jones. Dead men, their bodies let go when they get killed," Sergeant Laabs said as he walked over. It didn't seem necessary to spit, but he did.

"So how come we couldn't smell poop on the boat when that Corporal got greased?" Jones said.

"Likely because you kiddies soiled your own diapers," Marino said. "Anyway, I smelled it on the boat. I just didn't say anything is all."

We'd hit the soldier only once it looked like, a round into his shoulder. The body looked shapeless, like a pile of laundry on the floor, but it was all still there.

"*Okaachan...*"

"Hell, he ain't all dead. He's talking in his Jap talk," Jones said.

There was a sound like a sock full of dimes hitting wet meat. Marino had shot the wounded Jap soldier again, at point blank range.

"Like it matters how. We're supposed to kill Japs," Marino said. "You know they only need two pallbearers at their funerals 'cause garbage cans only got two handles. Anyway, I've seen worse shit back in the neighborhood."

"Marino, watch your mouth, you're still talking to a goddamn officer," Laabs said. "Lieutenant, sir, a word?"

"Good job, um, Marino. Okay, Sergeant Laabs, over here. Rest of you keep an eye out," I said.

Laabs and I walked a few steps away in what was becoming our ritual. The men kept looking at the dead guy, lowering their voices like they were worried they might wake him up.

"Goddammit Lieutenant, Marino shot a wounded man we should've taken prisoner. You didn't need to condone that," Laabs said. "You don't have to be much of a leader, sir, just be one. The men watch you to see how they should act. It matters out here, sir, a lot."

"I wanted to look tough in front of the men," I said.

"I understand, sir, I get it, I really do. You want it to be simple, you want it to make sense, but it was just wrong. Hey sir, that a stain on the front of our trousers?"

"Nope, rice paddy water, Sergeant."

"Ground's frozen, sir."

"YOU SEE ME GREASE that guy?" Marino said to the men. "What was he saying before he died anyway?"

"Sounded like *okaachan*."

"What's that mean?" Jones said. "Burke, you got that Japanese phrase book?"

"I'm savin' it for when we see the *geishas*."

"You ain't never gonna see no *geishas*. Gimme the goddamn thing," Marino said. "*Okaachan*. It means 'mama.'"

"Same as the Corporal. The guy from Indiana, too, in the landing craft. They all said mama."

Laabs and I walked over to where the rest of the men had flopped down on the ground, acting like one dead enemy soldier had made for a good day's work, and it was time to settle back a bit.

"On your feet, contact right." It was Polanski this time who saw it first.

"Relax, it's just a Jap girl, waving a white flag," Marino said.

The girl probably would have been scared to see a full meal in her house; she looked like a marionette, arms and legs all spider thin. She shouted something over her shoulder we didn't understand, and an old Japanese man came out of the woods. "Yankee, come friend," he said, pointing toward the village.

We had been told a lot of things about the Japanese people, mostly along the lines that they were fanatics who were going to resist us to their last breath, fighting with sticks and kitchen knives if necessary, suicidal samurai. It happened a few times during the earlier landings on Kyushu, at least we'd heard that from some guy who knew someone that'd been there. And everybody knew about the Sasebo Massacre, where the crazy ass Marines killed 50 unarmed civilians, some women, when they wouldn't surrender. But after that, there weren't many more. It got so when a couple of crazed farmers came at our guys with pitchforks, they'd fire a few shots over the farmers' heads and get behind a wall or something until the old men tired themselves out. Turkey shoots are only fun at first, then you feel sorry for the birds.

Still, according to the field manuals, if it was to be a massacre, this would be the time.

I could see everyone's breath condensing in the air. Lined up along both sides of the single unpaved street were dozens of Japanese, mostly women and children, a few old men. You couldn't tell how old the women were closer than somewhere between 15 and 80. No young males of military age, no *geishas*. They all mostly looked like sacks of bones loosely wrapped with skin, a medieval scene out of some picture book. We were the most powerful military on Earth and we were greeted by the poorest Japan had to push up against us. We stood with our rifles, and they stood silent. Both sides were encountering this situation for the first time, and neither knew what to do.

The war had certainly been here ahead of us. A few houses had been spared, maybe by fate as reminders of what more this war still had left to eat. Some others had burned; they were made mostly made of wood and paper and straw, almost purpose-built to be taken by our firebombs. But the houses that startled me most looked as if they'd just had their legs kicked out from under them. The heavy tile roofs sat more or less intact on top of broken furniture and pieces of wood. From the skeletons of the places, they built them here with roofs too heavy for the wood beams holding them up. Our concussion bombs had their way with that. What kind of boneheads built houses out of paper and wood? Even in Ohio we knew better than that.

A few of the children looked up into our faces, then the women looked, and finally even a few of the old men. Without an order, my men lowered their rifles.

"Sergeant Laabs, move the men back, and be ready to lay down covering fire. Jones, come forward with me," I said.

"You going to do whatever the hell this is without backup, Lieutenant?" Laabs said.

"Sergeant, rank has its privileges. C'mon, Jones."

THE FEW YARDS DEEPER into the village were a long walk.

"Bang! Bang! *Boku ga Amerika-hei o uttan da yo.*"

"Lieutenant!"

"Jones, stop, lower your weapon. It's just another damn kid. He was playing, shooting at you with a stick. Be easy, Jones. They're scared."

"Well, how you think I feel, Lieutenant?" Jones said. Just a farm boy likely out of state for the first time, you could hear the soil in his voice. I remembered now seeing him aboard ship, his lips moving as he read a paperback Western on deck. A man ought to be remembered for something more than that, even Jones.

An old man startled everyone by falling to his knees and bowing until his head touched the ground.

"*Makoto ni moshiwake gozaimasen deshita.*"

"What's he saying? Anybody in this village speak English?" I said.

"Yes, I." It was the same man. "But I wanted apologize Japanese first. Now we can talk English, a little, because I was a merchant sailor. I sailed Kobe to San Francisco. And back, too. My village asked me to talk you, for them."

"What the hell are you people doing? Why the hell did we almost shoot a child down there? Who was that old soldier who nearly killed me?" I said.

"Please, slow. A long time since English. So now, we are surrendering to you."

"You can't surrender, we just liberated you," I said.

"Sorry, there is some 'liberate' on your shirt," the old man said.

I looked down. Blood from the Japanese soldier, or maybe from one of my men killed on the boat—who could tell, red is red. Then an old woman screamed something in Japanese so sad that I knew it was her husband, the old soldier, we'd shot.

"What about the child down there? Was she trying to surrender?" I said.

"We were afraid of how to contact you after you shot the old soldier. The man you talked to down below said he was not scared, so he sent his granddaughter while he hid in the weeds."

"What is wrong with you people? We could've killed her, for God's sake," I said.

"We have lost many children already to your bombs and planes. Now, we ask only for our lives." The old man stood up, putting his hands on his knees to push himself vertical.

"We're Americans. You're free now, dammit. Don't you know that? Don't you understand what we've done for you? Let's start over, old man. Any soldiers here?" I said.

"Only the one you killed. He is no longer here."

"Why was there only one soldier defending a whole village?" I said.

"He was not defending us," said the old man. "The old soldier served with the Imperial forces in Manchuria long ago. He could barely see. He was not a danger man for you. About one month ago, real Japanese soldiers came here and instructed us to fight to the death when the *kichikubeei*, 'The Devil's Farm Animals,' came. That is you. It is not a nice word. They said that *ji ji* old soldier had an obligation to prepare us. He made us sharpen bamboo sticks to use against your guns. He told us to shave the heads of our women so you would find them ugly. He made me teach them to say 'syphilis' in English to scare you away."

"Old man, how come these kids all look so hungry?" I said.

"We do not have much meat. We even ate the dogs, or they ran away."

"I had to stop my men from killing one we ran across this morning," I said.

"A dog? If you had shot it we could have fed our children tonight."

"It was just a puppy. What was that you said before about the old soldier and obligation?"

"Mister soldier, we Japanese believe life is controlled by *otsutome*. I am not sure how to explain it to people like you—maybe, 'obligation is everything,'" said the old man.

"And so the old soldier had to die to fulfill his obligation to the Emperor? That it? That *banzai* thing?" I said.

The old man explained things to me like if I was a child. He said the soldier saw us, so tall, so well fed, and knew he had been wrong to try and convince the villagers to fight. They would have all died because of him, and so he did what he had to do. They were weak and I wasn't. I realized I could do anything I wanted to these people. They couldn't stop me, only I could do that, and only if I wanted to. None of the rules from home, church, the cops, the consequences, mattered. The war would bury any crime.

Marino had killed the Japanese soldier. Then I said it was okay. Without that second guy—shit, me—it's just something bad in isolation. But real evil's participatory. It's the condoning that makes it cross over into something you learn in church you shouldn't do.

I didn't know what to do next, but I knew the others would just stand by when I acted. I could do anything I wanted.

"Jones, give these people some of your rations," I said.

"The ones you wouldn't let me give to the puppy?" Jones said. "To them, sir? The enemy?"

Skirmishes

Chapter 21: The Real Lesson from Major Yamada

Eichi Nakagawa: Kyoto Train Station, 1946

AFTER I WATCHED OLD Man Tanaka die inside his home, I welcomed the army recruiters taking me. We traveled to the largest train station in the area, in Nishinomiya itself. It was a two story brick building that used to be a maroon color, the same as the others that were built in all the big cities during the Emperor Meiji's time. It was just gray now, as there was only soft coal left for heat and the air was smoky.

I remembered train stations from when I was a child. Outside then were always vendors. You could buy snacks and *bento* lunches for long trips, *omiyage* souvenirs and so much more that my eyes would spin. At times my parents would allow Naoko to come along with us, or I would go with her and her mother. When her mother would reach into her purse and hand us a few sen—one yen was too large a sum for such things—I always knew what to buy, running with Naoko to the candy man for the fruit drops we loved, called Sakuma.

The same area now was filled with soldiers. A mother was waving goodbye as our train pulled away. She shouted, "Come back to me." Such emotions were to be unspoken in wartime; we Japanese were expected to bear our burdens silently. It was considered an honor to give up a son to the war. A police officer grabbed her and shoved her into a telephone pole, opening a gash that bled into her eyes. "You are lucky I do not arrest you for sedition, old woman," he said. "You should be congratulating your son, and be grateful the nation will take him. You are a disgrace, go home." I knew it was her son near me in the train carriage when he looked away.

I understood then there are horrors apart from death. I stayed on the train.

Eichi Nakagawa: Japanese Imperial Army Training Center, North of Nishinomiya, 1946

I WANTED TO SHAKE myself like an animal to tear off the rain, but whenever anyone moved, a soldier would come and slap him. As we became colder and our movements not our own, the soldiers would punch us, and I could see blood run from the nose of the boy next to me, and just as quickly be washed away by the steel of the rain. I had never paid attention to how red fresh blood is. What a strange thought, and what strange things I was learning!

We stood on the muddy parade ground, so close in ranks that I could feel the breath of the boy behind me on my neck. The rain had so softened the earth so that each boy's weight pushed him deeper into his own puddle. Around us were the barracks we would live in. They were wood, with tar paper roofs, thrown-together structures standing intact enough to say we were perhaps worthy of shelter, but not of comfort.

An officer walked forward, his uniform crisp somehow. I believed the rain was afraid to fall on him. He demanded we bow, which we did as a group. We had long practiced such signs of respect while in school, readying us for this moment as if it was an entrance exam. The officer's voice was harsh, and he used a command form of Japanese we had only heard before aimed at slow-moving farm animals. He had so much army in his blood. I wished to be him. I could see the others were afraid, but I was not, not of the officer. My only fear was failing him.

"I am Major Yamada. Here are two rules for your survival. You have a mouth but you cannot say what you wish. And you have a brain but you cannot think as you wish. Now you. How old are you?"

"I am 48, sir," one of the other recruits said.

"Why are they sending me old men?" Major Yamada said.

"My factory burned down and I had no work so I was sent here."

Major Yamada looked down, testing the ground for its worthiness, then spat. The rain quickly washed it away.

"And you? Are you the factory man's baby boy?" he said.

"I am already 17-years-old, sir," I said. "My name is Eichi Nakagawa. My father has a small shop, sir."

"Peddler's sons for the Emperor. I guess we cannot be too strict any more in who we must use as consumables," Major Yamada said. Without warning, he slapped me. "Do you think I care about you, Nakagawa?"

"No, sir." He slapped me again, removing his glove this time and using it like a whip against my face. The rain hid what the pain caused to well up in my eyes. I tasted blood from where my teeth tore inside my cheek.

"You are wrong. I do care," Major Yamada said. "I care because I am ordered to do so by my superiors. I was told to prepare children to defend Japan. You will become a game piece in the hands of others. So I care about a pustule like you without regard for my own feelings. That is why I am here. Why are you here, Nakagawa?"

"To serve my country," I said.

"Wrong. There is only a single correct answer: You wish to feel the blood of an American run down your bayonet blade. Repeat that out loud, you little bastard," Major Yamada said. "Are you ready to learn what I must teach you, Nakagawa?"

"I will fight, sir."

"Fighting is what boys do in the schoolyard. I am going to train you to die, Eichi Nakagawa. That is *gyokusai*, striving for an honorable death. When you are ready to not fail at that, your training will be over and you may then be able to contribute something to this country with your wretched life. Let us start. Nakagawa, you are a dog."

"Yes, Major," I said.

"Now bark."

"Yes, Major," I said.

"Do not say 'Yes Major,' bark, dammit, let me hear you. Ah, good. Do you know why you are a dog, Eichi Nakagawa?"

"No, Major," I said.

"Why do you not know?"

"Because you have not told me yet, Major," I said.

"Hmm. Fine answer. I shall keep my eye on you, Nakagawa."

"PSST... NAKAGAWA, ARE YOU AWAKE?" It was one of the other recruits, speaking to me from the top bunk. "Nakagawa, tell me, are you afraid?"

"Of Major Yamada?"

"No stupid, of the Americans," he said. "I am afraid of the Americans. When I was little, my daddy worked for a trading company and we were stationed in Singapore. An American warship made a port call and daddy took us to see it. They wore those white hats that look like trumpets. I remember how tall their sailors were."

"No, they just look tall. I think when we see them up close they will be just our size," I said.

"Nakagawa, they are tall. Don't tell anyone, but I have seen them very, very close. Not in Singapore."

The boy told me before he was sent to our training camp he had been staying with relatives on Kyushu, and had been trapped there for a long time after the Americans invaded. One day, some Japanese soldiers came to his relatives' home and took him away. They brought him to a hidden spot in the woods, within sight of an American camp. They told him to walk up to the Americans, carefully counting his steps, and ask for chocolate. If he was not killed, he should walk back, carefully recounting his steps.

"I did exactly as I was told. And you know what the Japanese soldiers said? They said that night they would attack the Americans with mortars, and now, because of me, they knew the precise range—73 steps—from their hiding spot to the American camp and would certainly be able to kill the men who gave me the chocolate. It was called Hersey's. I remember it tasted like things from before this war. I never told anyone, not even my parents."

"I lay here at night thinking about my parents. I worry the Americans will harm them," I said.

"They are safe near Kyoto, though, right? Mine are in Osaka. They live on a hillside and say sometimes the fighter planes come at eye level right past them, dive bombing the city."

"They did everything for me and I cannot bear the thought of all of that being lost because the Americans came to our country," I said.

"But my daddy says it could not be unexpected," he said. "Do you want to be here, Nakagawa?"

"I like it here," I said. "I just have to eat and train. Nothing more. I only have to think at night."

"I envy you, Nakagawa. But I wish I was home now."

"When I can kill one of them, I want to not hesitate. Just a week ago I worried about a spanking from Uncle," I said. "Now, look at me, I am allowed a real rifle. Every time Major Yamada makes me do physical training in the cold, I think about what will happen to my parents. It makes me mad, and that makes me warm. Now I wish to kill one hundred of the Americans. I cried about killing one frog once, you know."

"I do not always understand you, Nakagawa. Are you being silly?"

"I no longer understand silly."

IT WAS AS IF it had never rained before in Japan, and now it was time to resolve that. As we did every day during training, we stood outside the barracks at attention, rifles on our shoulders, until our uniforms were soaked. The sergeants then inspected us, pushing and shoving shivering boys into straight lines, knocking off the caps of those who had forgotten to buckle their chin straps, and then screaming at them for not wearing a cap. I never imagined properly wearing a cap would become the focus of my being.

The way the caps themselves were designed added to our discomfort. Because so much of the war had been fought in the jungles of Asia, and because there were few resources worth devoting to our comfort, each cap still had a flap on the back that was supposed to shield our necks from a blazing sun. One might have thought the flap would also help keep us warm, but in fact having a wet cloth held against our necks did not accomplish that.

Once the sergeants had either tired of their sport or grew cold themselves, they would notify Major Yamada. He would march out from his office and take charge of us. Some days he had us drill for hours. Some days we took shooting practice. Other days we conducted physical exercise, missing the midday meal, and then marched until daylight failed. Should a soldier need to defecate or urinate, he would have to wait until the alloted time. Should he violate the order to wait and soil his pants, he would be made to clean them in front of the group, using his hands if in the back, his tongue in the front. We learned not to question orders.

On one of the last mornings of training, Major Yamada singled me out. It was an odd day, a rare time when the sky was blue with high clouds. The Major inspected my rifle, ensuring it was loaded. He handed it back to me, and had me pull back the bolt to prepare it to fire. As he heard the bolt click into place, Major Yamada took a deep breath, looked into that sky, ordered my bunkmate, the boy who had eaten the Hersey's chocolate, forward, and placed the barrel of my rifle against that boy's forehead.

"Kill him," the Major said. The boy met my eyes, though I kept them empty. He cried, prompting a slap from the Major.

"Kill him, Nakagawa. That is an order."

I could smell the soil beneath me, and nearly hear the clouds moving above. My finger was firmly against the trigger, and I paused when I realized how smooth the metal had been machined. We two had been expertly made to serve a purpose.

"Kill. Him. Now." The Major was at my side, watching the boy and I. The boy's eyes were seeing something far away.

I stood still.

"Lower your weapon, Nakagawa," the Major said. He was close to my face, and I could smell *sake*.

"Why did you not kill him? You heard my order."

"Sir, a soldier must strive for an honorable death. He must die fighting the enemy, or he must die by his own hand if he is able to accomplish a proper death through that means. If I had fired I would have violated those orders and denied this boy a chance to die through duty to our nation."

The Major walked around me, a narrow circle, until he was directly behind.

"Had you pulled that trigger, Nakagawa, you would have disgraced yourself, and this army, and I would have been bound to strike you dead as you stood." The Major squeezed my neck, pressing muscle against bone. "I would have pitied you enough to have used my sword, and of course to save a bullet for the Americans."

Even though it was still hours until the midday meal, the Major dismissed us to our barracks and walked away.

THOUGH IT WAS AS late as night can be, he allowed only a single bulb. The dim light made his skin look like tired leather. He was behind his desk, and nodded as I entered and assumed the position of attention. His stiff uniform collar was undone, his sword unsheathed on the wooden surface that I could see had once been polished. There was an empty bottle. Another full one was awaiting his orders. I bowed deeply to Major Yamada.

"Do you want?" Major Yamada said. "*Sake*. This."

The Major refilled his own drink, the *sake* gurgling out of the bottle as if he had squeezed the neck. *Sake* is usually taken in small porcelain cups, but the Major had a full water glass in front of him.

"Sir, I do not drink, I mean, I have never drunk, except only at the New Year, when my father allowed me a small sip," I said. "Sir, pardon me, am I being tested once again? Is it not against regulations to drink on duty?"

"Am I on duty here, Nakagawa?" Major Yamada said. "Am I violating regulations?"

"I am not sure, sir."

"Well, as your senior officer, am I ever wrong?"

"No, sir."

"Let us test that. Are you still a dog, Nakagawa?"

I barked.

"Good, good. This *sake* is from my hometown. About a day's walk from Nishinomiya."

"It must be very good, sir."

"It tastes like urine. My father worked in this brewery. I told you I was from a family of warriors. That is not true."

"Yes, sir," I said.

"Do not agree I am wrong. Only I say that, but I am never wrong. Now bark again, Nakagawa, dammit. Outstanding, your bark is still strong. Did you know my father died in some filthy part of Korea, guarding a small bridge. In the letter we received from my father's superior months later, he referred to it only as 'a bridge,' no name. Is that not enough warrior blood for you, Nakagawa?"

"Yes, sir."

"My father's war is now his son's war. Your mother was still wiping your ass for you when this began." He looked down at a sheaf of papers in front of him, squeezing his eyes to focus on the tiny characters. "Nonetheless, we must continue. We are somewhat short of officers due to the unfortunate present situation in our nation. It has thus been ordered units once led by those trained in our finest staff college will now be led by non-commissioned officers, mere sergeants. You recall I had the men count off by ten before summoning you to this office. What was your number, Nakagawa?"

"Ten, sir.

"As a number ten, you are now to become a non-commissioned officer, a sergeant, in His Majesty the Emperor's Imperial Land Army. Congratulations. Those who called out number nine are being sent to become *kamikaze* pilots."

Major Yamada tried twice before successfully coming to his feet. He picked up his sword and ran his eye along the blade's edge, looking at the small nicks. The steel glowed angry in the room light.

"Sergeant Nakagawa. God, even saying that title in front of your name makes me bitter. You have not been trained enough to clean a field privy well."

"Sir, you have trained us well, to kill," I said.

"I trained you to hate. The killing part comes easy after that."

Like pounding a frog into the dust. I remembered now.

Major Yamada looked again at the sword, seeing something I could not. "Do you know my final test at staff college, when we truly cared to train our men? After we were issued our swords—this sword, this goddamn sword—they marched us out to where some Chinese prisoners were trussed up. We always used

Chinese as raw material instead of American prisoners, they were more... vulnerable? Our commandant showed us how to cut off their heads in one stroke. I braced and swung. The sword slid through the boy's neck, as I was precise. Two fountains of blood shot up from the vessels on each side of the stump, then faded in their arcs. I will remember it always. It was the finest experience of my life. I loved the smell of the blood... it smells like copper, but you would not know, would you? I was no longer a recruit at that moment. I was the sword."

"Yes, sir."

"Afterwards, we cooked and ate his liver under a banner that read THE MORE WE EAT, THE BRIGHTER WILL BURN THE FIRE OF OUR HATRED FOR THE ENEMY. Could you do what I did, Nakagawa? Even today when I see a man, I think, oh, that one has a strong neck, or, his neck would slice easily. Like yours, thin and weak. It is the stringy type of muscle that makes it troublesome. The bones themselves cleave easily. Ah, I am wasting my time telling you this, like trying to explain music to a deaf man. Nakagawa, do you know what happened to our nation?"

"We were told the Americans are in Japan, sir," I said.

"All military tell their young men about duty and tradition. Why otherwise would a young man strive to die before he is eighteen? How else can we convince the sons of farmers and trainmen and peddlers to fight? How else can I make you wish to please me by barking like a dog? Do you understand, Nakagawa?"

"I am not sure, sir. Do you wish me to bark again?"

"You will soon die, Nakagawa. I am trying to shove something important into your thick peasant skull. Why would you want to live past this war? Give me a reason."

"My parents, sir. I am their only son," I said.

"My father is dead now, Nakagawa, and you are selfish to wish for what I do not have. My only brother died when his warship sank off the Philippines. My mother said she would never remarry, fearful of ever birthing another son. 'I no longer wish to work for the military,' she said. If I had a living son, he would be your... Nakagawa, listen closely. You can kill as many Americans as you like and it will not make a difference to this war. But you, you cannot live if you forgo obligation, and you cannot die well if you forgo obligation. This is thus not about your life, Nakagawa, but about your damn soul. So that is duty. Be better than me at that."

Major Yamada picked up his glass. He screwed up his face as the *sake* burned.

"You have a girl who is arranged for you to marry?" he said.

"No, sir. My parents could not afford it. But when I was a boy there was a girl named Naoko I cared for very much. She left with her father for her safety, but perhaps I will find her. I will protect her from the Americans," I said.

"Perhaps, Nakagawa, perhaps. Perhaps this Naoko has already has run off with an American soldier who gives her chocolate and nylons, yes? Perhaps your parents are already dead. What will you die for then?"

Major Yamada threw himself back into his chair, bumping the desk and sending his sword clattering to the floor. He pushed aside his glass and drank directly from the bottle. Looking at the label, he dribbled the last bit of liquor he held in his mouth down his unshaven chin.

"Want to see what a professional officer in His Majesty's Army does now? Watch, with my seal impressed on this document, I have just certified every member of your group as

Class A, ready for duty, even the 48-year-old who can barely climb stairs. Now, I disgust myself talking with you further. Get out, Nakagawa. Tomorrow I have to kill myself. But until then, my obligation is to this bottle."

Chapter 22: On the Thin Ice of the Day

Lieutenant Nathaniel Hooper: Japan, 1946

WE WERE STUCK UNDER a sky the color of dirty ice, coming to terms with the reality that we were a helluva a long way from home. The breeze had picked up, chilling us in our wet uniforms, and we needed to move off the beach to stay warm, if nothing else. We climbed, all of us this time, over the seawall and turned inland. My face felt heavy under the helmet, greasy from the gun powder that hung in the air. Never mind the cold, I was sweating part of my uniform black.

It wasn't fifty steps before I stood in front of the skeleton of the Japanese pillbox, defecated on just a few minutes earlier by naval gunfire. There were pieces of the Jap machine gun itself left, almost not enough to even tell it had been a thing trying to kill me minutes before. As we passed, Laabs took a playful swing at the gun barrel, then quickly let off a string of ripe profanity, pulling his hand to his mouth to suck at the burn caused by the still-hot metal.

Bodies had been thrown up into the trees, hanging like Christmas ornaments. The enemy soldiers on the ground were a mix of stories. Most you'd need a spoon to gather up. But one, there was too much of him left. He still had his glasses on somehow, one lens shattered. I felt like Dougie Dietz, who used to beat me up in school back in Ohio.

After passing through the trees, we came into a kind of open space, half-sand, half-dirt, with weedy sea grass about waist high, thick as hair. The grass whispered soft enough to lull as we walked through, but never let us see more than a few feet ahead. The sweat started in that one spot in the small of my back. Nothing good ever followed when that happened.

"Hey, Sarge, movement in the grass," Marino said. We didn't have guys like him back home, but we knew about them from the preacher: Marino was a hood, shrewd and sour, dangerous to boys from Ohio.

"It's a dog, knucklehead," one of the other men, Polanski, said. How'd I miss this guy aboard ship, with that face like a potato, teeth the color of root beer?

"It's a dog, sir," Burke said.

"I can see it's a dog. Keep your heads down," I said. I wasn't sure what keeping our heads down had to do with a dog, but it sounded like a thing a leader would say. Nobody put their head down.

"Can I shoot it? I wanna shoot something in Japan," Marino said.

"It's just a dog," I said.

"But it's an enemy dog," Marino said. "Sir."

"Listen to the Lieutenant, rank has its privileges. And it's a goddamn puppy, not a dog," Sergeant Laabs said. "And you, Marino, ease up on your dago mouth, you're acting like John

Wayne with a hard-on. Dammit, you, Private Jones, put that ration can away."

"Dog looks hungry, and if we ain't gonna shoot it, we probably should feed it," Jones said.

"Wait for the Lieutenant to make a decision," Laabs said. I could swear I saw him wink at Smitty before he turned to me. "What should we do here, sir, you being in charge and all?"

"I think I see a village up ahead. Maybe it came from there," I said.

"Sir, you want Sergeant Laabs to call out to the ships, get a Navy spitball on that village?" Smitty said. He already had the handset out, waving it toward Laabs, and, as a mean afterthought, back at me. I needed time to sort out being in charge of everything, including, apparently, a stray dog. Dammit, not a dog, a puppy. A puppy—as I stood there, I found myself slipping away, smelling the sweet Ohio clay turned over in the spring, seeing the field behind Reeve Primary School, looking past the electrical lines leading off forever...

"Goddammit, we are not here to care about dogs, we are here to, um, liberate Japan," I said.

"Sir, Sergeant Laabs said it was a puppy, not a dog, so—"

"Jones, be quiet. Sergeant Laabs, get the squad ready to move toward that village. We'll check it out on our way inland."

"Can I at least throw a rock at the puppy, Lieutenant, scare it away?" Jones said.

"Fine, throw the damn rock, Jones, but don't hit the puppy," I said. It was the first decision where my mistakes weren't counted in lives.

"Jeez, Sergeant, you see one day of this and start praying you never see another."

"Oh my, that is true, Lieutenant."

THINGS WERE QUIET ENOUGH I could imagine someone had reached for a big knob and turned down the volume on the war. Out in the distance it was repetitions of low ridges, leading to higher hills. This might be a pretty country someday. We crossed a frozen rice paddy, moving inland to check out the village I'd seen, maybe where the dog had come from, and to connect up with our own forces. At home I skated on ponds sort of like this paddy. I wondered when the last time someone else had. Maybe those people from the village.

We were strung out like links in a chain. The distance between each of us was supposed to be a couple of paces, for safety in case we were shelled, but the men bunched up so they could talk. Having survived the landing and the puppy, everyone was in what passed for a good mood, and the men stomped on the thin ice, just for the fun and the sound as they teased and cursed each other.

"Steiner, wait up. I got a joke for you. You hear the one about the midget and the horse?" Jones said.

"It's a midget, a horse and a drunk, asshole," Marino said. "Your jokes go over like a lead balloon."

"Whatever. How's it go?" Steiner said. He had a smile on that said he probably had heard a lot of off-color stories in his time. A dead cigarette dangled from his lip. He clicked open his Zippo to light it with one hand.

There were American artillery rounds passing overhead, reaching inland—even I could tell the incoming from outgoing now—followed by our Navy fighters, Bearcats, in their blue-almost-black paint, aluminum birds that had migrated here alongside us. Up higher, the sun glinted off the silver fuselages of the B-29s. They were bombing out of our new bases on Kyushu, commuters, two trips a day, to empty their bowels on some Japanese city. Enemy couldn't touch us up there. All along the horizon, smoke was rising like exclamation points. It made me feel safe, as my war had pleasantly settled into a spectator sport.

"Lemme tell the joke, Marino, will ya?" Jones said. The three men paused while the rest of the squad moved forward. Better keep moving, Laabs said, but I stopped too, wanting to hear the joke myself.

"C'mon, tell the damn joke, Jones, some of us ain't got all day," Marino said.

"So this midget, a horse," Jones looked at Marino, "...and a drunk... walk into a bar, and the midget says 'Gimme a drink for my horse,' and the drunk says, 'That ain't no horse, that's a—'"

Three pops.

Pop. Pop. Pop.

There was no echo. Instead, in place of each pop was a pink mist. That was the three boys up ahead, the ones who hadn't stopped for the midget, the horse, and the drunk, who just stepped on three land mines, which destroyed their bodies with such efficiency that everything but a little bit of what they used to be was gone. Their mist blew through me, kids to ghosts in the space of a breath I sucked in, taking them inside me. The others who kept the pace count were okay; the mines were specific in their work.

The dead hadn't been with us even long enough to have acquired wartime nicknames—no Tex, no kid with red hair we would have called Rusty. They were three guys whose names didn't matter because no one knew them, and because they ended up in front of the rest of us. Walking killed people here.

The metal top plate of Japanese mines was thin and brittle, like the ice, so the explosive underneath would shatter steel into flesh. The boys who stepped on them weren't killed by the explosion—it was only a pop after all—but by a spray of hot steel projected up through their flesh faster than they could shout out their deaths.

Laabs had the squad look around for the dead men's dog tags. Everybody had two sets; one to bury with the body, one to bring back to account for the lost man. A lot of guys kept one set around their necks, and another tucked into the laces of their boots, so there'd be a second chance of IDing them if they got whacked. Laabs explained the boots usually got blown off and you could find them a short distance away, no matter what had happened to the legs.

"Hey, Jones, lookit this, steak for dinner," Marino said.

"C'mon, Marino, show some respect," Jones said.

"Aw, relax. Jeez, some people can't take a joke," Marino said.

Chapter 23: Getting to Know You

American Lines, Mess Tent, 1946

"HEY, POLANSKI, WHERE YOU from anyway?" Jones said.

"Chicago. Where you from, Jonesy?"

"Tulsa. Well, near Tulsa. That's Oklahoma. I don't think it's too far from Chicago."

"Sure, close enough, Jonesy," Polanski said.

"Aw, Chicago ain't much of a city," Marino said. "Kind of a shithole." His remark quieted the room. Cups were put down and plates pushed aside as everyone waited to see if Polanski would take up the challenge.

"You know, Marino, you got a mouth only a fist could love. Where you think you're from anyway?" Polanski said.

"Flatbush. Brooklyn."

"How the hell many people in Brooklyn? Every damn outfit I pass through's got someone from Brooklyn. The Army ever draft anybody from anywhere else?" Polanski said.

"Some kid from the Bronx I heard, but I never saw him around," Marino said, with enough of a smile that people picked up their cups, and forks went back to digging deep into scrambled eggs.

"Smitty, you?"

"Ohio, a big city, Toledo."

"Ohio is Ohio. If you ain't from Brooklyn you can take a hike," Marino said.

"That kinda talk is gonna bite you in the ass someday, buster," Polanski said.

"Nah, ain't nobody that hungry," Marino said.

"You're a charmer, Marino," Polanski said. "But how come you're the only red haired kid in your family, huh? Better ask your mom about that Irish postman."

"Guys, stop kidding around, Marino don't have red hair. And I sorta got a bad feelin' about this war," Jones said.

"Jones, I got a bad feeling about you. Like this war'll be over twice and you'll still never have learned to handle your liquor like a grown man," Smitty said.

"Hell, Jonesy here, he ain't no teetotaler. Tell him, Jonesy, about Chinatown, in Waikiki," Marino said.

"Yeah, I ain't no teetotaler, guys," Jones said. "Sort of."

"Old Jonesy here met a bowlegged bar girl, the best kind. She kept making him buy drinks so she'd stick around and talk with him," Marino said. "Tell them her name, Jonesy."

"Her name was Jenny."

"Tell 'em how you know her name was Jenny," Marino said.

"Because after I told her my girl back home was named Jenny she said her name was Jenny, too. What'd you think of that coincidence, fellas?" Jones said.

"I bet old Jonesy's girl back home is real Oklahoma, major-league tits with bush-league brains," Marino said. He added in a hand gesture like he was holding two basketballs in case his point wasn't clear enough.

"Jenny, the one back home, she ain't no backseat girl, she's nice. And anyway, my bar girl was prettier than yours, Marino," Jones said.

"Yeah, the one I was with was nothing special, but then again, I know quality tail from street meat. Got more ass back home than a toilet seat," Marino said. "But you gotta make do when traveling."

"Sure, Marino. But you seemed happy enough. Jeez, when you were kissing her, it sounded like my mom stirring macaroni and cheese on the stove. And she couldn't even speak English. You had to tell her kid hanging around the bar what you wanted to say so he could translate," Jones said.

"Yeah, well, that kid spoke damn good English for a little Chinaman. I gave him an extra buck and he taught her to say 'I love you,'" Marino said, scratching his pimple-studded nose with a middle finger everybody but Jones saw. "Anyway, Jonesy, tell 'em how you can't hold your booze any better than a schoolgirl."

"Marino, no, not now," Jones said.

"So yeah, what happened with 'Jenny' next?" Burke said.

"Jonesy, he's at the bar with whatever the hell her name was, and I'm over in the corner getting to know my little cookie real up close," Marino said, grinning for effect. "Next thing I know, Jonesy's girl is laughing and cursing at the same time. So I step over to see what the commotion is, and Jones tells me he just upchucked a week's pay worth of gin all over the place."

"You ain't so nice, Marino," Jones said. "You wasn't supposed to tell anyone that. You promised."

"Yeah, Jones? Well, you're just some hick anyway."

"I, um, I ain't that, Marino," Jones said, chewing on the neck of his undershirt.

"C'mon Marino, give the kid a break, and stop reminding the rest of us why we don't like you," Polanski said.

"I saw you Polanski, you don't fool me. What were you smiling about over there while I was telling the story, huh?" Marino said.

"Nothing."

"Bullshit. You were staring way out there, and I seen a smile, just enough of one. What's your little piece of sugar's name? She from Chinatown?"

"No way," Polanski said. "And especially not for you, Marino. One more crack outta your mouth and I'll give you a knuckle sandwich to chew on."

"Take your shot, Polanski," Marino said. He was on his feet. While a couple of G.I.s stepped away, about twice as many got closer to watch the fight.

"C'mon, easy guys. So, other than the girls, what'd you guys miss from back home? Being warm? Your folks?" Steiner said. He was on his feet, hands on Polanski's shoulders, guiding him without much resistance back down into his seat.

"Not me, I mean my dad, he died when I was young. It was pretty rough on me as a kid," Polanski said. He fingered the hole where a good tooth once had been. "My mom changed my first name, you know, legal and all, after he died, so I became a junior. She said I'd remember him better that way. Then every time we went to the cemetery I saw my goddamn name on the headstone."

"Back home in Brooklyn we lived in a railroad flat, so my old man was always just on the other side of a curtain, no bedroom wall," Marino said. "Snores like a dragon when he's drunk.

Which was every night. Not a speck of nice in him after the booze neither. At night, we'd listen for his keys when he came home from the bar. If the old man was sober enough to get the key in the lock, it'd probably be okay. If he couldn't and Ma didn't open the door fast enough, it'd be a bad night. Sometimes I'd try and make him pissed at me, call him the bastard he was, so he'd beat on me instead of Ma. Helluva thing."

"So?" Steiner said.

"So it was rough on him as a kid, nitwit," Polanski said. He rubbed his arm right near those little round burn scars.

"So he slapped the shit outta my mom and when she ran off, he kicked the shit outta me until I ran off. Booze and kicking, like peanut butter and jelly for him. You ever fight some old perv behind the bus station over a cardboard box to sleep in? You ever not win a fight like that and know what happens to a kid? I only remember one good Christmas, we got Chinese takeout from the place on 93rd, in them white paper cartons. Here ya' go son, have a fortune cookie, merry freaking Christmas. You ain't got that in happy land, do you, Jones?"

"Aw, shut up, Marino. What do you know anyway? And it don't matter. We're all gonna get plenty of Chinese food here in Japan anyway. And you ain't so special. One way or the other we all got drafted and now we're here."

"Maybe you got drafted, Jones, probably right off your mama's tit. I volunteered, to get away from my old man. Even in Brooklyn you gotta have a better excuse than I had to whack someone."

"That's it, I've had enough for one war, I'm gonna go to the latrine," Polanski said. "Any of you palookas got any toilet paper?"

"Not for you, Polanski," Marino said. "Say goodbye to one of your socks."

THE BASE CAMP WAS starting to empty out, except for the brass who stayed behind in what I found a new reason to call the rear. The rest of us were being sent off to sleep in the snow and walk across the paddies and do the fighting.

The men were gathered in front of the briefing tent when I came out from meeting Captain Christiansen. In the center of the group was Laabs, cleaning his M-1. The smell of oil and solvent must have been a permanent part of him, like a guy who sold fish. I cleaned my rifle, too, everybody did, but I watched as he oiled it like an artist at work, then drew a cloth patch and a stiff brush through the bore, and worked the action click-clack back and forth in a nervous tic. One speck of dust was a score that needed settling for that guy. Next to him was Jones, chewing gum like he was the squad's rhythm section. Polanski, Marino, Steiner, Burke, and Smitty, with the radio. They all saw me and drifted in.

"See what we got now, sir? A BAR, a real live Browning Automatic Rifle," Polanski said. The weapon could put out a lot of lead, probably the most dangerous one-man firearm we had.

"Who signed the hand receipt for that?" Laabs said. He shot a glance over at Jones. "See, Lieutenant, every piece of U.S. government property has to be signed for. There are ten thousand clipboards running this war, as I figured you knew, from your officer training and all, and you'd want to do things by the book. Sir."

Laabs appealed for an ally with a raised eyebrow aimed at Jones. The shot missed.

"We put your name on the receipt, Lieutenant Hooper," Jones said. He was grinning. It was easy to imagine him back home somewhere, grease on his face, working with this dad in the garage, same grin. A pause to see if he was in trouble with me, but the smile endured.

"You sure you chiselers didn't just steal it?" I said.

"How could it be stolen? It's right here, sir," Burke said.

"Fair enough for now, jokers. Marino, is that pile of stuff over there sleeping bags? Grab enough of them for us all," I said.

"Oh yeah, those are sleeping bags, Lieutenant, sure thing, special just for you," Marino said.

"If your bullshit was water we'd all drown, Marino," Polanski said. "Sir, those are body bags."

"Alright, enough fellas, save it for the enemy. Sergeant Laabs? A word in private, please," I said. I felt like a kid trying to live up to his older brother. I wanted to clear the air with Laabs, start over if I could. "Hey, the Captain mentioned something about you being able to speak a few words of Japanese. From on Okinawa."

"No, sir, only some stuff I learned from this Nisei girl in Waikiki."

"Sergeant Laabs, er, Jason, right? Look, I may have made some mistakes this morning. I wanted you to hear that before we headed out," I said.

"Mistakes are expected, Lieutenant. That's why they put erasers on pencils."

Chapter 24: You've Arrived at the Ashiya Beachhead

Lieutenant Nathaniel Hooper: Japan, Ashiya Beachhead, 1946

THERE WAS A HAND-LETTERED sign out front, WELCOME TO JAPAN, YOU'VE ARRIVED AT THE ASHIYA BEACHHEAD, COURTESY OF THE U.S. SIXTH ARMY. We made it to our first objective, this beachhead, where I'd been told I'd get my next set of orders.

Underway was the well-practiced dance of bringing ashore the beans and bullets. To see all this happening just a couple of hours after landing made me feel like Superman. It looked like the industrial Midwest had gathered up a lung full of air and spat out everything it made all at once: bundles of bandages, crates of K-rations, cartons of powdered milk, pallets of tires, truck parts, mess gear, rifle parts, mechanics' tools, pin-up posters, howitzers, mortar tubes, sleeping bags, typewriters, toothbrushes, condoms, Jeeps, and artillery pieces, all bound up with spit, baling wire, Yankee ingenuity, frontier spirit and Wild West know-how. It smelled of wet khaki and axle grease and leather, all overlaid with a smog of diesel fumes. The ground was a slush that made sucking sounds out of my boots, even as the trucks muled up the slopes churning more of the semi-frozen mud into slop while they aimed their horns at me. A dozen generators buzzed, and Sherman tanks moved inland. America had arrived in Japan.

And everywhere, crates of ammunition, wooden boxes big enough for howitzer shells and small enough for pistol rounds, all bound together with steel straps. Hundreds of thousands of them, maybe millions, maybe that number after millions. Inside every box, all those rounds next to each other, kind of keeping each other warm until someone needed to pull them out of the dark and kill Japs.

At the same time, we'd already accumulated a tremendous trash pile, all sorts of wooden pallets and empty cardboard boxes hauled across the Pacific to be dumped here, their job done. Our guards had figured out the Japanese civilians coming to pick through it all were harmless and left them alone, just kids rooting for food scraps and seam-faced old women using our discarded tin cans as little stoves, starting cooking fires inside with pieces of our scavenged wood. I'd heard the Japanese were industrious people; hell, they were already starting to clean up after us.

Our artillery fired from not too far away. We could use shells heavier than one guy could lift to chase away a single enemy sniper a mile distant. The smoke columns rising in the distance looked like the arms of God reaching down to pound him. If we could do this halfway across the world, what couldn't we do? We were gods, the only nation in human history that'd never lost a war and probably never would. I thought there must be more Americans in Japan by this time than Japanese, and we were dumping supplies ashore so fast you might have thought the place would sink under the weight.

And towering over it all was the American flag, all 48 proud stars, flying off a flagpole we'd pounded deep into the Japanese ground. This place was ours, it said, we took it. It all had a feel of temporary permanence, a place never meant to exist but that had accepted its role. I suspect if I could have seen it from the air it'd look like an island floating inside Japan.

Sergeant Laabs took the men for chow. That was about the extent to which I knew my job at this point—let Laabs do it. I heard the men pass another group of soldiers, equally self-conscious in a new place, but greener than us by all of about two hours. Our group bragged like a rival sports team over killing a single machine gun on the beach, while the newer guys stared in awe.

There was as much confusion as snow lying over the base camp. Nobody had heard of the Captain Christiansen I was supposed to report to. I found a soldier who pointed me toward another soldier who said some captain or another could be found either over there, or over that way. I tried both directions and found him in a third place.

Lieutenant Nathaniel Hooper: Ashiya Beachhead, Captain Christiansen's Tent, 1946

"NO, YOU LISTEN TO me, goddammit. The first man who brings me a Jap skull today gets a three-day pass," Captain Christiansen said into a field telephone. I could practically see the steam rising off him as we stood there in the cold. And that voice—like he'd been chain-smoking Luckies since nursery school. Here was a man who needed war the same way Baptists need sin. He dropped the handset back into its holder and looked at me. "Who the hell are you?"

The inside of the tent was as empty as a place with only a coffee pot, a radio, some maps and a small desk could be. A police blotter description of Captain Christiansen would say it didn't matter what color his eyes were or what he weighed. He was a fist of a man wrapped around a regular body for convenience. At the same time, it was odd, he had a kind of baby face, smooth skin that made you wonder if the inside matched the outside. He looked down at a list on his desk.

"Lieutenant, um, Hooper, right? I kinda expected you to be dead by now. Grab a cup o' joe over there and take a load off. You want in on my Jap skull game? Get you into a Manila whore house lickety-split if you win."

The coffee was the first hot thing I'd put down the pipe since I threw up breakfast. We'd been served the traditional American pre-invasion meal of greasy steak, greasy powdered eggs and coffee that somehow tasted greasy, the Navy mess cooks making us feel cared for, at least until the one old timer made a joke about fattening me up for the slaughter. "Ya get a last meal 'fore the electric chair, too," another said, not smiling back even after I grinned a bit.

"Hooper, pass me a cup of that coffee willya, hell, I think this is my tenth already this morning. No, twelfth. Who's counting? Cheers, to better days and happier endings. So, this your first rodeo, Hooper?"

"Sort of, Captain. I was on Kyushu for Operation Olympic, rear wave. Guard duty mostly, trying to meet some of the local girls, but they didn't speak American money. A joke there, sir."

Captain Christiansen curled down his bottom lip to show he'd heard it and would not be laughing.

"Sometimes I'd get a Jeep and a translator and visit some village we were making hold an election. I'd hand out some pamphlets, and then mark it off a list as having been democratized," I said. "I was bored to death, tell you the truth, so I asked to get into some real action here."

I saw the tendons wiggling in his wrist, and thought he was going to throw the last of his coffee at me, but then he looked deep inside, through the bottom of the cup, and drank it instead.

"Real action? Hooper, how the hell'd you end up here?"

"I was studying agriculture, Ohio, sir, for after the war when we'd start back in on the farm, when I got, um, sort of called. The Army saw I had some college, even though it was studying agriculture, and said they needed more Second Lieutenants. So I guess I was a victim of my own potential. Another joke there, sir." The Captain didn't smile. "And, um, my dad had been in the Army, too."

"Good for him, but that's not what I asked you. How'd you end up here?" Christiansen said.

"Well, sir, it wasn't much of a choice, at least not my choice. I didn't have much training, sort of like they just said 'score more home runs than the other team,' but didn't explain how to hit or pitch. Another joke, sir, last one, sorry, I'll stop. Then the war in Europe was over and I got promoted to real lieutenant."

"First Lieutenant, Hooper, for the love of God and this man's army, not 'real lieutenant.' Jesus, son, did you fail potty training, too? I better get myself out to Ohio and give your mother a son she can be proud of. Who's the poor sergeant that's stuck keeping you out of trouble, First Lieutenant Hooper from Ohio?"

"Laabs, sir," I said.

"Sergeant Jason Laabs? Shit, you're luckier than a bull with two dicks, Lieutenant. Much sweat and beer between me and

Laabs. Bravest man I know. He'd bleed on the flag to keep it red."

"I sorta guessed. You look at him and say, 'I bet he killed a lot of men,'" I said.

"You don't have to be brave to kill, that just takes a steady aim. Laabs, Jesus. So we're on Okinawa, sweating like whores in church. The Japs honeycombed damn near everywhere with caves, and we had to dig the yellow bastards out. Only after the first couple of times when we poured flamethrowers in, we found some of the caves were full of goddamn women and kids, not troops. The Nip soldiers had been telling them for weeks we planned to kill them and eat them, or some stupid shit about throwing them into the sea alive to drown in front of their kids, and so they hid. Sometimes they'd be in there with grenades, waiting for the last moment to blow themselves all to hell."

"I read about Okinawa in *Stars and Stripes*, tough business," I said.

"Jesus, Hooper, do you squat when you pee? Go on into a cave with the walls painted with baby, and then tell yourself to shut the hell up 'cause you know nothing. Laabs had one of the squads under me with some butter bar like you, the LT all piss and vinegar to hose out another cave, but Laabs said he hadn't seen them take any fire out of that one. So against his lieutenant's orders, Laabs belly crawled into that cave and in some sort of baby-talk Japanese, got twenty women and their kids out alive."

The Captain's hand was shaking enough to nearly put out the match he'd struck. He gave up on it, steadied himself, and lit his next cigarette off the end of the previous one still burning in the ashtray. Christiansen looked like he was going to say something more, but let me cut him off instead.

"I'll be sure to ask Sergeant Laabs about Okinawa when I get back to my unit, sir."

"You'll be smart and do nothing of the sort, Hooper. You need to know a man like Laabs keeps a lot inside. Let it stay there. But Lieutenant, and mark this down, if Laabs says something to you, he's right and you're not, because you know about as much about war as a pig knows about Sunday. Pay attention. Do that and you'll get yourself and most of your men home from this, because you either learn fast or they die fast. Pick one."

The Captain spat out the words like he was prosecuting me. He turned, hovered over his maps, then seemed to surprise himself reaching for another cup of coffee. He was now holding two cups, one in each hand, and drinking back and forth from them both. Halfway through the swallow he took from the one in his right hand, he noticed I was still in the room.

"Sir, really, I'm sorry, I don't want to start off on your bad side," I said.

"You don't need to be sorry, Hooper, you just need to be quiet. And I don't have a good side, so stop worrying. Look, this is rough on all of us, son. No hard feelings, it's just been a tough week this morning. Okay?" Indifference maybe, but no weakness in the apology.

"You mean regular okay, or here kind of okay?" I said. I could smell the Captain's disgust at being on the other end of a question.

"You lose some men this morning?" Captain Christiansen said. Something weary in his voice.

"Nine, I think, I'm not sure." I was so tired I needed to use my fingers to count. "Two in the boat, three more on the beach, and three to mines crossing a frozen rice paddy. So, no, eight."

"And you feel responsible?"

"I do, sir. I was in, am, in charge. On the beach I picked which three men died," I said. "I mean, it could've been three others, or nobody at all."

"You're gonna get used to it. You die a little when your men die, but then the Army sends you some new ones and you start over. Grieving can get to be a bad habit in this job," Captain Christiansen said. He waited, but I didn't say anything. "War can be about a lot of things, my young Lieutenant, but it's always about the crappy things that happen to people. So when I hear somebody back home use the word unforgettable, well, his nightmares have no idea. 'Eviscerate' is not just a good Scrabble play. He's never seen a thousand maggots in the shape of a human body, and I have."

There was never a longer pause in my life.

"I hope I'm not making this sound too romantic for you, Hooper," Captain Christiansen said.

"I get it, sir, but I can't shake it," I said.

"Shake it, Lieutenant, on the double, 'cause you gotta start being a real soldier man now. You have an obligation to bring the rest of those men home, and yourself to whatever chubby Ohio girl you think is waiting for you. Hike up your skivvies, get your head right, and do your job."

"Yes, sir. Captain, you mind if I talk to the Chaplain? I have a few, you know, religious kinds of questions. About all this," I said.

"Be my guest, Lieutenant Hooper, but watch yourself. Old Chaps, well, you could say his cheese has slipped off the cracker a bit."

As I started to leave, Captain Christiansen waved me back, waiting until I got close to his desk before he spoke. "And

Lieutenant? War ain't so bad. Where the hell else is a kid like you gonna have the chance to be a hero?"

Lieutenant Nathaniel Hooper: Japan, Ashiya Beachhead, Chaplain's Tent, 1946

"SIR, YOU'RE CHAPLAIN SAVAGE?" I said.

Tight glasses over eyes the color of the dirt under his still-clean boots. Only man in the entire Army with his collar buttoned.

"Yes, yes." Chaplain Savage said. "And I like to pronounce it as in the French, with a rising intonation." He finished with a shallow smile.

The Chaplain had pores the size of craters, and an uncomfortable face, like my dog when his ass itched. The guy probably hoped I'd feel more at ease despite him fidgeting with the things on his table, olive drab crosses, a metal box with screw-on legs labeled ALTAR, RELIGIOUS, TYPE CHRISTIAN, OLIVE DRAB, PORTABLE, and a handbook called *Interdenominational Last Rites.*

I told him about the men that had died already.

"Were they Buddhist? Atheists? I'm a Christian Chaplain is why. Those others have their own God. Not even in the handbook, I think." He leafed through the book, wetting his finger to turn the pages.

"I just wanted to know about those men, the ones I got killed. Are they okay now?" I said.

"Oh, I doubt it. That's pretty much the same in any religion. No, wait, I think Buddhists believe in reincarnation, heathens," the Chaplain said. He tossed the handbook aside. "So that's settled, son." He looked at me like a bored school teacher, and got up before I wanted him to and motioned me towards the way out.

At the flap of his tent Chaplain Savage asked if I wanted him to bless my rifle. I shook my head no.

"Okay, then. Go see Major Moreland, everyone has to, before we fan out and win the war, and he can get promoted to Colonel. He's in the tent next door, though he calls it a command post, watch that if you want to score some points. And Lieutenant, a word just between us believers, eh. The Major isn't like me, in fact I think the old bastard's got a screw or three loose, if you know what I mean."

Lieutenant Nathaniel Hooper: Japan, Ashiya Beachhead, Major Moreland's Command Post, 1946

"LET'S MAKE THIS QUICK. I'm sure you're anxious to get out into the field anyway, marching to the sound of the drums and all," Major Moreland said. He spoke without looking up.

If not for the uniform, he might be that rounded guy who won't stop restarting a conversation on the train. And for a guy in a hurry, Major Moreland didn't have much in front of him but a form with a long list of names. He ran his finger down into the H section, and drew a line through one of them.

"Harper?"

"Hooper." Major Moreland erased the line he'd drawn and then crossed out a different name.

"Hooper, of course, just know this is the Jap's Waterloo, his Götterdämmerung. Oh, don't speak German? There's no need to speak Japanese either. By the time we have anything to say to each other, the locals will have learned English. 'War is a terrible thing but God I love it so.' You know who said that, Lieutenant? It was the great American general William Tecumseh Sherman, while he burned the great American city of Atlanta to the ground during the Civil War to liberate it from the Confederates. A general who loved his men, and who was loved by his men."

Major Moreland was now arched over his desk, way past the centerline at this point, to emphasize some part of what he said. I was afraid he'd tip over. But about all I could focus on was his nearly perfect circle of a bald spot, and the unhealthy scraps of red hair I now hated uncombed on the sides.

"You getting to know your men, Lieutenant, er, what is it, Hooper, dammit?" Major Moreland said. Every word was wrapped in the smell of bad teeth. He leaned forward even further as I leaned away.

"Yes, sir, Hooper. But no, sir, the men keep getting killed before I can get to know them."

"All the more reason to get ahead of the curve, son. You'd better start learning their names now, while they're still alive, much easier that way I've found over my years at this game. You'll need to write death letters to their parents. See, I keep a list. There's your name."

"I don't want to know them, Major, not until this is over and I know which ones are still gonna still be alive."

"I knew we saw eye-for-an-eye on all this. Top-notch work so far, son. You'll get the hang of this, road to success is always under construction and all that, right? And oh, yes, one more thing, Harper, I'm telling all the men, be careful with the local ladies. Every one's a looker."

"You really think I'll get to know any Japanese girls out here?" I said.

Major Moreland smiled. "Who knows, Hoover, you may even meet the girl of your dreams."

Chapter 25: Come Hell or High Water, Invading Japan

Lieutenant Nathaniel Hooper: Pacific Coast of Japan, American Landing Craft, 1946

THERE IS NOWHERE TO go in a landing craft except where it takes you. I was in that oily half light of dawn, under a sky dug in so low I felt I had to stoop. The cold was a hammer. Chunks of steel destroyed boys. Gear scraped against buckles. Cellophane crinkled as soldiers pulled rifles from waterproof bags. I watched someone I didn't know torn apart.

"Lieutenant Hooper, who was that? Who the hell was that?"

"The Corporal, he fell on me, oh God, Lieutenant Hooper."

"Lieutenant Hooper, get down or you're in the soup with him."

The soup—the mix of seawater, vomit, and now warm blood around my ankles. I saw the face, first a red blur, then the color of school chalk, everything and his last sound grabbed away. The torso stood upright in our landing craft, then tried to fall, a leaning drunk on a crowded bus. I couldn't tell who was shouting. Their helmets made them look like identical mushrooms.

Aboard ship they told me it was my job to lead boys I didn't know into a kind of combat I'd never experienced. Don't worry, they said, you'll get to know them like brothers. Years from now you'll still be saying those names at reunions and weddings.

"He said he wanted his mother."

"He's still bleeding, Lieutenant Hooper."

"Give him water."

"No water, no water. Morphine."

"Don't you understand, he's already dead."

"Lieutenant Hooper, you're in charge."

"The guy from Indiana, the back of his head—"

Jesus, his head snapped back like one of those red rubber balls attached to a paddle, stopping only when his spine held. Someone's severed arm was loose in the bottom of the boat now. I crouched to keep my own head below the rusted sides of the boat. Aboard the transport ship I wondered if I'd see much fighting, while all along my war was waiting. I reached to steady myself touching something too wet and soft.

A *kamikaze* in a steep dive, scream of the damned over a fierce whistle. Missed, breaking apart on impact and showering the boat. I saw the pilot's face above the water, his mouth open in a pantomime scream as the fuel on the water's surface burned his flesh even as the ocean swallowed him. People back in Ohio were buried wearing suits after they died quietly in their beds.

"Sergeant, I don't know what to do," I said.

"Don't say that, never, sir, that's quicksand," the Sergeant said.

"Stop the boat, make the Lieutenant stop the boat, we're all gonna die," a soldier said.

"Lieutenant can't stop the boat, nobody can stop the boat. Boat can't stop the boat," another of them said.

Screeching metal-on-metal, the ramp dropped and everyone ran forward, the only direction they could. The near-freezing water pushed my balls up into my belly, and my uniform turned wet-black. Minus a Corporal whose name no one knew and whoever the guy from Indiana had been, we went ashore, the Sergeant ordering us to take cover in the dirty sand behind the seawall to our right. That was all I could hear, the sounds pulled away by the wind, except the sing-song of "Lieutenant! Lieutenant! Lieutenant! Lieutenant!" hitting me in the face like well water.

I pressed myself into that seawall like it was my pillow back home during a wicked dream. The wall held apart the sand on the beach and me, and the sand inland and them. We needed to cross over that wall, move a few miles and then link up at the Ashiya Beachhead with the rest of the American forces. All I could see of Japan out there from under my helmet were the tops of scorched trees that looked like black licorice stuck into the ground. Nearby what I saw were boys hugging each other with the empty joy of still being alive.

"Look, Lieutenant, out the other way," the Sergeant said. "Those dots? More ships, just off shore. We're gonna be okay, no dirt nap for us." We watched two *kamikazes* lance from the sky, just missing a troop ship. "Probably."

I knew about the ships. From the landing craft at sea level below them you had to bend your neck all the way back to see the tops, like looking up at buildings. The ships had their bellies full of former county clerks and farmers and car salesmen and butchers and other boys like me from Ohio and New York and Oklahoma playing at being what we hoped to be. The ships didn't even have names, just APA-101, painted in white numbers on their hulls.

"Sergeant, you know much about these men?" I said. I was almost afraid to talk with him, his tough as jerky voice and me sounding like a student asking questions to kill time. In a crowd, this was the guy you noticed first and then looked nowhere else.

"No, sir, about the same as I know about you. I got assigned to your landing craft after my first one was blown out of the water," the Sergeant said. Laabs dropped his voice and the war silenced around us. "You haven't done this before, have you, Lieutenant?"

"No. Sort of. Well, I came ashore on the southern island, Kyushu, five days after the first part of the invasion back in November. No Japanese anywhere near us then. You been out before, right?"

"Saw a little action on Okinawa."

"You... shoot anyone?" I said.

Laabs nodded. That was it. I think he could tell I wanted something else.

"Nothing more worth saying. You won't understand. You're still thinking of them as people."

"Sergeant, I'm Lieutenant Hooper, Nathaniel Hooper. Nate sometimes."

"Sergeant Laabs, sir."

Machine gun rounds skimming overhead, I stuck my hand out to shake like back home. Sergeant Laabs reached out to me, but his eyes never stopped scanning the beach, the seawall, flicking like a lizard, on guard, searching for a fight.

"How old're you, Sergeant Laabs?"

"Sir, I was a stray who lied about his age to join up. I'm only 17. Believe that?"

His face already had the first thousand lines of a story. He didn't smile; those kinds of lines were missing.

"Me, I'll turn 19 in a few months," I said. "Already feeling too old for this."

"I know what you mean, sir. My birthday's in a week."

"Helluva day, Sergeant, and it's only 6 a.m."

"Yes, sir. Should've slept in."

WE STAYED CROUCHED BEHIND the seawall playing hide and seek with the war. The Japanese machine gun rounds overhead were accomplishing nothing for all the noise but to remind me of the size of the mistake I'd made coming here. Their weapon was up above us, on ground we couldn't see, over the seawall. I could spot other squads of our guys on the beach, and I could see the dead sprawled out like they were napping. But for me, all that mattered were these few yards of sand I was occupying. It made no sense to move left or right. I couldn't go forward and the ocean made sure I couldn't go back. That was the world. Plus that Jap machine gun.

Laabs said how the Japs were fighting harder than a hair stuck in a biscuit, and it was only a matter of time before some Japanese officer got the idea of sending infantry around to flank us, drawing in the sand with his finger how the attack would look. Laabs explained what our next move should be, but I desperately wanted to show him I had a handle on this. I ordered the nearest three men who would listen to go over the seawall with me. Sergeant Laabs and the others would stay where they were to provide covering fire while the four of us rushed the machine gun.

It surprised me when the men I'd selected threw themselves up and over the wall to attack the machine gun head-on. When I tried to imitate them, my boot failed to catch hold, me tied up in wet web gear, a soaked knapsack, a raincoat, a first-aid kit, shaving gear, 60 rounds of pistol ammunition, a shelter half, tent pegs, and a nine pound rifle. Jesus, I had tent pegs. My knees buckled, my legs went light, I fell backwards, my glasses flew off, and I landed on my ass right about where I started.

Grenades thrown by Sergeant Laabs and guys whose name tapes said they were Marino and Steiner exploded far over the seawall, but instead of the sounds of dying Japanese, I heard shrapnel ping off concrete; the machine gun was inside something solid none of us could've seen from behind the wall. I couldn't watch the three anonymous men I'd ordered over the wall die.

"Hey, Lieutenant, Lieutenant, it's me, Sergeant Laabs. Look, I know you're in charge and all, but we gotta try something else. We are well into this and it's turning into a real shit show. I was thinking, maybe with all those ships out there, one of them might want to kill that Nambu machine gun, you know, let the Navy do a little work for us." Laabs waited for me to say something. "Lieutenant, you need to call out to the ships, sir. Sorta now or we're likely to die right here. We gotta get off this beach."

"Okay, okay, I got it. What's your name, Private?" I said to the kid closest to me.

"Jones, Alden Jones. People at home call me Alden, Lieutenant." He stretched it out, "Lew-ten-naut," like he was leaning against the side of a barn somewhere. Christ.

"Nobody here wants to know your goddamn first name, Jones. Go find the radioman," I said.

"Over here, sir. Smith—Smitty—radioman. Here's Burke and Polanski with me."

"Smitty, gimme the handset, I'm going to call in Navy fire on that machine gun," I said. Our SCR-300 Galvin radios were monsters, over 30 pounds, plus the extra lead batteries, and, like everything else in my life now, olive drab. It took most of Smitty's not-inconsiderable strength—he was what we called back home "country strong"—to horse the thing alongside all his other gear. Even so, it nearly bent him in two as he scuttled closer. I realized I hadn't even fired my own rifle yet, so I thought this was the way to do something more than worry about where my glasses were.

Smitty crouched over the radio, one hand holding his helmet from slipping forward, the other at the end of an arm hanging over the radio, making him look like an elephant adjusting the settings with his trunk. He held out the handset. My hands were shaking, and somehow all I could focus on was the line of black dirt under each of my nails. We all heard the empty hiss coming through the speaker.

"Oh, for the love of Christ, we gotta move this right along now before we really shit the bed," Laabs said. He reached across me for the handset.

"Lieutenant?" Smitty said.

"Sergeant Laabs, I'm making the decisions on this beach." But I didn't reach for the radio.

"We'll sort it out later, sir, decisions are easy, it's the consequences what're hard," Laabs said. He grabbed the handset: "Break, break. Inferno, Inferno, this is Lancer Six, hell, Lancer Six Actual. Fire mission, priority, Ashiya Beach, Sector Packard, grid NF3 QXF3. Between us and the tree line, I got eyeballs on him. Aim well, my friend, we're danger close. Light 'em up."

"Naval gunnery on the cruiser Alaska here. Roger that, Lancer Six, we aim to please. This one's gonna be a fastball DiMaggio couldn't touch, so heads down. Over."

"Joltin' Joe can kiss my ass, I'm a Dodgers fan. Out," Sergeant Laabs said. He threw down the black plastic handset, with a quick glance at me. It wouldn't have surprised me if he'd bitten the end off it instead, but he said, "It's that easy, Lieutenant, kid could do it."

For a moment there was nothing but that last burst of static. Then real sound cracked the sky. It was that easy; you said a few words into the radio and shells were summoned to blow away all to hell somebody you couldn't even see. It was black magic.

Something stood me on my head and almost shook all the fillings out of my teeth as the naval gunfire tore apart the machine gun emplacement, concrete that might as well have been flesh, leaving that smell of cordite in the air Laabs called war perfume. The sound of the shells deafened me for a long moment. I dug a finger into my ear to try and clear the ringing. My hearing fuzzed in as the heat from the explosion came and slapped me back onto that beach.

"Smells sorta like meat on the grill," Burke said. It was hot and sticky for a smell.

I asked Laabs how many we'd killed, and he said later we'd count up the arms and legs and divide by four. It was that kind of day.

"I told you boys, I'd kill more Japanese with this here radio than I ever would with a rifle," Smitty said, patting his gear. "Most dangerous weapon we got. Oh, and hey, Lieutenant, here's your glasses. Found 'em in the sand."

Child's Play

Chapter 26: Memories of Naoko

Eichi Nakagawa: Rural Japan, Before the American Invasion

NAOKO WAS OUR NEIGHBOR'S daughter. We played together. We ran through the woods and pretended there were ghosts at the old temple near our homes. There was morning, after lunch, and then night. No sense of time was our silent friend.

The shops were full of special things to eat. My father told me that because Japan had freed Korea and China from the west, our markets were flooded with new goods from those far away places. Mother especially loved the Korean plums, quietly insisting they were juicier than the Japanese ones, even as my father would shush her for fear a neighbor might overhear her being what he said was disloyal.

There was a traditional Japanese sweet maker in town, but his candy was not so tasty. The candy we liked best was made somewhere else by a factory. It was called Sakuma, fruit drops that came in a metal tin. Naoko and I fought over the red ones, but neither of us liked the green ones that burned our tongues. Some days Naoko's mother shook out a drop at random into our hands, some days she put some out into her own palm and let us choose. We would beg Naoko's mother to send us off to the store with a few coins to buy another full tin.

The thing we looked forward to all year was the summer festival at the old temple. Everyone would dress up in summer kimono, *yukata*. The men would wear ones all of one color, while the women would have designs of flowers on theirs. We would all wear our clog shoes, *geta*, and the sound they made clomping on the stone streets called us to summer, same as the night noises of the cicadas and the soft wind chimes everyone hung by their doors. At the festival, the men would gather off to the side and drink *sake*, turning beet red. I do not think I remember my father ever laughing except then.

Naoko and I would say we wanted to drink *sake*, too, because whatever was in it made people happy. We never got to try it, well, I had a small sip every New Year's Day for tradition, but it burned my throat more than it made me laugh. Still, the *sake* would somehow make my father reach inside his *yukata* and pull out money for us to buy the things children buy, like shaved ice with flavored syrup. We also liked to play the catch the goldfish game, *kingyosukui*. Everyone knew it. A man with bushy eyebrows we pretended to be afraid of would set up a low tank with tiny goldfish swimming around. For a few *sen*, he gave you a tissue paper scoop. If you could scoop up a fish and transfer it to a cup, you could keep the fish. But almost always the paper scoop would dissolve and fall apart before you could catch a fish, and you would have to pay to try again and again until you ran out of money. Only one time I did get a fish, but I forgot to add water to the cup the next day. Naoko laughed at me for that, but I did not like that it died.

A special thing that last summer was that a photographer came to the festival, and set up a little booth. No one we knew had a camera of their own, but people could get their picture taken for not much money. That summer, Naoko's mother had our picture taken together, just Naoko and me. We stood very close.

After that photo was taken, Naoko's father Professor Matsumoto would spend a lot of time looking at me closely. Sometimes when we were together he would look just as closely at Naoko. He was like my father in a way, not warm, but unlike father he did not become warm even after *sake*. He was always serious, wiping his little glasses with a handkerchief when he explained things to us about the world. There would be a big war, he said, maybe with England. Naoko knew a few of the foreign words. When she said them, that was the only time her father smiled.

On warm days through the spring and summer Naoko and I would tug off our clothes down to our underwear and wade out into the Kamogawa River. The water was always cool, because of the willow trees that shaded it. I knew I wanted to hold her hand. But I did not understand the day I felt a stirring and had to stay with the water over my waist for a long time before I could leave the river. Naoko had already gone to the bank to sun herself while I stood in the river looking at the drops of water drying on her skin. I think my lips turned blue even with an unfamiliar warmth inside the rest of me.

Naoko's father, until the bombing made the rail lines dangerous, took a long trip from where we lived to his work. But they eventually moved. That was the last I ever saw of her before I was sent away.

The best I can do to remember how I was when she left was when my father took me and my friends to a warehouse near his job. Fathers like to scare their children, so once inside he turned off all the lights. We knew others were there, but we could not see each other.

When I stepped back outside the sky was blue, cloudless, with no airplanes.

Chapter 27: A Hunger

Eichi Nakagawa: Rural Area in Japan, Before the American Invasion

THE FIRST FOOD SHORTAGE everyone noticed was white rice. To be able to eat white rice was a sign of prosperity; before the war, only poor people could not afford it. Before the war, we were sometimes served brown rice for our school lunches as an example, accompanied by a lecture from teacher on how our ancestors had to eat this every day until they worked hard enough to afford white rice.

However, once the war started, the best rice went to the soldiers. So most of what we got was sent out brown and to we Japanese, *misuborashi*, shabby. It was a sacrifice we were required to make to ensure victory.

I began dreaming in rice. I went to mother saying I was hungry, and she had to turn away. The fish man would open his doors only when fish was available, the bread store when they could get enough flour. Fish in particular was very hard to find, father explained to us, because the boats could no longer be safe from the Americans. Whenever people saw a line forming outside a shop, they joined, even if they had no idea what they were waiting for.

Buying anything on the black market meant risking a beating from the economic duty police. Still, late at night, men would come in from the farms with an egg or two here, a rib with a little meat on it there, only such tiny amounts that they could still make their quotas when the military procurement teams would descend. My father would often tell us he was going out for a walk, taking with him something of value. That is how mama lost grandma's kimonos she said she did not want anymore and father said we could not eat anyway. The farmers did not want actual money that could lose its value, my father said. The deals were terrible, gold for near-rancid pork, but trading much for little was seen as part of our obligation to the war effort. It also allowed us to eat.

The *Bi-nijuku*, the American B-29s, attacked day and night. None of us could believe there were so many airplanes in the world. So, like many children in Japan, I was sent away by my parents to *doinaka*, the distant countryside. Father joked I had to move away to make room for the war. It was actually to save us from the Americans, but also for at least a little longer from the Army recruiters, who were banging on doors for younger and younger boys. I lived out in the countryside with people I called Auntie and Uncle, but to be honest, I do not think they were relatives. We all had been educated to bear any burden for Japan. So when children arrived at night from the cities—during the day it was too easy for the Americans to attack our trains—we were taken in. That was the first night I ever slept away from home.

We ate at a long table, the adults and ten children, strangers and me mixed together. We boys fought over second helpings, and punched and kicked each other under the table before running off. Our meals with Auntie and Uncle were simple, that brown rice mixed with barley and *daikon* radish, and maybe some of the small frogs we caught in the rice paddies for meat. See, every hog was counted by the government and in birthing season, every piglet. The frogs they could not count, and so we ate a lot of those.

One morning I woke up to a breeze coming through the window to tickle my bare feet. I wanted it to be Mama, telling me my part of the war was already over and she would take me home.

WE ALL WORE UNIFORMS to school. Japanese boys had been wearing them, dark blue with brass buttons, and stiff collars we hated to fasten, since our Emperor was restored to the throne in 1868. Everyone in Japan knew that date from history class as we knew our own birthdays. The uniforms, we were taught, were copied from the Prussian style of that time, a reminder of how Japan beat its enemies by using western weapons in a Japanese way. Everyone had his head shaved to the skin, and we were inspected by teacher each day. If your hair was too long, he would trim it to the proper length. There was blood.

At my school outside of Kyoto, our teacher left to volunteer for the war, so we had a lot of time to play at first. Then this gimpy man showed up as a replacement and we had to go back. He was old, too, so his face looked like a peach pit. When he walked out of the room, we mocked him, dragging our legs and tipping over chairs. We thought he was weak and we were not.

One day we assembled on the sports playing field and a squadron of real Japanese fighter planes flew low over us—we could even see the pilots waving from their open canopies. Every one of us could identify the different types of aircraft we saw, competing over who could shout out the model number. The ones that day were Mitsubishi A5M's, Type 96, and I said it first. We also knew the names of the warships pictured in the newspaper articles we collected. The Yamato was my favorite.

Every day after that, teacher lined us up in the hall, two rows facing each other, and screamed at us to slap the boy across in the face. Then the other row hit back at us. If you did not strike the other boy hard enough, teacher delivered the blow to you. Learn to hit harder than you have been hit, he said. He was surprisingly strong for a gimp. One of the boys once raised his hand back to teacher, and was dealt with severely. Still, I think I saw the gimp smile at what we had learned.

Our victory at Pearl Harbor was seen almost as the end of the war. How could the Americans ever recover from such a thrashing? The newspapers featured story after story of our successes, from the Philippines to Malaya to Hong Kong, and we boys studied them all. Who could care about arithmetic or old books?

We had a large map in the classroom, and teacher selected boys with the highest test scores and best martial spirit to paste small Japanese flags on countries as they fell, each victory announced on the radio to the sound of the "Battleship March." We were told by our teacher that Japan was leading its younger brothers in Asia away from whatever the colonial domination of the West was.

At some point there were fewer new flags to paste on the map, and some of the more senior boys were pulled away for the Army before graduation. Sirens warning of American bombers replaced the exciting flyovers of our own Japanese planes. We pledged ourselves to the flag each morning. We memorized slogans such as "Deny One's Self to Serve the Nation."

This was all part of our patriotic education. They said we were empty bags that they were filling with *Yamato Damashi*, the spirit of the original Japan. Ships and airplanes, we were taught, were only symbols. We were the true tools of war. It was an exciting time.

Real soldiers came to our school and told us how they learned to shoot and showed us their pistols. They explained that our weapons and training were superior, and that we would never be hurt, but if we were, sacrificing ourselves for the nation in this cause was a perfect way to die. They said one day we would have to stop playing. They told us the Americans would come.

Chapter 28: Old Man Tanaka's House

Eichi Nakagawa: Rural Area in Japan, Before the American Invasion

THE WAR CAME in the form of American planes. They did not bomb us, but the nearest town instead. We did not know what in that town had to be destroyed by planes that came all the way from America. Someone in that town would call the single telephone in our village, owned by the man who was also in charge of our *tonarigumi*, the civil defense group, to warn us the planes were nearby. He would spend most of his days sitting near the phone, drinking cup after cup of tea. The man would leap up when the phone rang, grab a hand bell, and ring it three times. Women and small children were to put on quilted bonnets with a short cape attached. Those were supposed to help protect against flying embers catching their hair on fire. Men and boys would fill buckets of water to use against a fire. Then we would all run to our shelters.

The only days everyone rested were the rainy ones, when the Americans did not fly. Uncle tried to cheer us up by saying the American pilots were like picnickers, waiting on nice weather. It was not funny, but I was not worried, even though my friend Kenta became scared of blue skies and would cry in the morning when he woke up without hearing rain. In fact, I thought hiding was stupid. The planes never bothered with us. Why should they, we were barely a speck below them, far away in the countryside.

Our shelter, under Auntie and Uncle's house, smelled like wet sweaters. There were all sorts of wooden tea chests down there, stuffed with handfuls of photos: Auntie in a kimono, Uncle fit and sharp in a military uniform with buttons and medals down the front from when he liberated Taiwan. Uncle would tell us to leave those damn photos alone, but Auntie always said, "Oh, let them look, it distracts them." One time my friend Kenta got a paper cut off one of the pictures, and on a dare we boys all tasted the blood. "To defend the nation," we sang, "Use the blood of Japanese men," the words from a popular song.

One late summer evening, after we tired of playing soldier, we set out to catch frogs. The flooded rice paddies in front of Old Man Tanaka's house were full of frogs. Tanaka would watch us from his window. He smelled funny, like old people do, but he was nice. One time he taught us to make whistles out of small pieces of bamboo.

It was easy to smack the frogs in the paddy with a stick when they came up to croak and snap at fireflies. Then Ring! Ring! Ring! The bell. The American airplanes were coming. But that night we were having too much fun to run for the shelter. They would always fly over us to bomb somewhere else anyway.

The frogs went silent.

My friend Kenta looked up and saw a metal cylinder falling under a small streamer. The cylinder did not appear so big, but when it crashed through Old Man Tanaka's roof, it shattered the ceramic tiles.

"Look," Kenta said. "More."

We counted three, four, then seven cylinders coming down. Some landed in the woods and, with a crack, started fires. Another fell behind us. Our shadows danced across the water as we ran. The embers from the house rose upward, chasing away the fireflies that had been over the paddy.

The planes continued high and away, like they always had. They did not know about Old Man Tanaka.

His home burned quickly. Men from the village ran toward us with their wooden buckets and *hitataki*, bamboo poles tipped with cotton cloth, and put water from the paddy on the house. The low clouds that had lit up orange became black again.

There was a sticky smell. The old man had not gotten out of the house fast enough.

"Kenta, what do you want? What can help?" I said. He would not stop crying as we watched the flames die out.

"I do not want to smell this. I want my mother to take me to the toy store when she goes to the market for rice and fish and buy me a toy. I want to see a coin in her hand and hear her say, 'You choose something and give the man this coin, Kenta.'"

For a week after Old Man Tanaka died, the cats did not come out from under the storage shed.

ON MY LAST AFTERNOON with Auntie and Uncle, I went out to try and play again with my friend Kenta, and we saw a frog hop out of the paddy. I brought my stick down as hard as I could on it, just like I had done before. But then I picked the already dead frog up, threw it on the ground, and hit it again and again until it burst open and its pink insides spilled. I pounded, over and over, until my arms were tired and the frog was a part of the dirt.

I didn't understand what was happening to me because of the war. How could I feel powerful and powerless at the same time? I was just a child, and wars were fought by adults, after all.

Chapter 29: The First Day

Former Lieutenant Nathaniel Hooper: Retirement Home, Kailua, Hawaii, 2017

I WAS BORN AND had always lived in a small town called Reeve, Ohio, spending my childhood outside and wrapped in dirt. I'd worn glasses since I was 10, and ended up losing a pair a year if I didn't break them first. Like nearly everyone in America, when I first heard about the attack on Pearl Harbor, I had to look at a map to double-check where it was. Hawaii wasn't even a state then. The war at first looked to affect us in Reeve like one of our Ohio summer storms, something coming from far away, grumbly and dark, but it might blow over.

I was 14-years-old in December 1941, sitting in an over-heated classroom hearing about Sherman's Burning of Atlanta and Pickett's Charge at Gettysburg, asking my equally bored teacher numbing questions about why we had to learn this stuff. Every minute dragged like a week's worth of Mondays.

Soon enough, though, some of the older kids started getting called up, then the juniors at the high school thinned out, then some teachers left for the service and most of the seniors graduated straight into uniform. Soon we couldn't get enough boys together to field a baseball team, and Reeve became a town of old men and kids trying to grow up fast. Then a few soldiers started to come home, not all alive and not all whole. Watch out for the Jared boy, Mom would say, especially after he'd been drinking.

As it looked like the time was coming for me to sign up, I had my own prewar goal to resolve, to go into the service a non-virgin. I refused to surrender to the belief that sex was merely enemy propaganda set loose to frustrate already frustrated boys like me, but I lost every skirmish in that war. The closest I came was one girl who was soft as a sweater. I liked how it felt foraging inside her mouth, tasting Spearmint gum, but for all the advances, there was no victory. I sent her a postcard from training at Fort Polk. Never heard back.

THE WORLD WE LIVED in then, we accepted it all. You could call it patriotism, or faith, or you could call it naiveté, but in the end you could call it whatever you wanted and it didn't matter. We'd been attacked at Pearl Harbor by an enemy that was beheading prisoners and was ruthless in serving their dictator emperor. They were out to wreck our way of life.

Nobody asked any questions about whether the war was right, because we were told it was. Though there was a draft, more than a third of the servicemen, like me, were volunteers. America was in trouble and we needed to help. We had been taught from a young age to stand our ground, and the time had come. It never occurred to us there'd be other wars, and dark men and women who'd waste our lives there.

We accepted that once our war started we would not just defeat the enemy. Nope, the war was to destroy them, to kill them all. We would crush their whole religion of Emperor worship and militarism. We were, in a literal sense, at war with the idea of them. We were a country that could accomplish anything, and that was what we were going to do with that power and our self-proclaimed authority to use it as we saw fit.

Reeve was all small-town life, neither misspent nor well-spent. Most days were as exciting as the grocery checkout line. We got along not because we liked each other so much, but because like people on a crowded bus we made adjustments to all fit in. It was easier in Reeve to learn the score of a baseball game than to buy a book. I found that out after I knew I was headed to the Army for sure and had to wait to buy one until I changed buses in Columbus on the way to basic. I ran into the big Lazarus department store outside the terminal and bought the thickest book on war with the smallest print they had. But it turned out there was nothing in it about Japan, and it ended up filling more of my suitcase than my head.

In Reeve you left the house in the morning always knowing you'd be back in time to wash up for supper. Everybody had a dumb dog; they'd been all together long enough that the brains had been bred out of them. I thought late August corn tasted that sweet everywhere. The last time I'd fought anyone was in 7th grade, a bully named Dougie Dietz, when I got a bloody nose, my ass kicked, and another pair of broken glasses.

It was a quiet day that I left home for the Army. A song I liked was playing on the radio. The morning felt as cool and sweet as a sip of lemonade. Rain was falling softly. If there was thunder, it was still far away.

Sometimes there are happy endings. Funny what you remember.

Afterwords

Fiction and Non-Fiction

NO ONE KNEW IF the atomic bomb would work.

The first full-on test was in July 1945, detonated on a static tower. Scientists were pretty sure the Bomb would work again, when air dropped, but weren't sure at what height the explosion would cause real damage to an entire city, as was desired. The effects of radiation, particularly how long it would take before people began to die from it under real-world conditions, were little understood. So even if Hiroshima and Nagasaki were totally destroyed, there was no assurance that the Japanese would surrender. Hence, planning for a land invasion of Japan continued up until the very surrender itself. Voluminous documentation exists for both sides on how that invasion and defense would have been carried out. You can read the original American plans, and some of the Japanese, at the U.S. Army Heritage and Education Center in Carlisle, Pennsylvania.

The scenes Lieutenant Hooper witnesses inside Kyoto after the fictional firebombing of the city are based largely on eyewitness accounts of the attacks on Coventry, Dresden and Tokyo, as well as from the August 1945 atomic bombings of Hiroshima and Nagasaki. Hooper's observation that survivors in Kyoto earned a few coins posing for photos with G.I.s actually took place, albeit in the ruins of Hiroshima. MacArthur outlawed the practice, in part because the effects of the atomic bomb were considered classified. Most photos and films of the atomic survivors were kept from the American public for "morale" reasons. It was not until many years later that Americans learned what had been done in their names.

Lieutenant Hooper in this book commands what was known then as a bastard unit. A typical World War II U.S. Army platoon consisted of up to 44 men, led by a lieutenant with a senior non-commissioned officer like Sergeant Laabs as second in command. That platoon would have been made up of two to four squads of about ten soldiers each. However, given wartime exigencies, incomplete units were thrown together, and that is what Lieutenant Hooper found himself taking into battle.

The soldiers in this story are young. When the American side of the war broke out in December 1941, the draft age was 21. It was quickly lowered to 18. Legally, one could enter the service voluntarily at 17-years-old, but in many cases the rule of thumb was someone who wanted to volunteer was as old as they claimed to be. In Japan, boys as young as 15 were conscripted.

The occasional mixing of war slang and terminology in this book ("hearts and minds" is a Vietnam-era term, for example) is to connect Lieutenant Hooper's experiences to the ones American soldiers encountered in later wars.

The use of firebombing against Japan had been set down in "War Plan Orange," written long before Pearl Harbor. As far back as the 1920s, U.S. General Billy Mitchell had said Japan's paper and wood cities would be "the greatest aerial targets the world had ever seen." Following the outline in War Plan Orange, the efforts during WWII in Japan were lead by the 20th Army Air Force, and its commander, Curtis "Bombs Away" LeMay. LeMay expressed his goal as "Japan will eventually be a nation without cities, a nomadic people."

LeMay's legacy was further tainted by his statement during the Vietnam War about bombing the enemy back to the Stone Age. Times had changed, and such remarks, celebrated during WWII, were less acceptable to the majority of Americans. The man many call the architect of the Vietnam War, Defense Secretary Robert McNamara, worked for LeMay during the WWII firebombing campaign. McNamara went on to order the use of napalm in Vietnam as Secretary of Defense.

Why Not Kyoto?

UNDERSTANDING WHY KYOTO WAS not bombed during World War II is based in large part on the debates among senior leaders in Washington, recorded by Secretary of War Henry Stimson in his diaries. You can read Stimson's diaries, written in his cramped handwriting, in the Yale University library.

Spared conventional bombing throughout the conflict, Kyoto was on the shortlist of targets for nuclear destruction. Consideration was based primarily on Kyoto's value as an untouched site, to allow a full evaluation of the Bomb's potential.

Stimson was no pacifist; when the Bomb was ready, he was very much in favor of using it. But he argued to President Truman against bombing Kyoto, a site of global cultural significance. Destroying the city, particularly after it had been ignored during the previous years of fighting, and destroying it with an atomic weapon, would influence world opinion against the U.S. after the war, as if the Nazis had dynamited the Louvre and burned the Mona Lisa on their way out of Paris. Stimson had been Governor-General of the Philippines in the 1920s and spent his honeymoon in Kyoto, so he knew the place better than most inside the government. If he'd honeymooned in Hiroshima instead, who knows how the end of the war might have gone.

Japanese Children's Evacuation

EICHI NAKAGAWA'S EVACUATION DEEP into the countryside is based on historical fact. The details in Eichi's story are derived primarily from personal interviews I conducted with now quite elderly Japanese who were sent away as children for their safety.

The government sponsored the movement of 350,000 elementary school boys and girls from a dozen cities into the countryside. Another 100,000 more were moved out of urban areas in March 1945. Some 300,000 children were relocated by their parents independently. For many children, it was an odd way to spend a war they only later learned in detail had been so tragic and devastating.

Food Shortages in Japan

THE ISSUE OF FOOD shortages among the Japanese population in the late-war period has received less emphasis in western scholarship than it deserves. Japanese historians, however, are clear on the impact hunger made on the nation's civilians.

A series of factors created the food crisis, including the American navy sinking or blockading supplies to Japan from its conquered territories, the lack of human capital to grow food as men disappeared into the armed forces, the diversion of foodstuffs to the military, and the havoc American air power wreaked on Japanese transportation infrastructure. The latter point was particularly important; Tokyo brought in 97 percent of its rice from outside the city.

Urban populations turned to a flourishing black market run by crime syndicates, the *yakuza*. The authorities, desperate to see the food shortages dealt with, turned a blind eye.

As the American occupation began, some 25 percent of the Japanese population suffered from serious nutritional deficiencies. The situation grew desperate enough that 150,000 people demonstrated in front of the Imperial Palace demanding food. Outright famine was avoided only after MacArthur, then ruling Japan as head of the occupation (the Japanese called him *Shogun*, after the samurai leaders), ordered thousands of tons of food to be imported. He reportedly sent word back to Washington to "send me more food, or send me more bullets."

The Debate Over the Bomb

THE DEBATE OVER WHETHER the atomic bombings of Hiroshima and Nagasaki were the only alternative to a land invasion of Japan is one of the most contested among modern historians.

The dominant narrative in the United States is the dead of Hiroshima and Nagasaki were a smaller price to pay than the greater loss of life anticipated under an invasion; in a grim calculus, the bombings were practically an act of humanity. Included in this view is that those killed were mostly Japanese anyway, while an invasion would have taken many American lives. The debate is framed as black or white, invasion or bomb.

The "we had no choice but to use the Bomb" argument is most strongly presented in Paul Fussell's (in)famous essay, *Thank*

God for the Atom Bomb. His premise is that absent those horrific shocks, Japan would have never agreed to surrender without a bloody invasion. And indeed the Bombs were dropped, and Japan surrendered. War is hell, and bigger bombs just made the work go faster, Fussell believed, stating matter-of-factly the U.S. had crossed any lines of morality anyway a long time prior. Himself scheduled to be in the invading force, Fussell, like every young man facing his own death, thought back then, damn straight, use the bigger bombs, and thank God we have 'em. I personally heard Howard Baker, a gentle and educated man, then U.S. Ambassador to Japan, make similar statements. Baker was assigned to pilot a landing craft in the invasion of Japan. Such reactions are understandable, even predictable, a survivor's quest for personal significance in what may otherwise be psychologically unprocessable.

There are tag-along arguments, all with at least some truth in them. One is the use of the Bomb was the end process of a technological roller coaster; it was built at great cost (the uranium enrichment plant at Oak Ridge, Tennessee, for example, used more electrical power in 1945 than all of Canada) and had to be used to justify that. Another is that the Bomb needed to be tested in combat ahead of the next war. Revenge for Pearl Harbor and racism ("dirty Japs") are also claimed by some as reasons. Some in the military argued in favor of destroying Hiroshima and Nagasaki as examples to the Russians of our atomic prowess. The war with Japan was almost over one way or another, and the Pentagon was thinking ahead to the next one.

Were the Only Choices the Bomb or an Invasion?

BUT WAS THERE A path that bypassed both the atomic bombings and a land invasion?

By summer 1945 Japanese leadership was divided over the best course of action. The loss of Okinawa made clear some version of defeat was inevitable. Despite much overt blustering in front of one's superiors, often via diplomatic cables that were not a place for contrary opinions, Japan's military professionals privately knew of both the unprecedented resources America was bringing to bear, and the pitiful reserves available to Japan. They also deeply feared the coming Soviet entry into the war.

The best result all but the most conservative of the Japanese hierarchy hoped for was indeed a peace settlement of some sort. The gap between what the U.S. expected out of an unconditional surrender and what the Japanese realistically hoped for out of a lightly negotiated one was not significant.

As a prelude to negotiations, in June 1945, a month before the Potsdam conference, and within hours of the Japanese commanding general's death on Okinawa, the Emperor directed the Supreme War Direction Council—his "inner cabinet"—to begin formal peace negotiations, if possible, through the "good offices" of Russia. Such negotiations, it was hoped in Tokyo, might also serve to keep the Russian army away from the Japanese home islands.

Japan wanted most of all to avoid a war crimes trial of the Emperor, fearing his imprisonment or execution. As one historian saw it, in perhaps a slight exaggeration, a public end to the Emperor, held by many in god-like status, would have been equivalent to the crucifixion of Christ.

The overvaluing of the atomic bombs in compelling surrender also overlooks that Japanese fear of the Soviet Union entering the Pacific War. While accepting defeat against the Americans, Japanese political elites did not want to cede large swaths of their northern territory, especially Hokkaido, to the Soviet Union, nor see the Soviets be part of any occupation. Events in Europe as the Red Army rolled toward Berlin were known to the Japanese.

The sequence of events is telling: After the bombing of Hiroshima on August 6, 1945, the Soviets declared war on Japan on August 8, and crossed the Manchurian border in force the morning of August 9, followed by the bombing of Nagasaki that same day (the near-simultaneous acts likely fueled Japanese paranoia, though history shows them unrelated.) Conventional bombing of Japan by the 20th U.S. Army Air Force continued for five full days after Nagasaki, until Japan accepted the modified "unconditional" surrender terms allowing it to retain the Emperor as head of state, on August 15.

Throughout the Pacific War the American mantra was Japan would never surrender. Then they did. How things would have played out with a week or two more of skilled diplomacy cannot be known, but it is clear there was a third alternative. To end the war, neither the use of nuclear weapons nor a land invasion of the Japanese mainland, was, at least, a possibility. Had such an option been pursued as aggressively as the martial ones, Lieutenant Hooper's story would have been different, as perhaps would have our own.

Acknowledgments

YOU WRITE ALONE, BUT you don't think alone. My thanks to early readers Lisa Ehrle, Joshua Patton, Lyn Liao Butler, Sarah Van Buren, Abigail Van Buren, Japanese language consultant Mari Nakamura, Chris Keelty and the New York Writers Critique Group, proofreader Laurie Russo, as well as Oliver Stone, Tom Englehardt, Jesslyn Radack, Kathleen McClellan, Helen Coster, the 79th Street Workshop, and Jim Hruska and Lisa Finkelstein, who helped me better understand PTSD. Once again my gratitude to the people at Luminis Books, especially Chris Katsaropoulos.

All errors are my own.

The quotation by Randy Brown is from his book, *Welcome to FOB Haiku: War Poems from Inside the Wire* (Middle West Press, 2015), and is used with his permission.

We all owe a great debt to the two greatest anti-war novels ever written, Joseph Heller's *Catch-22* and Kurt Vonnegut's *Slaughterhouse Five.*

About the Author

PETER VAN BUREN is a 24-year veteran of the State Department. He lived in Japan for ten years and speaks Japanese.

Following his first book, *We Meant Well: How I Helped Lose the Battle for the Hearts and Minds of the Iraqi People* (Metropolitan, 2011), the Department of State began judicial proceedings against Van Buren, falsely claiming he exposed classified material. Through the efforts of the Government Accountability Project and the ACLU, Van Buren instead retired from the State Department on his own terms.

Van Buren's second book, *Ghosts of Tom Joad: A Story of the #99Percent* (Luminis, 2014), traces the rise of the working poor and the destruction of the middle class. The novel tells the story of one Midwestern blue collar family across three generations.

Peter's commentary has been featured in *The New York Times*, Reuters, *Salon*, NPR, Al Jazeera, *Huffington Post*, *The Nation*, TomDispatch.com, Antiwar.com, *The American Conservative*, *Mother Jones*, MichaelMoore.com, *Le Monde*, *Asia Times*, *The Guardian*, and others. He has appeared on the BBC, *All Things Considered* and *Fresh Air*, Fox News, VICE, Japanese NHK, Democracy Now!, Voice of America, and more.

Follow Peter @wemeantwell and at www.wemeantwell.com

Praise for Peter Van Buren's *Ghosts of Tom Joad:*

"Politicians come and go, but the critical issues tearing at our society do not. In his new book *Ghosts of Tom Joad,* Van Buren turns to the larger themes of social justice and equality, and asks uncomfortable questions about where we are headed. He is no stranger to speaking truth to power, and the critical importance of doing that in a democracy cannot be overestimated. Standing up and saying 'This is wrong' is the basis of a free society. The act of doing so must be often practiced, and regularly tested."

—Daniel Ellsberg, whistleblower, *The Pentagon Papers*

"A lyrical, and deeply reported look at America's decline from the bottom up. Though a work of fiction, *Ghosts of Tom Joad* is—sadly, and importantly—based on absolute fact. Buy it, read it, think about it."

—Janet Reitman, contributing editor, *Rolling Stone*, author of *Inside Scientology: the Story of America's Most Secretive Religion*

"At the State Department Peter Van Buren was a pioneer blowing the whistle in defense of human rights by challenging torture. In this novel, he blows the whistle in defense of America's roots by challenging the dehumanizing consequences when big business abandoned the Rust Belt in Ohio. This tale of a mythical Earl's relentless quest for an American dream that has become a mirage is worthy of the voices that inspired it, from Woody Guthrie to John Steinbeck to Bruce Springsteen."

—Tom Devine, Legal Director, Government Accountability Project

"Van Buren is passionate about the truth, and his new book *Ghosts of Tom Joad* is a masterpiece, a must-read about the decline of our economy and social structure, an inspirational story showing how one man and one nation can claw its way back to greatness."

—Kathryn Milofsky, Producer Reporter ITV (UK) / Executive Producer of "The Brian Oxman Show" (US)

"A twenty-first century *Grapes of Wrath,* this memorable volume documents in a concrete, personal, often moving way the despair among many in America today due to economic and family hardships. In the words of its fictional but all too real narrator—Earl, from a rust-belt small Ohio town, unable get a permanent job or start a family —'they took away the factory, but left the people; this ain't a story, it's an autopsy.'"

—John H. Brown, Adjunct Professor of Liberal Studies, Georgetown University

"In Peter Van Buren's *Ghosts of Tom Joad*, things do not always look better in the morning. In this autopsy of the new depression, you turn a page and keep reading, hoping the story's left-behind people catch up . . . because one way or another, they're us."

—Diplopundit

"In *Ghosts of Tom Joad*, Peter Van Buren invokes his powerful story-telling gifts to portray a job-starved Ohio community. This gripping, contemporary novel in the tradition of *The Grapes of Wrath* is more real than real—and a worthy successor to Van Buren's reporting about Iraq in his courageous *We Meant Well*."

—Andrew Kreig, Director, Justice Integrity Project

"*Ghosts of Tom Joad* is a powerful and provocative tale of the working poor. Although the story is fiction, the themes are anything but. In a lively yet serious manner, Peter Van Buren tackles one of the most important issues of our day—how can a free society deal with the costs associated with creative destruction? *Ghosts of Tom Joad* is required reading for all concerned with the future of our country."

—Christopher J. Coyne, F.A. Harper Professor of Economics, George Mason University

"*Ghosts of Tom Joad* takes a hard, honest look at where millions of Americans are today: living a marginal existence, a no-exit life of grinding poverty. What Peter Van Buren is able to show through his gritty, close-to-the-ground prose, is how capitalism destroys the human spirit, leaving its victims devoid of any purpose in life. Those of us in our sixties and seventies are completely bewildered at where the America of our youth—a very different sort of place from today—went. The answer is contained in the pages of this book: the values of 'the market' finally swamped everything else, destroyed any values except those of rapaciousness and self-interest. 'I think God owes us an apology,' says the central character of this novel. No, I'd reply; but America certainly does."

—Morris Berman, historian and author of *The Twilight of American Culture, Dark Ages America: The Final Phase of Empire* and *Why America Failed: The Roots of Imperial Decline*

"I can't tell you what an impact this book had on me. The writing is beautiful, but the story is brutal. I grew up in and around these places, and to say it is grim is an understatement. *Ghosts* captures everything—the human complexity and the profound cultural/economic damages. The story stuck with me long after I stopped reading."

"I grew up and later worked in a 'Reeve, Ohio.' While experiencing a visceral recognition, Van Buren's intimate portrait of this dying town made me feel like a stranger peeking in on places many Americans have no idea exist. I will never again drive by the old manufacturing towns of my youth without wondering about the shadows within, as drawn so mesmerizingly in Van Buren's relentlessly vivid portrayal. As Steinbeck's *Grapes of Wrath* made a place for the Dust Bowl in our literary canon, *Ghosts* aims to do the same for the devastating industrial decline of the late-American 20th century."

—Kelley Vlahos, *The American Conservative*

"Bottom line: It's accessible and compelling, a mix of *Canterbury Tales* meets *Grapes of Wrath* meets *American Beauty*."

—Charlie Sherpa, military blogger, *Red Bull Rising*

"Have and have-nots have always existed. *Ghosts of Tom Joad* brings this conflict so often touched upon in literature into a modern day, down-turned economy. Riveted with a bit of nostalgia for the rosier '70s and '80s, the story manages to find humor in an otherwise dismal life. When you choose to ride this bus with Earl, you'll find yourself reminiscing with him, rooting for him, and yearning for the release he strives to find."

—Lisa Ehrle, Teacher-Librarian, Aurora, Colorado.

"Haunting and a kick in the gut, Peter Van Buren's first novel, *Ghosts of Tom Joad*, lays bare the brutal and very personal reality of America's Great Recession. In his first book, *We Meant Well*, Peter blew the whistle on the catastrophic effects of American policy in Iraq; now Peter turns his necessary and just attention on the effects of American policy at home. Want to understand the true and honest nature of our modern society and the American way of life? Then read *Ghosts of Tom Joad*."

—Matthew Hoh, Peace and Veterans advocate, former Marine

"Peter Van Buren has an amazing ability to draw the reader into his stories. That the author of the definitive work on the debacle of our post-war reconstruction of Iraq has now set his sights on the debacle of our post-industrial America makes perfect sense. Many of the actors are the same, with the same intent."

—Daniel McAdams, Ron Paul Institute

"Like his heroes in Steinbeck and Agee before him, the author takes us on an unflinching tour of America's 'broken places,' yet true to his predecessors Van Buren never loses sight of his rough characters' resilient humanity, their deeply held yearning for the grounding connection of family and community, their stubborn hope for a better life. An urgent, important story, and an incredibly necessary book."

—James Spione, Academy-Award nominated documentarian, *Incident in Baghdad* and *Silenced*